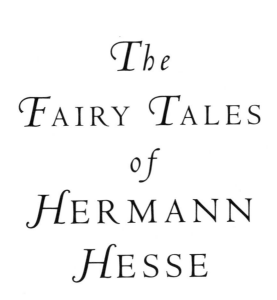

The
Fairy Tales
of
Hermann
Hesse

Translated and with an
Introduction by Jack Zipes

Woodcut illustrations by
David Frampton

Bantam Books
New York   Toronto   London   Sydney   Auckland

THE FAIRY TALES OF HERMANN HESSE

A Bantam Book / November 1995

Book design by Caroline Cunningham
Cover illustration and interior woodcut illustrations by David Frampton

Library of Congress Cataloging-in-Publication Data

Hesse, Hermann, 1877–1962.
[Märchen. English]
The fairy tales of Hermann Hesse / translated and with an
introduction by Jack Zipes.
p.   cm.
ISBN 0-553-10023-8 (hc)—ISBN 0-553-37776-0 (pbk.)
I. Zipes, Jack David.   II. Title.
PT2617.E85A287   1995
833'.912—dc20   94-49166
                                              CIP

Bantam Books are published by Bantam Books, a division of
Bantam Doubleday Dell Publishing Group, Inc. Its trademark,
consisting of the words "Bantam Books" and the portrayal of a
rooster, is Registered in U.S. Patent and Trademark Office and in
other countries. Marca Registrada. Bantam Books, 1540 Broad-
way, New York, New York 10036.

PRINTED IN THE UNITED STATES OF AMERICA
FFG   10 9 8 7 6 5 4 3 2 1

For Bette and Dave Dines,
two special people

CONTENTS

Contents

HERMANN HESSE'S FAIRY TALES AND THE PURSUIT OF HOME

By Jack Zipes

*H*ermann Hesse's fairy tales are not really fairy tales in the traditional sense of the term, and yet they are deeply embedded in both the Western and the Oriental traditions of fairy tales. Written between 1900 and 1933, Hesse's unusual narratives record his endeavors to experiment with the fairy-tale genre and to make his own life as an artist into a fairy tale. He failed as far as his life was concerned because he could never achieve the ideal state he desired, but his tales were successful exactly because of this failure: They are filled with the inner turmoil of a writer desperately and seriously playing with aspects of a literary genre to find some semblance of peace and perfect harmony. To know Hermann Hesse's fairy tales is to know the trauma, doubts, and dreams of the artist as a young man in Germany at the beginning of a tumultuous century. Like many other European writers, Hesse perceived the events around him—the rapid advance of technology, the rise of materialism, the world wars, the revolutions, and the economic inflations and depressions—as indicative of the decline of Western civilization. It was through art, especially the fairy tale, that Hesse sought to contend with what he perceived to be the sinister threat of science and commercialism.

Born in Calw, a small town in Swabia, on July 2, 1877, Hesse was raised in a religious household. His father, Johannes, who had been a pietistic missionary in India, continued to work in the ministry when he returned to Germany. His mother, Marie, was an assistant to her own father, Hermann Gundert, director of the Calw Publishing House, one of the leading pietistic book companies in Europe. Both parents were highly educated and totally dedicated to their religious beliefs, but they were not overly sectarian. Hesse found his pietistic home with its conservative routines to be oppressive, and early in his childhood he rebelled against the traditional ways of his parents and resisted authority of any kind. At one point in 1883, after his parents had moved to Basel, Switzerland, they gave serious thought to institutionalizing their son because he was so contrary, but fortunately for him he became more compliant and adjusted to the Swiss elementary school system. Three years later, in 1886, his parents returned to Germany to assume charge of the Calw Publishing House, and Hesse once again showed signs of rebelliousness. For the most part, however, he adhered to the pietistic principles of his parents and seemed prepared to pursue the highly regimented course of studies established in Germany.

In 1890 he was sent away to a private school in Göppingen,

another small Swabian city, so that he could prepare for the entrance examinations required for admission to one of the Protestant schools in this region. Yet as soon as he started his studies at an exclusive academy in Maulbronn in 1892, he began suffering from headaches and insomnia and ran away from the school. His parents then sent him to an institution for mentally disturbed children, but Hesse continually resisted help from doctors and teachers as well as his parents, whom he thought had deserted him, and even contemplated suicide. For over a year, Hesse went in and out of different schools, homes, and sanatoriums, until his parents brought him back to Calw in October 1893.

During the next two years, he appeared to gain control over his moods. He helped his father at the Calw Publishing House, worked in the garden, and had brief apprenticeships in a bookstore and a clock factory. By this time, Hesse, who was an inveterate reader, was already writing poems and stories and wanted to dedicate himself to a literary career. However, his father refused to give him permission to leave home to try his luck as a writer. Then in October 1895 he was finally allowed to begin an apprenticeship as bookseller at the Heckenbauer Bookshop in Tübingen, a university city with a famous cultural tradition.

In Tübingen, free of family constraints and the pressure of formal schooling, Hesse began to sense the direction that he wanted his life to take as a writer. He formed important friendships with other young writers and underwent his own literary apprenticeship by reading medieval literature, the German romantics, and Oriental works. During this period he also published his first book of poems, *Romantic Songs* (*Romantische Lieder*, 1898), and his first book of short prose pieces, *An Hour after Midnight* (*Eine Stunde hinter Mitternacht*, 1899).

Most important, Hesse began to replace the Pietism of his parents with his own personal religion—aestheticism. If there ever was a creed that he devoutly followed, it was the German romantic Novalis's notion that *"Mensch werden ist eine Kunst"*—to become a human being is art. For Hesse, art—the ultimate self-fulfillment—meant connecting with a profound, essential feeling associated with "home." But this home was not the home of his parents. Home was something intangible that was linked to aesthetic intuition and nurturing maternalism but was unique to each individual. It was both a return and a moving forward at the same time, and it could be attained only through art, through the artful formation of the self.

In 1899, Hesse accepted a position as an assistant bookseller in Reich's Bookshop in Basel, where he was to spend the next five years. Here he pursued his literary activities and made many new acquaintances, although he regarded himself more as an outsider and loner. In December 1900 he published *The Posthumous Writings and Poems of Hermann Lauscher (Hinterlassene Schriften und Gedichte von Hermann Lauscher)*, which showed the strong influence of E.T.A. Hoffmann and other romantic writers. He continued writing poems and book reviews and in 1903 had his first major success with the publication of *Peter Camenzind*, a novel in which the young romantic protagonist eventually turns his back on the cosmopolitan world to dedicate himself to art. It was somewhat the opposite with Hesse, who at this point in his life was learning more and more to enjoy the company of literary circles. In 1904 he married Maria Bernoulli, a gifted photographer, and since he was now able to support himself through his writing, they moved to a farmhouse in a village called Gaienhofen near Lake Constance on the Swiss-German border, where he and Maria hoped to be closer to nature and dedicate themselves to writing, painting, music, and photography. However, the period that Hesse spent in Gaienhofen, 1904–1912, was anything but idyllic.

To be sure, Hesse continued his prolific writing. He published *Under the Wheel* (*Unterm Rad,* 1904), an autobiographical novel about the brutality of educational institutions and authoritarianism in Germany; *This Side* (*Diesseits,* 1907) and *Neighbors* (*Nachbarn,* 1908), two collections of stories; *Gertrud* (1910), a novel; and *Underway* (*Unterwegs,* 1911), a volume of poems. He became an editor for an important cultural and political magazine, *März,* founded in 1908, and wrote numerous reviews for various German newspapers and journals. He also became the father of three boys, Bruno in 1905, Heiner in 1909, and Martin in 1911; won literary prizes; and formed friendships with well-known musicians, artists, and writers. He was not happy in his marriage with Maria, however, who was nine years older than he was and too self-sufficient and independent for him. Within a short time after their move to Gaienhofen, they each began going their own way and soon had very little in common except for the children. Hesse felt more and more lonely and isolated in the country, and he often took trips by himself or traveled to give lectures. But leaving home only exacerbated his anguish and ennui. In efforts to assuage his discontent, he tried vegetarianism, painting, theosophy, and the religions of India. In 1911 he took a trip to Ceylon, Sumatra, and Malaya, hoping that he would find spiritual peace on the subcontinent. However, he never reached India because of dysentery and because he was upset by the poverty in Asia and the commercialization of Buddhism. He returned to Gaienhofen sick, exhausted, and still unhappy in his marriage. In another endeavor to change these conditions, he and Maria decided to move to Bern in 1912.

Unfortunately, the change of environment did not help Hesse, and certain events led to increasing psychological stress in his life. His son Martin was stricken by mental illness and had to be placed in a foster home in 1914. He and Maria barely communicated. His father's death in 1916 led to great feelings of guilt. And after the outbreak of World War I, he gradually found himself at odds with most of his German compatriots. Though he sympathized with Germany, he took a public position against war, for which he was constantly attacked by the German press. Since his eyesight had prevented him from serving in the army, he cared for German prisoners of war in Bern for over two years. In 1917 he suffered a nervous breakdown and went to Sonnmatt, a private sanatorium near Lucerne, where he underwent electroshock therapy and numerous analytic sessions with a Jungian psychologist. Finally, in the spring of 1919, he separated completely from his wife, moved to the village of Montagnola in the Italian part of Switzerland, and appeared to be coming out of his depression.

It is astounding that despite—or perhaps because of—all his psychological troubles, Hesse wrote some of his best works during this painful time. In 1913 he published his diary, *Out of India (Aus Indien)*, about his journey to the Far East, followed by the novel *Rosshalde* in 1914. During this year he also published his provocative essay, "Oh, Friends not these Tones!" (*"O Freunde nicht diese Töne!"*), a pacifist tract, which enraged numerous Germans, who had become extremely militaristic. Until this time Hesse had been the "classic aesthete" and had rarely participated in politics. The war had awakened him, however, and though he never became a political activist, his writings began to assume a new political dimension that can be traced in his essays and fairy tales of the period, especially "A

Dream About the Gods" (1914), "Strange News from Another Planet" (1915), "If the War Continues" (1917), and "The European" (1918). Time and again, Hesse courageously stood up for his pacifist convictions and often exploded with frustration, as one of his letters to his friend Hans Sturzenegger in 1917 clearly demonstrates:

> They laugh about the conscientious objectors! In my opinion these individuals constitute the most valuable symptom of our times, even if a person here and there gives some strange reasons for his actions. . . . I have not been wounded, nor has my house been destroyed, but I have spent the last two and a half years taking care of the victims of the war, the prisoners, and just in this sector, in this small part of the war, I have learned all about its senselessness and cruel horror. I could not care less that the people are seemingly enthused by the war. The people have always been dumb. Even when they had the choice between Jesus and the murderer, they decided for Barabbas with great zeal. Perhaps they will continue to decide for Barabbas. But that is not a reason at all for me to go along with their decision.

While the dominant theme in Hesse's works continued to concern art and the artist, his collected fairy tales, *Märchen* (1919), reveal a shift from a solipsistic position to a consideration of the responsibility of the artist in society. At the same time, Hesse wanted to provide counsel for young readers in Germany, and works such as *Demian* (1919)—published under the pseudonym Emil Sinclair, who appears in "If the War Continues"—and *Zarathustra's Return* (*Zarathustras Wiederkehr*, 1919), dealing with ways to overcome chaos and nihilism, were clear gestures of reconciliation with his German readers after the destruction and turmoil of World War I.

It was from his retreat in Montagnola that Hesse felt, paradoxically, that he had enough distance to become more open and engaged with social and political problems. He was never inclined to align himself with a particular ideology; he was still the searcher, the artist on a quest to find himself. But by now he had found some tentative answers that he was willing to impart in his writings. Hesse had completely broken from his Christian and bourgeois upbringing and had been strongly influenced by Nietzsche, the German romantics, and Oriental religions. He now sought to combine these strands of thought in his own existentialist philosophy, concerned with finding the path home and discovering the divine within the essential nature of each individual. The book that perhaps best expressed his thinking at this time was *Siddhartha* (1922), a fairy-tale journey of rebellion and self-discovery, exuding the peace of mind that Hesse desired for himself.

The 1920s were not entirely peaceful for Hesse, however. In 1923, due in part to the continual harsh criticism of his works in the German press, Hesse became a Swiss citizen. This was also the year when he ended his marriage to Maria. In 1924 Hesse married Ruth Wenger, who was twenty-five years younger than he was. A sensitive young woman, she was a talented singer and dedicated to her career, but her health was very fragile and she suffered from tuberculosis. Given the differences in their ages and temperaments, this marriage was bound to fail, and within eleven weeks they parted ways. Again Hesse went through a major psychological crisis and contemplated suicide. But then he made a conscious decision to overcome his despair and introverted nature by frequenting taverns, dance halls, and places in Zurich and Bern where he had never before spent much time. To a certain extent, Hesse recorded these experiences in his famous novel *Steppenwolf* (1927), and the publication of this work seemed to cathartically release the wildness within him and enable him to settle down again in Montagnola to focus on his writing. During this time he met Ninon Dolbin, an art historian, who began living with him in 1928 and married him in 1929. A remarkably independent and wise person, Ninon Dolbin had a steadying influence on Hesse throughout the rest of his life, and although his difficulties with women and his own sexuality were not put to rest with this marriage, Hesse was able to establish a rapport with her that he had not been able to have in his other relationships.

With this marriage Hesse entered the mature period of his writing. He had begun numerous stories and novels during the 1920s and continued to publish literary essays and reviews in Germany and Switzerland. By the beginning of the 1930s he finished two important works he had begun earlier, *Narcissus and Goldmund* (*Narziss und Goldmund*, 1930) and *Journey to the East* (*Die Morgenlandfahrt*, 1932). The two books rounded out many of the existentialist, romantic, and Oriental ideas with which he had been experimenting during the 1920s. Now, in 1932, he was ready to begin his magnum opus, *The Glass Bead Game* (*Das Glasperlenspiel*), which would take him ten years to complete.

Although Hesse had always enjoyed traveling and lecturing and visiting such Swiss cities as Basel and Bern, he felt great pleasure in his large home in Montagnola. During the next twelve years, he rarely left his Swiss retreat, where he followed a set routine with Ninon. Mornings and afternoons were devoted to painting, gardening, and correspondence, while evenings he read and wrote. Over the years

Hesse had become a respected watercolor painter and had illustrated some of his own books; he continued to develop his talents as a painter during the 1930s and 1940s. Meanwhile, there was also another talent that he cultivated at this time, that of playing "host."

During the Nazi period numerous political refugees and friends fled Germany, and Hesse spent a great deal of his time helping them and providing them with a place to stay. However, he never published an official or public condemnation of Hitler and Nazism during the 1930s and 1940s. He still smarted from having been burned during World War I and the Weimar period for his public stand in behalf of peace. He firmly believed that the artist could not change society, but that politics could ruin an artist's perspective, perhaps even destroy it. The artist's role was to remain true to his art and not be influenced by ideologies on either the Right or the Left. Of course, in his private correspondence and in the reviews he wrote for various journals in Sweden and Switzerland, he made his position against Nazism quite clear. And yet he would issue no public declaration of opposition to German fascism. This refusal is clearly explained in a letter of 1936 to his editor at the Fischer Verlag:

> If I ask myself what more do you expect from me, then I find the following: You expect that I, as writer, should finally show a minimum of heroism once and for all and reveal my colors. But my dear colleague, I have done this continually since 1914, when my first essay against the war led to my friendship with [Romain] Rolland. Ever since 1914 I have had those forces against me that seek to prohibit religious and ethical behavior (and permit the political). I have had to swallow hundreds of

attacks in newspapers and thousands of hate letters since my awakening during wartime, and I swallowed them, and my life was made bitter because of this, my work was made more difficult and complicated, and my private life went down the drain. And I was not always attacked just by one side and then protected by another, but since I did not belong to any party, both sides liked to choose me as a target for their barrages. So, once again I am now being vilified simultaneously by the emigrants and the Third Reich. And I firmly believe that my place is that of the outsider and that of the man without a party, a place where I have my little bit of humanity and Christianity to show.

These views and many other reflections about art and education were incorporated into *The Glass Bead Game*, which was first published in Zurich in 1943 and subsequently in Germany in 1946. It was to be his last novel, and fittingly, it encompassed the wide range of issues that had been central to his writing since the turn of the century. *The Glass Bead Game* reads like an autobiographical novel of development. The young protagonist, Josef Knecht, is chosen to attend an elite school in Castalia, a province dedicated to intellectual and aesthetic pursuits. Like many of Hesse's other young "heroes," he must undergo an apprenticeship under the guidance of a wise man, in this case the Magister Musicae of Monteport, who teaches him to comprehend dreams and to embrace life's opposites—to play with them and become one with them. Once Knecht has achieved everything he possibly can as the grand Magister Ludi in this spiritual realm, he decides that he wants to leave Castalia and make a more practical contribution in the outside world. He had been bothered by the esotericism and elitism of Castalia and felt that a Magister of his stature should assume more social responsibility. Knecht's tragic death at the end of the novel reflects Hesse's own ambivalent attitude toward the social commitment of the artist as well as his self-questioning position in regard to aestheticism. By contrast, Hesse never questioned the value of art as a means of maintaining social values and imparting wisdom against the barbarism of his times.

After World War II, Hesse's own artistic productivity declined out of choice. He preferred to spend his time responding to demands from the outside world while trying to lead a "normal" private life. After 1945 Hesse had suddenly become famous and was sought out by critics, the media, and literary societies, not to mention numerous friends who could now travel freely in Europe. Nor could he avoid controversy. First came a difficult period in which it seemed that Hesse's works might be banned by the American occupying forces simply because they had not been banned by the Nazis. This censorship never occurred, and Hesse wrote numerous political essays about the necessity for moral regeneration in Germany and for overcoming the militaristic mentality. Four of his most important essays of the immediate postwar period were later published in *War and Peace (Krieg und Frieden)* in 1949.

Hesse always suspected that his admonishments would not be taken seriously in Germany. Immediately following the war, however, he was so disappointed and embittered by the continuation of certain forms of fascist and materialist thought in Germany and by his disputes with the Allied authorities that his nerves became frayed. Even though he received the Goethe Prize in 1946, followed by the Nobel Prize, also in 1946, he became so depressed that he again withdrew to a sanatorium for treatment. Only in March 1947 did he feel sufficiently healthy to return to Montagnola, where he spent the last fifteen years of his life following his artistic pursuits and nursing his frail health.

Although many writers, politicians, and friends called upon Hesse to take an active role in politics in the name of peace, he continued to refuse to commit himself to any one party, country, or ideology. In reviews, essays, and letters, he wrote about both the dangers of American capitalism for Europe—what he called the Americanizing of Europe—and the totalitarian threat of the Soviet Union. It was clear that his non-involvement had a great deal to do with his "politics" of nonviolence. Hesse refused to compromise his integrity or support causes that might be manipulated for nefarious ends. Humanity came first for him, not a political party or movement, and he believed peace could be achieved only if people were given freedom to realize their humanitarian impulses.

As the cold war escalated in the 1950s, Hesse withdrew from the world's stage and kept his opinions to himself. Except for writing some short stories, he spent most of his time painting, maintaining a vigorous correspondence, and fighting various debilitating illnesses. He had always suffered periodic spells of depression and physical exhaustion; after 1950 his eyes began to weaken, and in 1955 a heart condition prevented him from leaving the area around Montagnola. At about this time the doctors discovered he was suffering from leukemia, which became virulent at the end of 1961. Thanks to blood transfusions, he was able to live fairly comfortably until his death on August 8, 1962.

. . .

In many respects Hesse's great achievement as a writer was in the domain of fairy tales and fantasy literature. He wrote his very first fairy tale, called "The Two Brothers" *("Die beiden Brüder")*, when he was only ten years old, and his first significant period as a writer, 1895–1900, was a time when he immersed himself in reading and emulating European and Oriental fairy-tale writers. Like no other writer of the twentieth century, all of Hesse's works drew in some way on the great fairy-tale traditions of Europe and the Orient. He was most successful as a writer when he combined different traditions with his own personal experiences and endowed them with an unusual lyrical and sometimes sentimental but nonetheless strong note of refusal.

Hesse was the fairy-tale writer of the "modern romantic" refusal par excellence, a notion conceived by the philosopher Herbert Marcuse to indicate the resolute unwillingness of individuals to yield to social and political forces that tend to instrumentalize them and make them into objects of manipulation. Hesse's heroes refuse to comply with the norms of bourgeois life, and they reject the hypocrisy and superficiality of European society corrupted by materialism. They are loners, rebels, poets, intellectuals, painters, and eccentrics who represent the soul of a humanitarian tradition under siege. It was in order to commemorate the struggles of such marginal types who survive on the fringes of society, alienated by the increase of industrialization and capitalism, that Hesse experimented with the fairy-tale genre. Like his characters, he was tormented by arbitrary social codes, the rigid Manichaean principles of the Judeo-Christian tradition, and the onslaught of technology.

It is possible to consider Hesse's tales in chronological order and demonstrate how each reflected a phase of his own life and how each of his protagonists was a variation of his own personality. Such an approach to his fairy tales, though defensible and valid, would do these works an injustice, however. Hesse was a remarkably conscious artist who used fairy-tale conventions to gain distance from his personal problems. He found the symbolic forms, motifs, and *topoi* useful for generalizing his experiences and endowing them with multiple meanings through plots reminiscent of ancient Oriental and German romantic tales.

One of the first fairy tales that he ever published is a good example of the technique that he would refine over and over again to realize his own peculiar form of the modern fairy tale. This fairy tale is actually a novella entitled *Lulu,* and it appeared as part of *The Posthumous Writings and Poems of Hermann Lauscher* (1900). On the one hand, the incidents in this fairy tale are related to a summer vacation that Hesse spent with friends in August 1899. On the other hand, the work is an aesthetic experiment that reveals his great debt to E.T.A. Hoffmann and the German romantics. The tale concerns the poet Lauscher and two friends who meet in a village during the summer. Both fall in love with a waitress named Lulu, who works in the village inn. They have strange encounters with an eccentric philosopher, who also seems to be strangely involved with Lulu. At the same time, one of the friends has had a fairy-tale dream about a princess named Lilia, who is threatened by a witch named Zischel-gift. Lauscher and his friends soon conflate the identities of Lulu and Lilia, and the boundaries between reality, dream, and fairy tale dissolve. Their pursuit of Lulu/Lilia is transformed into a pursuit of the blue flower, a well-known romantic symbol of ideal love and utopia. Lauscher and his friends are brought back to reality, however, when a fire breaks out in the inn and Lulu and the philosopher mysteriously disappear.

This fairy-tale novella contains poems by Lauscher and his friends and is written in a hyperbolic sentimental manner that makes the story and characters at times appear contrived. Yet despite this artificiality, the novella is the key to understanding the narrative technique that Hesse developed more artistically in the fairy tales that followed. Like the German romantic writers Wilhelm Heinrich Wackenroder, Ludwig Tieck, Novalis, Joseph von Eichendorff, and E.T.A. Hoffmann—all major influences on his work—Hesse sought to blend the worlds of reality and imagination. All kinds of experiences assume startling symbolical meanings that demand interpretation if the Hesse protagonist is to know himself. Only by seeking to go beyond the veil of symbols can the essence of life be grasped. But first the ordinary has to be appreciated as extraordinary through the artful transformation of experience, and this is the task of all of Hesse's heroes. The obstacles confronting them are not the traditional witches, ogres, tyrants, and magicians but rather science, materialism, war, alienation, and philistinism. Like the German romantics before him, Hesse chose the fairy-tale form paradoxically to demonstrate how difficult it is to make life into a fairy tale, and he preferred tragic and open endings to the uplifting harmonious endings and perfect closure of classical fairy tales. Yet he did not abandon the utopian "mission" of the traditional fairy tale, for even though many of his narratives are tragic, they leave us with a sense of longing, intended to arouse us so that we might contemplate changing those conditions that bring about the degradation of humanity.

In his early tales, such as "The Dwarf" (1904), "Shadow Play"

(1906), and "Dr. Knoegle's End" (1910), Hesse described the process by which harmless individuals with poetic sensibilities are crushed by narrow-minded people. The central question in all his writings concerns whether the individual with a poetic nature, who represents more than Hesse himself as an artist, will be able to come into his own when social conditions are adverse to the arts and humanity. In only a few of his tales, such as "The Beautiful Dream" (1912), "The Poet" (1913), "Flute Dream" (1914), "The Forest Dweller" (1917), and "The Painter" (1918), did Hesse portray young men who rebel, seek, and realize their full potential as artistic human beings. Yet even after successfully undergoing hard experiences and apprenticeships, they are alone in the end, never married, never wealthy. The poet appears to be totally isolated and able to find fulfillment only in his art. Other characters similar to these poet types—like Martin in "Shadow Play" (1906), Augustus in "Augustus" (1913), the climber in "The Difficult Path" (1917), Anselm in "Iris" (1918)—lead terribly painful lives and must come to terms with their alienation. They find solace in death by returning to what appears to be home or the eternal mother.

To a certain extent it is embarrassing to read Hesse's portrayal of women and their roles. Like many German writers of his genera-tion, Hesse depicted women either as gentle muses who have a mysterious wisdom that men do not possess, or as strong and sensitive martyrs who are in contact with the source of knowledge. When female characters appear in his tales—and very few have any substance—they are generally there to save the men from themselves. Whether young or old, they are associated with eternal harmony, Isis, Maya, truth, and home. All are artificial constructs that seem to smack of an infantile fixation on the mother; yet they represent more than Hesse's oedipal attachment to his mother or the Oedipus complex itself.

For Hesse, the mother figure and home represented lost innocence, a feeling of oneness with nature and one's own body that is destroyed by the alienating process of civilization, often represented by norms of material success and science. Given the cruel nature of the institutions of socialization and civilization, which were governed mainly by men, Hesse believed that conformity to their rules and regulations would lead to the perversion of humanity. Adjustment to a sick reality was in itself a sick thing to do. Therefore his protagonists break away from society, often aided by sagacious elderly men on the margins of society. But these men do not suffice because, nonconformists themselves, they cannot help the young men achieve a harmony of opposites. They can only point out the direction that the protagonist must take, often toward a "mystical mother." The return to the mother at the end of some of Hesse's tales is a recognition of what has been lost in the process of "civilization" and a refusal to go along with this process any longer. The mother figure is consequently a symbol of refusal to accept a "masculine" or "logical" way of regarding the world that leads to war and destruction.

As we know, Hesse was a staunch opponent of the military, masculine aggressiveness, and war. Some of his very best fairy tales—such as "A Dream About the Gods" (1914), "Strange News from Another Planet" (1915), "If the War Continues" (1917), "The European" (1918), and "The Empire" (1918)—contain passionate critiques of the barbaric mentality and the conditions that engender violence and conflict. Hesse believed, as one can glean from both "The European" and "The Empire," that nationalism is the most dangerous force because it can inspire people to obsessively seek power and become caught up in war for war's sake. He never pointed his finger at any particular nation as the major perpetrator of wars. Rather, Hesse believed that there are certain cycles in the world—portrayed in "The City" (1910) and "Faldum" (1916)—that reflect general conditions that either enhance the potential for developing humane societies or lead to barbarism. As his stories reveal, he was convinced that the divisive forces of technology, nationalism, totalitarianism, and capitalism were most detrimental to individual freedom and peaceful coexistence. Therefore his fairy tales repeatedly point to the possibilities of individual refusal and the goal of inner peace.

Taken together, Hesse's fairy tales, written between 1900 and 1933, record both his own personal journey and the social and political conflicts in Europe of that period. Although he often followed the traditional form of the folk tale in works like "The Three Linden Trees" (1912) or used some of Hans Christian Andersen's techniques, as in "Conversation with an Oven" (1920) and "Inside and Outside" (1920), he generally preferred to break with the plots and conventions of classical fairy tales to experiment with science fiction, the grotesque and macabre, romantic realism, and dreams, thereby generating his own unique form and style. Here, too, Hesse followed in the tradition of romantic refusal. To be sure, some of his aesthetic experiments lapse into narcissistic musings, as in "A Dream Sequence" (1916), but Hesse's best tales are filled with a keen sense of longing for a home that is the utopian counterpart to the horrors we continue to witness in our present day and age.

A Note on the Texts

~❦~

*M*ost of Hesse's fairy tales were printed in journals or newspapers before they appeared in book form. Only eight were gathered together for publication in *Märchen* (1919). Since he himself would have refused to categorize which of his tales were "truly" fairy tales, it would be foolish here to try to make clear-cut distinctions as to which of his narratives properly fit the genre. The present volume is an endeavor to collect as many of his tales as possible that were obviously associated with the modern fairy-tale tradition. Due to difficulties in obtaining permission for five of the tales, this is not a complete edition of Hesse's fairy tales, but it is the first English edition to include the majority of them, many of which have never appeared in translation before.

The following bibliography lists the original German title, the journal or newspaper where it was first published, and the date of publication of each tale.

The Dwarf—*Der Zwerg,* first published as *Donna Margherita und der Zwerg Filippo,* in *Die Rheinlande* (1904)

Shadow Play—*Schattenspiel,* in *Simplicissimus* (1906)

A Man by the Name of Ziegler—*Ein Mensch mit Namen Ziegler,* in *Simplicissimus* (1908)

The City—*Die Stadt,* in *Licht und Schatten* (1910)

Dr. Knoegle's End—*Doktor Knögles Ende,* in *Jugend* (1910)

The Beautiful Dream—*Der schöne Traum,* in *Licht und Schatten* (1912)

The Three Linden Trees—*Drei Linden,* in *Die Alpen* (1912)

Augustus—*Augustus,* in *Die Grenzboten* (1913)

The Poet—*Der Dichter,* first published as *Der Weg zur Kunst,* in *Der Tag* (1913)

Flute Dream—*Flötentraum,* first published as *Märchen,* in *Licht und Schatten* (1914)

A Dream About the Gods—*Ein Traum von den Göttern,* in *Jugend* (1914)

Strange News from Another Planet—*Merkwürdige Nachricht von einem anderen Stern,* in *Neue Zürcher Zeitung* (1915)

Faldum—*Faldum,* first published as *Das Märchen von Faldum,* in *Westermanns Monatshefte* (1916)

A Dream Sequence—*Eine Traumfolge,* in *Die weissen Blätter* (1916)

The Forest Dweller—*Der Waldmensch,* first published as *Kubu,* in *Simplicissimus* (1917)

The Difficult Path—*Der schwere Weg,* in *Die Neue Rundschau* (1917)

If the War Continues—*Wenn der Krieg noch zwei Jahre dauert,* first published as *Im Jahre 1920,* in *Neue Zürcher Zeitung* (1917)

A Note on the Texts

The European—Der Europäer, in *Neue Zürcher Zeitung* (1918)

The Empire—Das Reich, in *Neue Zürcher Zeitung* (1918)

The Painter—Der Maler, in *Vossische Zeitung* (1918)

The Fairy Tale About the Wicker Chair—Märchen vom Korbstuhl, in
Wieland (1918)

Iris—Iris, in *Die Neue Rundschau* (1918)

ACKNOWLEDGMENTS

As in other instances, Linda Gross has been the guiding spirit and force behind this book. Not only did she encourage me to develop the Hesse project, but she also did a superb job of advising me and editing the manuscript throughout its different phases. In addition I should like to express my gratitude to Janet Biehl, whose thorough copyediting improved the translation immensely, and to Carol Dines, my wife, who read through various drafts and added "magic" touches to the tales.

JACK ZIPES
Minneapolis, 1995

The

Fairy Tales

of

Hermann

Hesse

THE
DWARF

One evening down on the quay the old storyteller Cecco began telling the following tale—

If it is all right with you, ladies and gentlemen, I shall tell you a very old story about a beautiful lady, a dwarf, and a love potion, about fidelity and infidelity, love and death, all that is at the heart of every adventure and tale, whether it be old or new.

Signorina Margherita Cadorin, daughter of the nobleman Batista Cadorin, was in her day the most beautiful among all the beautiful women of Venice. The poems and songs dedicated to her were more numerous than the curved bay windows of the palaces on the Grand Canal and more plentiful than the gondolas that swim between the Ponte del Vin and the Ponte della Dogana on a spring evening. Hundreds of young and old lords from Venice and Murano, and just as many from Padua, could not close their eyes for a single night without dreaming about her; nor could they wake up the next morning without yearning for a glimpse of her. Moreover, there were few among the fine young ladies in the entire city who had not been jealous of Margherita Cadorin at one time or another. Since it is impossible for me to describe her, I shall content myself with saying that she was blond, tall, and slender like a young cypress, that her hair flattered the air, and the soles of her feet, the ground, and that Titian, when he saw her, is said to have wished that he could spend an entire year and paint nothing and nobody but this woman.

With regard to clothes, lace, Byzantine gold brocade, precious stones, and jewels, the beautiful signorina lacked nothing. On the contrary, her palace was rich and splendid. The oriental rugs were thick and colorful. The closets contained plenty of silver utensils. The tables glistened with their fine damask and glorious porcelain. The floors of the rooms were filled with beautiful mosaics, and the ceilings and walls were covered partially with Gobelin tapestries made of brocade and silk, and partially with bright and attractive paintings. In addition, there were plenty of gondolas and gondoliers.

Of course, all these expensive and pleasant things could also be found in other houses. There were larger and richer palaces than hers, more abundantly filled closets, more expensive utensils, rugs, and jewels. At that time Venice was very wealthy, but young Margherita possessed a gem all to herself that was the envy of many people richer than she. It was a dwarf by the name of Filippo, a fantastic little fellow, just about three feet tall with two humps on his back. Born in Cyprus, Filippo could speak only Greek and Syrian when Vittoria Battista brought him home one day from a trip. Now, however, he spoke such a pure Venetian dialect that it seemed as if he had been born on the Riva or in the parish of San Giobbe. As beautiful and slender as his mistress was, the dwarf was just that ugly. If she stood next to his crippled figure, she appeared doubly tall and majestic, like the tower of an island church next to a fisherman's hut. The dwarf's hands were wrinkled, brown, and bent at the joints. His gait was unspeakably ridiculous; his nose, much too large; his feet, wide and pigeon-toed. Yet when dressed, he walked like a prince garbed in pure silk and gold.

Just this outward appearance made the dwarf a gem. It was perhaps impossible to find anyone who cut a figure stranger and more comical, not only in Venice but in all of Italy, including Milan. And many a royal king, prince, or duke would certainly have been glad to pay gold for the little man, if he had been for sale.

Now there may have indeed been dwarfs just as small and ugly as Filippo at certain courts or in rich cities, but he was far superior to them with regard to brains and talent. If everything depended on intelligence alone, then this dwarf could easily have had a seat on the Council of Ten or been head of an embassy. Not only did he speak three languages, but he also had a great command of history and was clever at inventing things. He was just as good at telling old stories as he was at creating new ones, and he knew how to give advice, play mean tricks, and make people laugh or cry, if he so desired.

On pleasant days, when Margherita sat on her balcony to bleach her wonderful hair in the sun, as was generally the fashion at that time, she was always accompanied by her two chambermaids, her

African parrot, and the dwarf Filippo. The chambermaids moistened and combed her long hair and spread it over a large straw hat to bleach it. They sprayed it with the perfume of roses and Greek water, and while they did this, they told her about everything that was happening or about to happen in the city: the deaths, the celebrations, the weddings, births, thefts, and funny incidents. The parrot flapped its beautifully colored wings and performed its three tricks: It whistled a song, bleated like a goat, and cried out, "Good night!" The dwarf sat there, squatting motionless in the sun, and read old books and scrolls, paying very little attention to the gossip of the maids or to the swarming mosquitoes. Then on each of these occasions, after some time had passed, the colorful bird would nod, yawn, and fall asleep; the maids would chatter ever more slowly and gradually turn silent and finish their chores quietly with tired gestures, for is there a place where the noon sun burns hotter or makes one drowsier than on the balcony of a Venetian palace? Yet the mistress would become sullen and give the maids a good scolding if they let her hair become too dry or touched it too clumsily. Finally the moment would arrive when she cried out, "Take the book away from him!"

The maids would take the book from Filippo's knees, and the dwarf would look up angrily, but he would also manage to control himself at the same time and ask politely what his mistress desired.

And she would command, "Tell me a story!"

Whereupon the dwarf would respond, "I need to think for a moment," and he would reflect.

Sometimes he would take too much time, so that she would yell and reprimand him. However, he would calmly shake his heavy head, which was much too large for his body, and answer with composure, "You must be patient a little while longer. Good stories are like those noble wild animals that make their home in hidden spots, and you must often settle down at the entrance of the caves and woods and lie in wait for them a long time. Let me think!"

When he had thought enough and began telling his story, however, he let it all flow smoothly until the end, like a river streaming down a mountain in which everything is reflected, from the small green grass to the blue vault of the heavens. The parrot would sleep and dream, at times snoring with his crooked beak. The small canals would lie motionless so that the reflections of the houses stood still like real walls. The sun would burn down on the flat roof, and the maids would fight desperately against their drowsiness. But the dwarf would not succumb to sleep. Instead, as soon as he exhibited his art, he would become a king. Indeed, he would extinguish the sun and soon lead his transfixed mistress through dark, terrifying woods, then to the cool blue bottom of the sea, and finally through the streets of exotic and fabulous cities, for he had learned the art of storytelling in the Orient, where storytellers are highly regarded. Indeed, they are magicians and play with the souls of their listeners as a child plays with his ball.

His stories rarely began in foreign countries, for the minds of listeners cannot easily fly there on their own powers. Rather, he always began with things that people can see with their own eyes, whether it be a golden clasp or a silk garment. He always began with something close and contemporary. Then he led the imagination of his mistress imperceptibly wherever he wanted, talking first about the people who had previously owned some particular jewels or about the makers and sellers of the jewels. The story floated naturally and slowly from the balcony of the palace into the boat of the trader and drifted from the boat into the harbor and onto the ship and to the farthest spot of the world. It did not matter who his listeners were. They would all actually imagine themselves on this voyage, and while they sat quietly in Venice, their minds would wander about serenely or anxiously on distant seas and in fabulous regions. Such was the way that Filippo told his stories.

Aside from reciting wonderful fairy tales mostly from the Orient, he also gave reports about real adventures and events from the past and present, about the journeys and misfortunes of King Aeneas, about rich Cyprus, about King John, about the magician Virgilius, and about the impressive voyages of Amerigo Vespucci. On top of everything, he himself knew how to invent and convey the most remarkable stories. One day, as his mistress glanced at the slumbering parrot, she asked, "Tell me, oh Know-It-All, what is my parrot dreaming about now?"

The dwarf thought for a moment and then related a long dream as if he himself were the parrot. As soon as he was finished, the bird woke up, bleated like a goat, and flapped its wings. Another time the lady took a small stone, threw it over the railing of the terrace into the canal, where it splashed into the water, and asked, "Now, Filippo, where is my stone going?"

Immediately the dwarf related how the stone in the water drifted down to the jellyfish, crabs, oysters, and fish, to the drowned fishermen and water spirits, imps and mermaids, whose lives and experiences he knew quite well and could describe in precise detail.

Even though Signorina Margherita, like many other rich and beautiful women, was arrogant and cold, she had great affection for her dwarf and made certain that everyone treated him nicely and honorably. Yet there were times when she herself took pleasure in tormenting him a little. After all, he was her property. Sometimes she

took all his books away or locked him in the cage of her parrot. Other times she would make him stumble and trip on the floor of a large hall. Since she did not do this out of meanness, Filippo never complained, but he also never forgot a thing, and sometimes he wove little allusions, hints, and insinuations in his fables and fairy tales, which his mistress tolerated with composure. She took care not to irritate him too much, for everyone believed that the dwarf possessed secret knowledge and forbidden powers. People were certain that he knew how to talk with many kinds of animals and that his predictions about the weather and storms were always correct. He kept silent for the most part, however, and if people bothered him with questions, he would shrug his sharp shoulders and try to shake his stiff head, and the questioners would soon forget their business out of pure laughter.

Just as every human being has a need to be attached to some living soul and to show love, Filippo was also attached, and it was not just to his books. Rather, he had a strange friendship with a small black dog that belonged to him and slept with him. It had been given to Signorina Margherita as a gift by one of her rejected suitors and had been passed on to the dwarf by his mistress under most unusual circumstances. On the very first day that the dog arrived, it had an unfortunate accident and was struck by a closing trap door. The dog had broken a leg and was supposed to be put to death. But the dwarf interceded on its behalf and received the animal as a gift. Under his care the dog recovered and, out of great gratitude, became deeply attached to its savior. Nevertheless, the healed leg remained crooked so that the dog limped and was thus even better suited to its malformed master. Consequently, Filippo was to hear many a joke about this.

Though this love between dwarf and dog seemed ridiculous to many people, it was no less sincere and warm for all that, and I believe that not many a rich lord was as deeply loved by his best friends as this bow-legged miniature hound was by Filippo, who named the dog Filippino and then shortened it to the pet name Fino. Indeed, he treated the dog as tenderly as a child, talked to him, brought him delicious treats, let him sleep in his little dwarf bed, and frequently played with him for a long time. In short, he transferred all the love of his poor and homeless life to the clever animal and was mocked for it a great deal by the servants and his mistress. But as you will soon see, this affection for the dog was not ridiculous at all. In fact, it led to a great disaster, not only for the dog and the dwarf but also for the entire house. So I hope that you are not annoyed by my talking too much about this small lame lapdog. As you well know, small things in life often cause the greatest catastrophes.

While many distinguished, rich, and handsome men cast their eyes on Margherita and carried her picture in their hearts, she herself remained so proud and cold, it was as if men did not exist. Indeed, until the death of her mother, a certain Donna Maria from the House of the Giustiniani, she had been raised in a very strict and rigid way. Moreover, she was born with a supercilious nature that was opposed to love, and she was justifiably regarded as not only the most beautiful woman of Venice but the most cruel. A young nobleman from Padua was killed in a duel with an officer from Milan on her account, and when she was told that the dead man's last words were intended for her, it was impossible to detect even the slightest shadow on her white forehead. She continually mocked all the sonnets dedicated to her. When two suitors from the most respectable families of the city ceremoniously asked for her hand at almost the same time, she compelled her father to reject them, in spite of the fact that her father was in favor of her marrying either of the men. A prolonged family dispute resulted from this affair.

But the tiny winged god of love is a cunning rascal and does not like to lose his prey, especially such a beautiful one. Now as we know from experience, proud and unapproachable women are precisely the ones who fall in love the fastest and with the most passion, just as the warmest and most glorious spring usually follows the hardest winter. So it was with Margherita, who lost her heart to a young cavalier and seafarer during a celebration in the Muranese gardens. He had just returned from the Levant, and his name was Baldassare Morosini. He soon caught Margherita's attention, and it was apparent that he was just as noble and majestic as she was. Whereas she was light and slender, he was dark and strong, and one could see that he had been on the seas and abroad for a long time and was disposed toward adventure. His thoughts flickered over his tan brow like lightning, and his dark eyes burned intensely and sharply over his aquiline nose.

It was impossible for him not to notice Margherita, and once he learned her name, he immediately arranged to be introduced to her and her father. And indeed, all this transpired with many flattering words and polite gestures. Then he stayed as close to her as propriety allowed until the end of the party, which lasted until midnight, and she listened to his words more eagerly than to the gospel, even when they were addressed to other people and not herself. As you may imagine, Baldassare was asked more about his voyages, deeds, and constant dangers than anything else, and he spoke of them with such decorum and serenity that everyone took great pleasure in listening to him. In reality all his stories were dedicated to one listener only, and she did not let one breath of his words escape her. With such ease did he talk about the strangest adventures that his listeners were led to believe they themselves must have actually experienced them. Nor did he place himself too much in the foreground, as seafarers, especially young ones, are wont to do. Only one time, when he was recounting a battle with African pirates, did he mention a wound—its scar ran diagonally across his left shoulder—and Margherita held her breath as she listened, fascinated and horrified at the same time.

At the end of the party he accompanied her and her father to their gondola, bade them farewell, and remained standing for a long time, gazing at the torch of the gondola as it glided over the dark lagoon. Only after he completely lost sight of the gondola did he return to his friends in the arbor of a tavern, where the young cavaliers, and also some pretty maids, spent the rest of the warm night drinking yellow Greek wine and sweet red. Among them was Giambattista Gentarini, one of the richest young men of Venice, who enjoyed life to the hilt. He approached Baldassare, touched his arm, and said with a laugh, "I had really hoped that you would tell us tonight about your amorous affairs during your voyages! Now there's probably no chance of this since the beautiful Cadorin has stolen your heart. But you better know that this beautiful lady is made of stone and has no soul. She's like one of Giorgione's paintings. Though you truly can't find much fault with his women, they're not made out of flesh and blood. They exist only for our eyes. Seriously, I advise you to keep away from her—or would you like to become the laughingstock of the Cadorinian family and the third to be rejected?"

In response, Baldassare only laughed and did not feel compelled to justify his actions. He emptied a couple of glasses of the sweet, oil-colored Cyprian wine and went home earlier than his friends.

The very next day at the proper hour, he visited old Signore Cadorin in his small pretty palace and sought as best he could to make himself acceptable and to win the father's favor. In the evening he serenaded Margherita with many singers and musicians and had some success—she stood listening at the window and even appeared for a short time on the balcony. Naturally, the entire city began talking about this right away, and the idlers and scandal-mongers knew of the engagement and the supposed day of the wedding even before Morosini put on his best suit to ask Margherita's father for her hand. In fact, he spurned the custom of that time, and instead of sending one or two of his friends to present his case, he appeared himself before the father. Soon enough, however, the gossips, who always know it all, could take pleasure in seeing their predictions confirmed.

When Baldassare went to Margherita's father and expressed his wish to become his son-in-law, Cadorin was, to say the least, most embarrassed.

"By almighty God, my dear young man," he said imploringly, "I don't underestimate the honor that your proposal means for my family. Nevertheless, I beg you not to proceed with your plans. It would spare you and me much grief and trouble. You've been away from Venice a long time on voyages, so you don't know how many problems this unfortunate girl has caused me. Indeed, she has recently rejected two honorable proposals without any reason whatsoever. She doesn't care about love and men. And I confess that I have spoiled her somewhat and am too weak to be severe with her and break her stubbornness."

Baldassare listened politely, but he did not retract his proposal. On the contrary, he took great pains to soothe the anxious old man and put him in a more cheerful mood. Finally, Signore Cadorin promised to speak to his daughter.

You can surely imagine how the lady responded. To be sure, she raised some minor objections and put on quite a show of arrogance in front of her father, but in her heart she had said yes even before she was asked. Immediately after he received her answer, Baldassare appeared with a delicate and valuable gift, placed a gold wedding ring on the finger of his fiancée, and kissed her beautiful proud lips for the first time.

Now the Venetians had something to gaze at, to talk about, and to envy. No one could remember ever seeing such a magnificent couple. Both were tall and had fine figures. The young lady was barely a hair's breadth smaller than he was. She was blond; he was dark; and both held their heads high and free. Indeed, when it came to a noble and superior bearing, they could compete with the best.

But one thing did not please the splendid bride, and it occurred when Baldassare told her that he would soon have to travel to Cyprus again in order to conclude some important business. The wedding was to take place upon his return. The entire city was looking forward to it already, as though it were a public celebration. In the meantime the couple enjoyed their happiness without much disturbance. Baldassare missed no opportunity to organize events for her, to give her gifts, to serenade her, and to bring about surprises, and he was with Margherita as often as possible. They even took some discreet rides together in a covered gondola, though this was strictly forbidden.

If Margherita was supercilious and a little bit cruel, it was not surprising given the fact that she was a spoiled young aristocratic lady. She was matched, however, by her bridegroom, who was basically arrogant and not used to being considerate toward others. Nor had his work as a sea merchant and his early successes in life made him any gentler. Though he had courted Margherita arduously as a pleasant and demure young man, his true character and ambitions surfaced only after he had attained his goal. Naturally impulsive and overbearing, as seafarer and rich merchant he had become completely accustomed to fulfilling his own desires and to not caring about other people. Right from the beginning it was strange how repulsive he found many of the things that surrounded his bride, especially the parrot, the little dog Fino, and the dwarf Filippo. Whenever he saw these three, he became irritated and did everything he could to torture them or to get them away from their mistress. And whenever he entered the house and his strong voice could be heard on the winding stairs, the little dog howled and fled and the parrot cried and flapped its wings. The dwarf contented himself with withdrawing and remaining stubbornly quiet. To be just, I must say that Margherita put in many a good word, if not for the animals then certainly for Filippo, and she sometimes tried to defend the poor dwarf. Of course, she did not dare to offend her lover and could not or would not prevent many small torturous and cruel acts.

In the case of the parrot, its life came to a quick end. One day as Signore Morosini was tormenting it by picking at it with his small cane, the enraged bird pecked his hand with its strong and sharp beak until a finger bled. In response, Morosini had the bird strangled and thrown into the narrow dark canal in back of the house, and nobody mourned it.

Soon after this, things did not go much better for the little dog Fino. Whenever the bridegroom entered Margherita's house, the dog hid in a dark corner of the stairs, as it had learned not to be seen when it heard the sound of this man's footsteps. But one time—when perhaps Baldassare had forgotten something in his gondola and did not trust any of his servants to fetch it—he turned around at the top of a flight and walked unexpectedly down the stairs. The frightened Fino barked loudly in his surprise and jumped about so frantically and clumsily that he almost caused the signore to fall. Baldassare stumbled and reached the corridor floor at the same time that the dog did, and since the frightened little animal scrambled right up to the entrance, where some wide stone steps led into the canal, Baldassare gave him a violent kick along with some harsh curses. As a result, the little dog was propelled far out into the water.

Just at this moment the dwarf appeared in the doorway. He had heard Fino's barking and whimpering, and now he stood next to Baldassare, who looked on with laughter as the little lame dog tried anxiously to swim. At the same time the noise drew Margherita to the balcony of the first floor.

"Send the gondola over to him, for God's sake!" Filippo yelled to her breathlessly. "Mistress, have him fetched right away! He's going to drown! Oh Fino, Fino!"

But Baldassare laughed and commanded the gondolier, who was about to untie the gondola, to stop. Again Filippo turned to his mistress to beg her, but Margherita left the balcony just at that moment without saying a word. So the dwarf knelt down before his tormentor and implored him to let the dog live. The signore refused and turned away from him. Then with severity he ordered the dwarf to go back into the house. He himself remained on the steps of the gondola until the small gasping Fino sank beneath the water.

Filippo climbed to the top floor beneath the roof, where he sat in a corner, held his large head in his hands, and stared straight ahead. A chambermaid came to summon him to his mistress, followed by a servant. But the dwarf did not move. Later in the evening, while he was still sitting up there, his mistress herself climbed up to him with a light in her hand. She stood before him and looked at him awhile.

"Why don't you get up?" she finally asked. He did not answer. "Why don't you get up?" she asked again.

Then the stunted little man looked at her and said, "Why did you kill my dog?"

"It wasn't me who did it," she sought to justify herself.

"You could have saved him, but you let him die," the dwarf accused. "Oh my darling! Oh Fino, oh Fino!"

Then Margherita became irritated and impatiently ordered him to get up and go to bed. He obeyed her without saying a word and remained silent for three days like a dead man. He hardly ate his meals and paid no attention to anything that happened around him or that was said.

During these days the young signorina became greatly troubled. In fact, she had heard from different sources certain things about her fiancé that upset her to no end. It was said that the Signore Morosini had been a terrible philanderer on his journeys and had numerous mistresses on the island of Cyprus and in other places. Since this was really the truth, Margherita became filled with doubt and fears and contemplated Baldassare's forthcoming voyage with bitter sighs. Finally she could stand it no longer. One morning when Baldassare was in her house, she told him everything she knew and did not conceal the least of her fears.

He smiled and said, "What they have told you, my dearest and most beautiful lady, may be partly false, but most of it is true. Love is like a wave. It comes, lifts us up high, and sweeps us away without our being able to resist it. Nevertheless, I'm fully aware of what I owe my bride and the daughter of such a noble house. Therefore you need not fret. I have seen many a beautiful woman here and there and have fallen in love with many, but there is none who can compare to you."

And because a magic emanated from his strength and boldness, she calmed down, smiled, and stroked his hard brown hand. But as soon as he left, all her fears returned to haunt her. As a result, this extremely proud lady now experienced the secret, humiliating pain of love and jealousy and lay awake every night for half the night in her silken sheets.

In her distress she turned once again to her dwarf Filippo, who meanwhile had regained his composure and acted as if he had forgotten the disgraceful death of his little dog. He sat on the balcony as he had before, reading books or telling stories, while Margherita bleached her hair in the sun. Only one time did she specifically recall that incident, and that was when she asked him why he was so deeply buried in his thoughts, and he replied in a strange voice, "God bless this house, most gracious mistress, that I shall soon leave dead or alive."

"Why?" she responded.

Then he shrugged his shoulders in his ridiculous way and said,

"I sense it, mistress. The bird is gone. The dog is gone. What reason does the dwarf have for staying here?"

Thereupon she seriously forbade him ever to talk like that again, and he did not speak about it anymore. Indeed, the lady became convinced that he no longer thought about it, and she once again had complete trust in him. Whenever she talked to him about her concerns, he defended Signor Baldassare and did not reveal in any way that he held anything against the young cavalier. Consequently the dwarf regained the full friendship of his mistress.

One summer evening, as a cool wind was sweeping in from the sea, Margherita climbed into her gondola along with the dwarf and had herself rowed out into the open sea. When the gondola came near Murano, the city was swimming like a white image of a dream in the distance on the smooth, glittering lagoon. She commanded Filippo to tell a story, while she lay stretched out on the black cushion. The dwarf crouched across from her on the bottom of the gondola, his back turned toward the high bow of the vessel. The sun hung on the edge of the distant mountains, which could hardly be seen through the rosy haze. Some bells began to ring on the island of Murano. The gondolier, numb from the heat and half asleep, sluggishly moved his long rudder, and along with the rudder, his bent figure was reflected in the water laced with seaweed. Sometimes a freight barge sailed close by, or a fishing boat with a lateen sail, whose pointed triangle momentarily concealed the distant towers of the city.

"Tell me a story!" commanded Margherita, and Filippo bent his heavy head, played with the gold fringes of his silk dress-coat, deliberated a while, and told the following tale:

"During the time my father lived in Constantinople, long

before I was born, he experienced something most remarkable and unusual. At that time he was a practicing doctor and consultant in difficult cases, having learned the science of medicine and magic from a Persian who lived in Smyrna and had gained a great deal of knowledge in both fields. My father was an honest man and depended not on deception or flattery but only on his art. Nevertheless, he suffered from the envy and slander of many a swindler and quack. So he kept yearning for an opportunity to return to his homeland. On the other hand, my father did not want to travel home until he had amassed at least a small fortune, for he knew his family and relatives were languishing in poverty at home. Although he witnessed numerous deceivers and incompetent doctors grow rich without effort, he himself did not enjoy any luck. Consequently he became more and more despondent and almost gave up hope of achieving success without tricking people. Although he did in fact have many clients and had helped hundreds of people in very difficult situations, they were mostly the poor and humble, and he would have felt ashamed to accept more than a small token from them for his services.

"As a result of this miserable predicament, my father determined it was best to leave the city. He planned either to leave on foot without any money or to offer his services on board a ship. He made up his mind to wait one more month, however, because judging from the astrological charts, it seemed still possible that he might encounter some luck within this time period. Yet the month passed without anything fortunate occurring. So on the last day, he sadly packed up his meager possessions and got ready to depart the next morning.

"On the evening of the last day he wandered back and forth along the beach outside the city, and you can certainly imagine how dreary his thoughts were. The sun had long since set, and the stars were already spreading their white light over the calm sea.

"Suddenly my father heard a doleful sobbing very near him. He looked all around, but since he could see no one, he became terribly afraid, as he believed that this was an evil omen regarding his departure. When the moaning was repeated even louder, however, he took courage and called out, 'Who's there?' Immediately he heard a splashing on the bank of the sea, and when he turned in that direction, he saw a bright figure lying there in the pale glimmer of the stars. Thinking that it was a shipwrecked person or a swimmer, he went over to help and saw, to his astonishment, the most beautiful, slender mermaid, white as snow, projecting half her body out of the water. Who can describe his surprise when the nymph spoke to him in an imploring voice. 'Aren't you the Greek magician who lives on Yellow Alley?'

" 'That's me,' he answered in a most friendly way. 'What do you want from me?'

"Once more the young mermaid began to moan, stretched out her beautiful arms, and implored my father with many sobs to take pity on her and prepare a strong love potion for her because she was pining away in futile desire for her lover. She looked at him with such beautiful eyes, pleading and sad, that his heart was moved, and he decided right then and there to help her. Before he did anything, however, he asked her how she intended to reward him, and she promised him a chain of pearls so long that a woman would be able to sling it around her neck eight times. 'But you will not receive this treasure,' she continued, 'until I have seen that your magic has done its job.'

"My father did not have to worry about this, for he was certain of the power of his art. He rushed back into the city, opened up his neatly packed bundle, and prepared the desired love potion with such speed that by midnight he was back at the bank of the sea, where the mermaid was waiting for him. He handed her a tiny vial filled with the precious liquid. Then she thanked him with great emotion and told him to return to the same spot the following night in order to receive the rich reward that she had promised.

"He went away and spent the night and the next day in great expectation. Though he had not the slightest doubt about the power and effect of his potion, he was not sure whether he could depend on the word of the mermaid. With such thoughts he proceeded to the same place at nightfall. He did not have to wait long until the mermaid appeared out of the nearby waves. But my father was overcome with horror when he saw what he had helped bring about with his art. As she drew closer with a smile on her lips and extended toward him the heavy pearl chain in her right hand, he saw the corpse of an extraordinarily handsome young man in her left arm. He could tell from his clothes that the man was a Greek sailor. His face was as pale as death, and the locks of his hair swam on the waves. The mermaid caressed him tenderly and rocked him in her arms as though he were a little boy.

"As soon as my father saw this, he uttered a loud cry and cursed himself and his art, whereupon the mermaid suddenly sank into the water with her lover. The chain of pearls lay on the sand, and since he could not undo the harm that he had caused, he picked up the necklace and carried it under his coat to his dwelling, where he separated the pearls in order to sell them one by one. By the time he left for Cyprus aboardship, he had plenty of money and believed that he would never have to worry about poverty again. But the blood of an innocent man had tarnished the money, and it caused him one misfortune after another. Indeed, he was robbed of his possessions by storms and pirates and did not reach his homeland until two years later, as a shipwrecked beggar."

During the telling of this entire story, the dwarf's mistress listened with rapt attention. When Filippo finished and was silent, she did not utter a single word and remained deeply absorbed in her thoughts until the gondolier stopped and waited for the command to return home. All at once she jumped, as if startled by a dream, and signaled the gondolier to return. As she drew the curtains together to conceal herself, the rudder altered their course quickly, and the gondola flew like a black bird toward the city. The dwarf still crouched on the floor and looked calmly and seriously over the dark lagoon as if he were already thinking up another new story. Soon they arrived at the city, and the gondola sped home through the Rio Panada and the other small canals.

That night Margherita had difficulty sleeping. The story about the love potion had given her the idea—just as the dwarf had envisioned—to use the same means to capture the heart of her fiancé completely and secure his love. The next day she began to talk to Filippo about this, but not directly. Rather, she asked him all kinds of questions and was curious about how such a love potion was made, even though the preparation of its secret ingredients was no longer commonly known. She asked him whether the potion contained poisonous and harmful liquids and whether its taste was such that the drinker would suspect something. The clever Filippo answered all these questions with a certain indifference and acted as though he did not notice anything of the secret wishes of his mistress, so that she had to speak even more explicitly about her desires and finally had to ask him directly whether there was someone in Venice who was capable of making such a potion.

Then the dwarf laughed and exclaimed, "You don't trust my skills very much if you think that I didn't learn such simple beginning steps of magic from my father, who was such a great wise man."

"You can actually make such a love potion?" the lady cried with pleasure.

"There's nothing to it," responded Filippo. "But I don't understand why you should need my art when all your wishes have been fulfilled and you have one of the most handsome and richest of men as your fiancé."

But the beautiful lady continued to insist, so that he eventually proceeded to prepare a potion while pretending to resist. She gave the dwarf money to acquire the necessary herbs and secret ingredients, and she promised him a stately gift later on if everything succeeded.

After two days he finished his preparations and carried the magic potion in a small glass bottle to the table of his mistress. Since Signore Baldassare was to depart for Cyprus soon, the matter was urgent. So when Baldassare proposed a secret pleasure trip to his bride on one of the following days—nobody took walks, due to the heat, during this time of the year—it seemed to Margherita, as well as to the dwarf, the fitting occasion to test the potion.

When Baldassare's gondola arrived at the appointed hour before the gate of the house, Margherita stood ready, and she had Filippo with her. He carried a bottle of wine and a basket of peaches into the boat, and after his mistress and Signore Baldassare climbed in, he proceeded to take his place in the gondola, sitting at the feet of the gondolier. Baldassare was not pleased that Filippo was accompanying them, but he restrained himself and said nothing. He thought it better to yield to the wishes of his beloved in these final days before his departure.

The gondolier pushed off. Baldassare pulled the curtains tightly together and dined with his bride in the cabin. The dwarf sat calmly in the stern of the gondola and regarded the old high, dark houses of the Rio dei Barardi as the gondolier navigated his vessel until it reached the lagoon at the end of the Grand Canal at the old Palace Giustiniani, where there was still a small garden in those days. Today the beautiful Palace Barozzi stands there, as everyone knows.

Occasionally muffled laughter, the soft noise of a kiss, or part of a conversation could be heard coming from the cabin. Filippo was not curious. He looked out over the water toward the sunny Riva, then at the slender tower of San Giorgio Maggiore, then back at the lion pillar of the Piazzelta. At times he blinked at the hardworking gondolier or splashed the water with a twig that he had found in the bottom of the gondola. His face was as ugly and impassive as always and revealed nothing about his thoughts. Just then he was thinking about his drowned puppy Fino and the strangled parrot. He brooded on how close destruction always was to all creatures, animals as well as humans, and he realized that there is nothing we can predict or know for certain in this world except death. He thought about his father and his homeland and his entire life. His face turned scornful for a moment when he considered that wise people serve fools almost everywhere and that the lives of most people are similar to a bad comedy. He smiled as he looked at his rich silk clothes.

And while he sat there silently with a smile, everything happened that he had been waiting for all along. Baldassare's voice rang out from beneath the roof of the gondola, and right after that

Margherita called out, "Where did you put the wine and the cup, Filippo?"

Signore Baldassare was thirsty, and it was now time to bring him the potion with the wine. So the dwarf opened his small blue bottle, poured the liquid into a cup, then filled it with red wine. Margherita opened the curtains, and the dwarf offered the lady peaches and the bridegroom the wine. She threw him a questioning glance or two and seemed edgy.

Signore Baldassare lifted the cup to his lips, but he cast a glance at the dwarf standing in front of him and was suddenly filled with suspicion.

"Wait a second!" he cried. "Scoundrels like you are never to be trusted. Before I drink, I want you to taste the wine first."

Filippo did not change his expression. "The wine is good," he said politely.

But Baldassare remained suspicious. "Well, why don't you drink it?" he asked angrily.

"Forgive me, sir," replied the dwarf, "but I'm not accustomed to drinking wine."

"Well, I order you to. I won't drink one drop of this wine until you've had some."

"You needn't worry." Filippo smiled. He bowed, took the cup from Baldassare's hands, drank a mouthful, and returned the cup to him. Baldassare looked at him, and then he drank the rest of the wine with one gulp.

It was hot. The lagoon sparkled with a blinding glimmer. Once again the lovers sought out the shadow of the curtains, while the dwarf sat down sideways at the bottom of the gondola, moved his hand over his wide forehead, and winced as if he were in pain.

He knew that in one hour he would no longer be alive. The drink had been poison. A strange sensation overwhelmed his soul, which was now very close to the gate of death. He looked back at the city and remembered the thoughts that had just absorbed his attention. Silently he stared over the glistening surface of the water and pondered his life. It had been monotonous and meager—a wise man in the service of fools, a vapid comedy. As he sensed that his heartbeat was becoming irregular and his forehead was covered with sweat, he began to laugh bitterly.

Nobody paid attention. The gondolier stood there half asleep, and behind the curtains the beautiful Margherita was horrified and worried, for Baldassare had suddenly become sick and then cold. Soon he died in her arms, and she rushed out from the cabin with a loud cry of pain. Her dwarf was lying dead on the floor of the gondola, as if he had fallen asleep in his splendid silk clothes.

Such was Filippo's revenge for the death of his little dog. The return of the doomed gondola with the two dead men shocked all of Venice.

Signorina Margherita went insane but still lived many years more. Sometimes she sat by the railing of her balcony and called out to each gondola or boat that passed, "Save him! Save the dog! Save little Fino!" Everyone knew her, however, and paid her no attention.

Shadow
Play

❦

The wide facade of the castle was made of light stone, and its large windows looked out over the marshes of the Rhine and, farther away, at a bright and breezy landscape of water, reeds, and meadows, and much farther away, at the blue mountains. This ridge of mountains formed a delicate swinging arch that the path of the clouds followed, and only when there was a warm wind could one see the light castles and farmsteads shining small and white in the distant mountains. The front of the castle was reflected in the gently flowing water, vain and content like a young woman. Its ornamental shrubs let bright green branches hang down into the water, and along the wall white gondolas rocked in the stream. The serene sunny side of the castle was not inhabited. Ever since the disappearance of the Baroness, the rooms had stood empty, except for the smallest one, in which the poet Floribert lived, as he had before. The mistress of the castle had brought shame on her husband and his castle, and now nothing was left of her large and merry entourage but the white pleasure boats and the silent poet.

After the Baron had been struck by this misfortune, he moved to the rear of the castle. Here a tremendous separate tower from Roman times eclipsed the narrow courtyard. The walls were dark and wet; the windows, narrow and low. Right next to the shady courtyard was the gloomy park with large groups of old oak trees, poplars, and birch trees.

The poet lived on the sunny side of the castle and was tranquil in his solitude. He took his meals in the kitchen and often did not see the Baron for days on end.

"We live in this castle like shadows," he said to an old friend who visited him one time and who was able to hold out for only one day in the inhospitable rooms of the dead house. In his time Floribert had written stories and gallant poems for the Baroness's company. After the dissolution of the merry entourage, he had remained there, unquestioned, because his simple soul feared the hard ways of the world and the struggle for bread more than the loneliness of the sad castle. It had been a long time since he had written any poems. Only when the west wind came, and when he saw the far circle of the blue mountains and the flock of clouds over the stream and the yellow reeds, and when he heard the tall trees rocking themselves during the evening in the old park, did he think up long poems. These, however, had no words and could never be written down. One of them was called "The Breath of God" and concerned the warm south wind, and one had the name "Consolation of the Soul" and dealt with the colorful meadows of spring. Floribert could neither sing nor recite these poems because they were without words, but he dreamed and felt them sometimes, especially in the evenings. Otherwise, he spent the majority of his days in the village, where he played with the small light-haired children and made the young women and girls laugh by tipping his hat to them as if they were aristocratic ladies. His happiest days were those on which he encountered the Lady Agnes, the beautiful Lady Agnes, the famous Lady Agnes, with the thin face of a girl. Then he would greet her with a deep bow, and the beautiful lady would nod and laugh, look at his embarrassed eyes, and move on with a smile on her face like a ray of the sun.

Lady Agnes lived in the only house that bordered on the neglected castle park. It had previously been the dwelling place of the cavaliers who had served the different barons of the family. At one point, Lady Agnes's father, who had been a forester, had received the house as a gift from the father of the present Baron because of some service he had performed. Lady Agnes had married young and had returned home as a young widow, and now, after her father's death, she lived by herself in the solitary house with a maid and a blind aunt.

Lady Agnes wore simple but beautiful new clothes made of soft colors. Her face was narrow like that of a young girl, and her dark brown hair lay in thick plaits wound around her fine head. The Baron had been in love with her even before he cast out his wife in shame, and now he loved her again. He met her in the mornings in the woods and conducted her in the evenings in the boat across the stream to a hut made out of reeds in the marshes, where her smiling girl's face lay on his beard, which had turned gray early, and her tender fingers played with his hard, gruesome hunter's hand.

Lady Agnes went to church on every holiday, prayed, and gave alms to the beggars. She visited the poor old women in the village, gave them shoes, combed the hair of their grandchildren, helped them with their sewing, and left the mild glow of a young saint behind in their huts when she departed. All the men desired Lady Agnes, and whoever pleased her and came at the right hour was guaranteed a kiss on the lips after the hand kiss, and whoever was lucky enough to be handsome might even dare to climb through her window at night.

Everyone knew this, even the Baron, and nevertheless the beautiful lady went her way smiling with the innocent look of a girl who could not be touched by the wishes of men. Sometimes a new lover appeared, courted her assiduously like an unattainable beauty, indulged himself in blissful pride upon conquering her, and was puzzled when the other men just smiled and showed no envy.

Her house stood quietly on the edge of the dark park. Covered by ramblers, it was isolated, like a fairy-tale house in the woods, and she lived there and went in and out, fresh and tender like a rose on a summer morning, a pure glow on her childlike face and the thick plaits of hair tied in a wreath around her noble head. The poor old women blessed her and kissed her hands; the men greeted her with a deep bow and smirked afterward; the children ran to her and begged and let her stroke their cheeks.

"Why are you the way you are?" the Baron would sometimes ask her and threaten her with imploring eyes.

"Do you have any rightful claim to me?" she would ask, surprised, as she braided her deep brown hair.

Of all the men, Floribert the poet loved her the most. When he saw her, his heart pounded. When he heard something bad about her, he became despondent, shook his head, and refused to believe it.

When the children talked about her, he would brighten up and listen as if he were hearing a song. His most beautiful fantasy occurred whenever he dreamed of Lady Agnes. Then he drew on everything he loved and considered beautiful—the west wind and the blue horizon and all the light meadows of spring. He envisioned her surrounded by all these things and placed all his longings and the vain fervor of his useless infantile life into this picture.

One early summer's evening, after everything had been quiet for a long time, some new life came into the dead castle. A horn blared in the courtyard. A coach drove in and stopped with a clatter. The Baron's brother had come to visit, with one servant. He was a large handsome man with a pointed beard and the wrathful eyes of a soldier. During his visit he swam in the rushing waters of the Rhine, shot at the silver sea gulls for pleasure, took frequent rides into the nearby city, and came home drunk. He teased the good poet at times and had loud arguments with his brother every few days. Indeed, he gave him advice about a thousand things. For instance, he proposed renovations and new additions to the castle and recommended changes and improvements. Of course, it was all very easy for him to talk, for he was rich, thanks to his marriage, while his brother, the Baron, was poor and had experienced mainly misfortune and trouble.

The brother's visit to the castle had been a whim, and he regretted it during the very first week that he spent there. Nevertheless, he remained and said nothing about leaving, even though the Baron would not have minded it in the least. But now his brother had seen the Lady Agnes and was pursuing her.

It was not long before the maid of the beautiful Lady Agnes brought her a new dress, which the visitor at the castle had sent as a present. It was not long before the maid was taking letters and flowers

from the visitor's servant, near the wall of the park. And after only a
few days had passed, the visitor met Lady Agnes in a forest hut at
noon on a summer's day and kissed her hand and her small mouth
and her white neck. When she went into the village, however, and he
encountered her there, he would take off his riding cap and salute her.
In turn, she curtsied to him like a girl of seventeen.

One evening shortly thereafter, when the visitor was alone by
the river, he saw a boat sail across the water carrying a rower and a
luminous woman. What the curious man could not discern for
certain in the dusk became clearer after a few days, and then he knew
more than he wanted to know. The woman whom he had held
passionately in his arms at noon in the forest hut and whom he had
ignited with his kisses, was the same woman who sailed in the evening
with his brother over the dark Rhine and disappeared with him
behind the shore of reeds.

The visitor became gloomy and had awful dreams. He had not
pursued and made love to Lady Agnes as if he were hunting a luscious
piece of game; rather he had treated her like a precious discovery.
With each kiss he had been surprised and overjoyed that so much
tender innocence had succumbed to his wooing. That is why he had
given her more than other women. She brought back his youth, and
he embraced Lady Agnes with gratitude, consideration, and tenderness—the very same woman who went down dark paths with his
brother at night. Now he bit into his beard, and his eyes were
inflamed with anger.

Untouched by all that was happening and by the invisible
tension mounting at the castle, the poet Floribert continued to
spend his days in peace and calm. He was not pleased when the
visitor teased and pestered him, although he was accustomed to

such behavior from previous visits. So he avoided the Baron's brother, spent entire days in the village or with the fishermen on the banks of the Rhine, and indulged himself with rambling fantasies in the fragrant warm evenings.

One morning Floribert noticed that the first tea roses were beginning to blossom along the wall of the castle. During the last three summers he had placed the first blossoms of these rare roses on the threshold of Lady Agnes's house, and he was now happy that he would be able to bring her this modest and anonymous greeting for the fourth time.

At noon on this same day the Baron's brother met with the beautiful lady in the birch woods. He did not ask her where she spent her evenings. He looked into her calm innocent eyes with a surprising glare that was almost cruel, and before he went away, he said, "I'm going to come to you this evening when it's dark. Leave a window open!"

"Not tonight," she said softly. "Not tonight."

"But I want to."

"Another time, all right? Not tonight. I can't."

"I'm coming tonight—tonight or never again. Do what you want."

She freed herself from his embrace and left him.

In the evening the visitor lay in wait by the river until it became dark. But no boat came. Then he went to the house of his beloved, hid in the bushes, and held his rifle over his knee.

It was quiet and warm. The jasmines smelled sweetly. The sky filled itself with small faint stars behind little white sweeping clouds. A bird sang deep in the park, a solitary bird.

When it was almost completely dark, a man came treading

softly around the corner of the house, almost creeping. His hat was pulled down over his forehead, although it was so dark that he really had no need of it. In his right hand he was carrying a bouquet of white roses that had a faint glow to them. The visitor, lying in wait, eyed him sharply and cocked the trigger of his rifle.

The man who had just arrived looked up at the house and saw that there were no lights burning. Then he went to the door, bent over, and kissed the iron handle of the lock.

Right at that moment there was a blaze, a crack, and then a weak echo inside the park. The man who had been carrying the roses fell to his knees, tumbled over backward onto the pebbles, and lay there quivering.

The marksman waited in his hiding place for a good while, but nobody came, and inside the house everything remained quiet. Then he moved cautiously to the door and bent over the man whom he had shot. The hat had fallen off his head, and the Baron's brother was astonished and upset to find the poet Floribert.

"Him, too!" he groaned and left.

The tea roses lay scattered on the ground, one of them soaked in the blood of the dead man. In the village the clock struck the hour. The sky covered itself more densely with white clouds, and against this background the enormous castle tower stretched like a standing giant that had just awakened from a sleep. The water of the Rhine sang softly in slow currents, and in the interior of the dark park the solitary bird sang and kept singing until after midnight.

A Man by the Name of Ziegler

‿᭡᭡᭡‿

There was once a young man by the name of Ziegler who lived on Brauer Street. He was one of those young men whom we meet every day time and again, but we never really notice his face because it resembles everyone else's, like a collective face.

Ziegler did everything that such people always do and was just like them. He was not untalented, but also not talented. He loved money and entertainment, liked to wear nice clothes, and was just as cowardly as most people. His life and actions were determined less by impulses and aspirations than by prohibitions and the fear of punishment. At the same time he had many honorable qualities and was in general, all things considered, a delightfully normal man who thought of himself as very nice and important. Indeed, he regarded himself, just as every person tends to do, as a unique individual, while he was really typical. He believed that his life and destiny were at the center of the world's attention, just as everyone does. He had very few doubts, and when the facts contradicted his views on life, he shut his eyes in disapproval.

As a modern man, Ziegler had an infinite respect not only for money but also for that other powerful force—science. Yet he would not have been able to say what science actually was. When he thought of science, he meant something like statistics and a little bacteriology. He knew very well how much money and honor the government gave to science. In particular he respected cancer research, for his father had died from cancer, and Ziegler assumed that this science, which had made great progress in the meantime, would not allow the same thing to happen to him.

In his appearance, Ziegler tried to distinguish himself by dressing somewhat beyond his means, and he always kept up with the particular fashion of the year. On the other hand, he looked down upon the trends of the month or season, for it would have taxed his pocket too much to keep up with them, and thus he regarded them as foolish affectations. He had great esteem for integrity and did not shy from cursing his supervisors or governments—but only among friends and in places where he felt secure. Actually, I am probably spending too much time on this description. Ziegler was truly a charming young man, and his loss is our loss. Indeed, his end came early and in a strange way that undermined all his plans and justifiable hopes for the future.

At one point, soon after he had arrived in our city, he decided that he would enjoy himself by spending an entire Sunday on an outing of some kind. He had not yet found the right companions to accompany him; nor had he joined a club, because he had difficulty making up his mind which one suited him. Perhaps this was his misfortune. It is not good for a man to be alone.

So he had no choice but to go sightseeing by himself and diligently inquired what was worth seeing in the city. After careful deliberation he decided to visit the museum of history and the zoo. The museum was free on Sunday mornings, and the zoo had a reduced price of admission in the afternoons.

Dressed in his new street clothes with a scarf that he loved very much, Ziegler went to the museum of history on Sunday morning. He brought with him his thin, elegant walking stick—a square, red-polished stick that made him look distinguished and important. To his dismay, however, the guard prevented him from taking the stick into the rooms of the museum, and he was obliged to leave it in the wardrobe.

There was a great deal to see in the large high-ceilinged rooms, and the pious visitor solemnly praised the omnipotent force of scholarly research, whose merits were on display here too, as Ziegler realized from the information printed on the exhibition cases. Indeed, these descriptions transformed old junk like rusty keys, broken copper necklaces, and similar things into astonishingly interesting items. It was wonderful to see how science took care of all this, how it controlled everything, how it knew how to control everything—oh yes, it would certainly find a remedy for cancer soon and perhaps eliminate dying altogether.

In the second room he found a glass case whose windows cast such a strong reflection that he could check his suit, haircut, collar, pleats, and tie with care and satisfaction for one whole minute. Now he could take a deep breath of relief and proceed to pay homage to some products of the old woodcutters. They were highly productive guys, he thought benevolently, even though they were very naïve. He looked at an old standing clock with ivory feet that had figures dancing a minuet at the stroke of the hour and gave it his approval. Soon, however, the entire affair began to bore him somewhat. He yawned and frequently took out his pocket watch, which he certainly could afford to show. It was made of heavy gold and was an heirloom from his father.

There was still a great deal of time before lunch, he noticed with regret, and so he went into another room that managed to arouse and recapture his curiosity. It contained objects of medieval superstition, books about magic, amulets, and the costumes of witches. In one corner there was an entire alchemical workshop with vinegar, mortar, test tubes, dried pig bladders, a pair of bellows, and many other items. This corner was partitioned off by a woolen rope. A sign indicated that the objects were not to be touched. People never read such signs very carefully, however, and Ziegler was all by himself in the room.

So without thinking, he stuck his arm over the rope and touched some of the strange things. He had heard and read a good deal about the Middle Ages and the odd superstitions held during that time. He could not understand how the people of that era could have been concerned with such childish stuff and why witches and all those other crazy things had not simply been banned. On the other hand, alchemy could certainly be excused, because it had given rise to chemistry, which became so useful. My God, if one thought about it, the goldmaker's crucible and all the ridiculous magical junk had perhaps been necessary. Otherwise, we would have neither aspirin nor gas bombs today!

Without thinking about what he was doing, Ziegler took a

tiny globule, something like a pill, in his hand. It was dried-out and weightless. He turned it between his fingers, and as he was about to put it down, he heard footsteps behind him. He turned around. Another visitor had entered the room. Ziegler was ashamed that he was holding the tiny globule in his hand, for he had definitely read the warning sign that prohibited such things. So he closed his hand, stuck it into his pocket, and left the room.

Only when he reached the street did he remember that he still had the pill. He pulled it out and thought about throwing it away. But before he did, he held it up to his nose and smelled it. Since it had a faint smell like tar that delighted him, he put the tiny globule back into his pocket.

Soon afterward he went into a restaurant, ordered something to eat, thumbed through some newspapers, adjusted his tie, and glanced at the other guests, sometimes with respect, sometimes with condescension, depending on how they were dressed. Since the meal was taking a while, Ziegler took out the alchemist's pill that he had inadvertently stolen and smelled it. Then he scratched it with the nail of his index finger. Finally he yielded to a childish desire and stuck it into his mouth. Within seconds it began dissolving, and since the taste was not unpleasant, he swallowed it down with a sip of beer. Right after this the waiter brought his meal.

At two o'clock the young man jumped off the trolley, went to the entrance of the zoo, and paid for a Sunday ticket. He went into the monkey house with a friendly smile on his face and stopped in front of the large chimpanzee cage. The big ape blinked, nodded at him in good humor, and spoke the following words in a deep voice: "How's it going, my dear brother?"

Repelled and horrified, the visitor turned quickly away and heard the ape cursing at him as he departed.

"The guy's still proud! Flatfoot! Idiot!"

Ziegler hurried over to the long-tailed monkeys, who were dancing uninhibitedly and screaming, "Give us some sugar, comrade!" But when he did not have any sugar, they became angry, mimicked him, called him a poor devil, and bared their teeth at him. Ziegler could not stand it. Stunned and confused, he fled the monkey house and headed for the moose and deer, whose behavior he expected would be much nicer.

A large splendid elk standing near the fence looked at the visitor. Now Ziegler felt deeply horrified, for ever since he swallowed the magic pill, he had understood the language of animals. So it was with the elk, who spoke with his eyes—two large brown eyes. His silent glance expressed majesty and mourning, and he showed the visitor how terribly he despised him and how superior he was to him. Indeed, Ziegler read in the silent majestic glance of the elk that he himself was nothing but dirt, a ridiculous and disgusting beast even with his hat, stick, pocket watch, and Sunday suit.

Ziegler fled the elk and went to the mountain goats. From there to the chamois, to the llama, to the gnu, to the wild boars, and to the bears. None of these animals insulted him, but they did show their disdain. He listened to them and learned from their conversations what they thought about human beings. It was terrible what they thought. They were particularly amazed that, of all things, these ugly, stinking, worthless, two-legged creatures were allowed to run around freely in their preposterous disguises.

He heard a puma hold a conversation with its cub that was full of dignity and objective wisdom seldom heard among human beings. He heard a handsome panther comment on the pack of Sunday visitors, and he was short and to the point, using speech in an aristocratic manner. He looked the blond lion straight in the eye and learned how large and wonderful the wild world was where there are no cages or human beings. He saw a falcon sitting on a dead branch, sad and proud, in torpid melancholy, and he saw the bluejays bear their captivity with dignity, a shrug of the shoulders, and humor.

In desperation, stunned and torn from all his usual ways of thinking, Ziegler turned once again to human beings. He looked for a glance that would show understanding of his predicament and anxiety. He listened in on conversations and tried to catch some consoling words, something comprehensible, something that would do him good. He observed the behavior of the numerous visitors at the zoo, trying to locate signs of their dignity, character, nobility, and superiority.

But he was disappointed. He heard their voices and words, saw their movements, gestures, and looks, and since he now saw everything through the eyes of an animal, he found nothing but a pretentious, lying, ugly society of creatures who seemed to be a preposterous mixture of different types of beasts.

Ziegler wandered frantically about, feeling completely ashamed of himself. He had long since thrown his square stick into the bushes, followed by his gloves. But when he now tossed his hat from his head, took off his boots, ripped off his tie, and pressed himself sobbing against the fence of the elk stable, he caused a great sensation, was taken into custody, and eventually brought to an insane asylum.

THE CITY

⁓⁒⁓

"We're moving onward!" exclaimed the engineer after the second
train arrived, full of people, coal, tools, and food, on the new tracks
that had been laid down the day before. The prairie glowed dimly in
the yellow sunlight. High mountain forests stood on the horizon in
the blue mist. Wild dogs and astonished buffalo watched as the
hustle and bustle began in the desolate spot, as flecks of coal and
ashes and paper and tin appeared in the virgin country. The first
airplane shrieked through the horrified land. The first rifle shot
thundered and echoed in the mountains. The first anvil sounded,
with a high pitch from the quick pounding of the hammer. A house
made of tin arose, and on the next day one made of wood, and others,
and every day new ones, and soon stone houses as well. The wild
dogs and buffalo stayed far away. The region became tame and

fertile. Already in the first spring there were rolling green fields filled with fruit. Farms, stables, and barns rose into the air. Streets cut through the wilderness.

The railroad station was finished and dedicated, followed by the government building and the bank. Hardly a few months had passed before new sister cities grew up nearby. Workers, farmers, and city people came from all over the world. Businessmen and lawyers, preachers and teachers came. A school was founded, three religious communities, two newspapers. In the west oil was discovered. The young city became rich. After another year there were pickpockets, pimps, burglars, a warehouse, a prohibition league, a Paris tailor, a Bavarian beer hall. The competition of the neighboring cities increased the tempo. Nothing more was missing, from movie theaters to associations of spiritualists. One could buy French wine, Norwegian herring, Italian sausages, English textiles, and Russian caviar in the city. Even second-rate singers, dancers, and musicians took their shows to this place.

And culture also came gradually. The city, which had been only a settlement at first, began to develop into a homeland with traditions. There was now a particular way to greet someone, to nod upon encountering someone, that was distinguished from such ways in other cities by its light and gentle manner. The men who had taken part in the founding of the city enjoyed respect and popularity. A small nobility beamed with pride. A young generation grew up. To them, the city already seemed to be an old city that had existed since eternity. The time when the first pounding of a hammer had sounded, the first murder had been committed, the first church service held, the first newspaper printed, all this lay far in the past— it was already history.

The city had risen to dominate the neighboring cities and became the capital of a large district. Solemn and venerable administrative buildings and banks, theaters and churches arose on the wide, cheerful streets, where the first house made of wooden planks and tin had stood next to piles of ash and puddles. Students sauntered to the university and the library. Ambulances drove cautiously to the hospitals. A deputy's car was noticed and greeted by onlookers. In twenty huge schoolhouses made of stone and iron, the founding day of the famous city was celebrated every year with songs and speeches. The former prairie was covered with fields, factories, and villages and traversed by twenty railroad lines. The mountains had moved closer and were connected by rail that went right into the heart of the ravines. In the mountains or far away on the seacoast, the rich people had their summer homes.

One hundred years after its foundation, an earthquake shattered and devastated the city. It sprang up once more, however, and all the wooden structures now became stone; everything small was now big; everything narrow, wide. The railroad station was the largest in the country. The stock market was the largest in the world. Architects and artists decorated the rejuvenated city with public buildings, parks, fountains, and monuments. In the course of this new century the city gained the reputation of being the most beautiful and richest in the country and a city well worth seeing. Politicians and architects, technicians and mayors of foreign cities took trips to study the buildings, water system, administration, and other institutions of the famous city. At this time the new city hall was built, one of the greatest and most glorious edifices in the world. Since this time of new wealth and municipal pride coincided fortuitously with an upsurge in popular taste, in particular a taste for architecture and sculpture, the quickly growing city became a brazen and appealing work of wonder. A broad green belt of splendid parks surrounded the inner district, whose buildings were all made out of an elegant bright green stone, and on the other side of this ring, the lines of streets and homes extended until they became lost in the vast open country. A tremendous museum had numerous visitors and admirers, and its hundred rooms, courtyards, and halls portrayed the history of the city from its origins until its most recent development. The first gigantic entrance hall of this building complex had showcases and rooms depicting the former prairie, with carefully cultivated plants and animals and exact models of the earliest impoverished dwellings, alleys, and institutions. The young people of the city strolled through this hall and observed the course of their history from the tents and wooden sheds, from the first uneven rails to the splendor of the large municipal streets. Guided and instructed by their teachers, they learned all about the glorious laws of development and progress, how fine things were made from raw material, how human beings evolved from animals, how educated people developed from wild ones, and how culture was formed out of nature.

In the next century the city reached the high point of its glory, which unfolded in rich opulence and grew rapidly until a bloody revolution of the lower classes set a limit to this splendor. The mob began by setting fire to the large oil works a few miles from the city, so that a great part of the country with factories, farms, and villages was either burned down or deserted. The city itself experienced slaughter and cruelty of all kinds, to be sure, but it continued to exist and slowly recovered once again in more sober decades. Still, it was never able to regain its earlier buoyant life. During its low period a distant country far across the seas suddenly began to flourish. It exported wheat and iron, silver and other treasures in plenitude, due to an inexhaustibly fertile soil that willingly provided everything. The new country was tremendously attractive to people of the old world, whose talents were not being adequately used, and it appealed to their wishes and goals. Cities bloomed there overnight. The woods disappeared. Waterfalls were brought under control.

The beautiful city gradually deteriorated. It was no longer the heart and brains of a world, no longer the market and stock market of numerous countries. It had to feel satisfied just keeping itself alive and not fading away in the hustle and bustle of the new times. The creative powers of business and industry, insofar as they had not moved to the distant new world, had nothing more to build and conquer and little more to trade and earn. Instead, an intellectual life took root in the now-old cultural soil. Scholars and artists as well as painters and writers were generated by this city, which had now become solemn. These individuals were the heirs of those who had at one time built the first houses on the virgin ground, and now they spent their days smiling and devoted to quiet intellectual pleasures and goals. They painted the melancholy splendor of old mossy gardens with weather-beaten statues and green waters and recited gentle verses about the distant tumult of the old heroic times and about the silent dreams of tired people in old palaces. Due to their labors, the name and the fame of the city resounded once again throughout the world. If outside the city people might be shaken by wars or occupied in carrying out great plans and works, one knew that peace reigned in this silent secluded spot and that the glory of sunken times faintly glittered in the dusk: in the quiet streets overhung with budding branches, in the facades of tremendous buildings with colors changed by the weather, in the noiseless squares, and in the crusts of fountains covered with moss run down by water playing in soft music.

For many centuries the dreaming city was venerable, a favorite place for the young world, sung about by poets and visited by lovers. However, the people felt a powerful urge more and more to move to other parts of the earth. In the city itself, the heirs of the old native families began to die out or become impoverished. Moreover, the last intellectual flowering had long since experienced its heyday, and only a decayed infrastructure was left. The smaller neighboring cities had also completely disappeared and had become silent heaps of ruin, sometimes inhabited by gypsies and escaped convicts.

In the wake of an earthquake that spared the city, the course of the river was shifted and a part of the ravaged countryside was turned into a swamp and another part into a desert. In the mountains, where the remains of ancient quarries and summer homes crumbled away, the forest climbed up—the old forest. It saw the vast region lying bare, and it began to envelop this land piece by piece, so that everything became part of its green circle. In one area it passed swiftly across a swamp of whispering green and then across a stony region with tenacious young pine trees.

In the end there were no more citizens living in the houses, only packs of vagabonds, wild churlish people who took refuge in the crooked sinking palaces of olden times and let their goats graze in the former gardens and streets. Even these last inhabitants gradually died from disease and insanity. Ever since the rise of the swamps, the entire countryside had been infested with fever and had fallen into neglect.

The remains of the old city hall, which once had been the pride of its time, were still enormous and stood very tall. They had been celebrated in songs in all languages and in numerous legends of neighboring peoples, whose cities also had long since been neglected and whose culture had decayed. The name of the city and its past glory, eerily distorted, appeared in children's tales, horror stories, and melancholy pastoral songs. Scholars of distant countries in the midst of their own golden age came sometimes to the site of the ruins on dangerous research trips, and the schoolboys of these distant countries eagerly discussed the mysteries of the old city. It supposedly had gates of pure gold and graves full of precious jewels, and the wild nomadic tribes of the region supposedly preserved the remains of thousand-year-old magic from fabulous old times.

But the forest climbed farther down from the mountains to the prairie. Lakes and rivers sprang up and dried out, and the forest moved on and gradually took over and covered the entire country, the remains of the old street walls, the palaces, the temples, and the museums. Foxes and pine marten, wolves and bears inhabited the isolated spot.

A young pine tree stood over one of the fallen palaces, not one stone of which could be seen. The pine had at one time been the most advanced messenger and precursor of the growing forest. Now, however, it looked out at the growth of young trees in front of it.

"We're moving onward!" cried a woodpecker, who hammered on the trunk of a tree and regarded the growing forest and the glorious, green progress on earth with satisfaction.

Dr. Knoegle's End

～✥～

Dr. Knoegle, a former high school teacher who had retired early from his profession and had devoted himself to private philological studies, would certainly never have come into contact with vegetarians and vegetarianism if signs of asthma and rheumatism had not at one time compelled him to follow a vegetarian diet. The result was so successful that, from then on, the teacher spent several months every year in some kind of vegetarian health spa or small hotel, mainly in the south. So in spite of his aversion to everything unusual and strange, he began mixing in circles and with individuals with whom he normally did not associate. Nor did he like their unavoidable visits to his hometown, even though they were infrequent.

For many years, Dr. Knoegle spent spring and early summer and even the autumn months in one of the many vegetarian hotels on the coast of southern France or at Lake Maggiore. He became acquainted with many different people at these places and accustomed to many things, such as people walking barefoot, long-haired apostles, fanatics who fasted all the time, and vegetarian gourmands. He made some good friends, especially among the latter, and he himself, whose ailments prevented him more and more from enjoying heavy meals, developed into a modest epicurean in the domain of vegetables and fruit. There was no way that he could be satisfied with your ordinary endive salad, and he would never have mistaken a California orange for an Italian. Otherwise, he did not take a great interest in vegetarianism, for to him it was only a cure, and if it appealed to him at all, it was sometimes due to the splendid linguistic innovations in this area that, as a philologist, he considered to be remarkable. There were vegetarians, vegetarianists, vegetabilitarians, the raw purists, the pulpists, and the mixed vegetarians.

According to the linguistic usage of the initiates, the doctor himself belonged to the mixed vegetarians, because he ate not only fruit and raw food but also cooked vegetables and even dairy products. It did not escape his notice that this diet was an abomination for true vegetarians, above all for purists, who observed a strict code of eating. However, he kept his distance from the fanatical debates conducted by disciples of true vegetarianism, and he demonstrated his status as a mixed vegetarian only through his actions, whereas many acquaintances—namely the Austrians—boasted of their particular status on their business cards.

As I said, Dr. Knoegle did not exactly fit in with these people. With his peaceful red face and broad body, he already looked much different from the disciples of pure vegetarianism, who were mainly lean and ascetic types, often dressed in fantastic clothes. Many had hair that flowed over their shoulders, and they went through life as fanatics, followers of a religion, and martyrs to their special ideals. Dr. Knoegle was a philologist and patriot. He did not support their ideas of humanity and social reform; nor did he share the strange lifestyles of his co-vegetarians. His appearance was such that the porters of the cosmopolitan hotels, who waited at the railroad stations and docks in Locarno and Pallanza and normally could smell every kind of "cabbage-head apostle" from a distance, would confidently recommend their hotels to him. They were always greatly astonished, however, when the man, who looked so respectable, gave his luggage to the porter of the Thalysia or Ceres hotel, or to the donkey master of the Monte Verita.

Nonetheless, Dr. Knoegle gradually became accustomed to the strange surroundings and felt at ease there. He was an optimist, almost an artist of life, and found many a peace-loving, red-cheeked friend among the plant-eaters of various countries. Moreover, he could sit side by side with them, consume his fresh salad and peach tranquilly, and have an agreeable table conversation, without having a fanatic of strict observance reproach him for his mixed diet or a rice-chewing Buddhist reprimand him for his religious indifference.

One time Dr. Knoegle happened to hear about the founding of the International Vegetarian Society, first through the newspapers and then through direct communication from his circle of acquaintances. This new society had acquired a tremendous piece of land in Asia Minor and had invited all the vegetarian disciples of the world to settle there permanently or to visit at reasonable prices. This undertaking was initiated by an idealistic group of German, Dutch, and Austrian plant-eaters, whose aspirations constituted a kind of

vegetarian zionism, for they aimed at recruiting followers and be-
lievers of their faith to establish their own country with their own
government somewhere in the world that already had the natural
conditions for the life that they envisioned as ideal. The settlement in
Asia Minor was just the beginning of their mission, for their appeals
were addressed to "all the friends of the vegetarian and vege-
tabilitarian lifestyle, of the nudist culture, and the movement to
reform life," and they promised so much and sounded so wonderful
that not even Dr. Knoegle could resist the nostalgic music from
paradise. He sent in his registration form to be a guest there in the
coming fall.

The land was supposed to provide plenty of fruit and vegetables. The kitchen of the large main house was directed by the author
of *Ways to Paradise,* and many people felt it was particularly nice that
they could lead their lives there without being subjected to the
mockery of the crude world. Every kind of vegetarianism and dress
reform was permitted, and there were no prohibitions except those
against meat and alcohol.

Strange refugees came from all over the world, partly to find
peace and comfort in a life suitable to their nature in Asia Minor,
and partly to earn a living and profit from those people eager for
salvation. Runaway priests and teachers from all kinds of churches
came, phony Hindus, occultists, language teachers, masseuses, mes-
merists, magicians, and faith healers. This small group of eccentric
people consisted less of swindlers and malicious types than of
harmless petty con artists, for there were no great profits to be
made and most were seeking a means to earn their livelihood—
which need not be much for a plant-eater living in a southern
country.

The majority of the people who had derailed themselves from Europe and America carried with them one single vice that many vegetarians had—they had an aversion to work. They did not want gold and pleasure, nor power and amusement. What they wanted most of all was to lead their modest lives without work and annoyances. Many of them had traversed Europe on foot numerous times as unassuming doorknob cleaners in the homes of well-to-do people who shared their ideas, or as preaching prophets and miracle doctors. When Dr. Knoegle arrived in Quisisana, he encountered many a former acquaintance who had visited him every now and then in Leipzig as a harmless beggar.

But above all, he met the great individuals and heroes from all the different factions of vegetarianism. Sun-tanned men with long wavy hair and beards arrived in white robes and sandals, as if they had just stepped out of the Old Testament. Others wore sport clothes made out of bright linen. Some venerable men walked around naked with loincloths made of wool that they had woven themselves. Various groups and even organized clubs were formed. The pulpists met at certain places, the ascetic fasters at other spots, and the theosophists and sun-worshippers at yet others. A temple was constructed by the flowers of the American prophet Davis, while the neo-Swedenborgians made use of a hall for their religious services.

In the beginning Dr. Knoegle did in truth feel some embarrassment as he moved about in this strange crowd. He attended the lectures of a former teacher from Baden named Klaber, who instructed his listeners in pure Allemanian about the fate of Atlantis, and he stared at the Yogi Vishinanda, whose name was actually Beppo Cinari, and who after decades of effort had managed to reduce the rate of his heartbeat by about a third through his own willpower.

In Europe this colony would have left the impression of a madhouse or fantastic comedy set between real political and professional happenings. In Asia Minor, however, everything seemed quite reasonable and not at all impossible. Sometimes newcomers walked around with bright spiritual faces and expressed delight that their fondest dreams had been fulfilled. Others could be seen with tears of joy and flowers in their hands, greeting everyone they encountered with a kiss of peace.

The most striking group, however, was made up of the pure pulpists. They had waived their right to have a temple, house, and organization of any kind and showed no desire but to become more and more natural. As they themselves stated, they wanted "to come closer to the soil." They lived in the open and ate only things that could be broken off trees and bushes. They completely disdained all other vegetarians, and one of them told Dr. Knoegle to his face that eating rice and bread was exactly the same disgusting thing as enjoying meat, and that there was no real difference between a so-called vegetarian who drank milk and any old drunk and toper.

Among the pulpists, the illustrious disciple Jonas towered above everyone else, for he was the most consistent and successful representative of this faction. To be sure, he wore a loincloth, but it was hardly distinguishable from his hairy brown body. He lived in a small wooded area, where he could be seen swinging through the branches with agility and quickness. His thumbs and large toes were in a miraculous process of reverting back to primitive form, and his mode of life and entire existence represented the most tenacious and successful return to nature that one could imagine. A few people made fun of him among themselves and called him the "gorilla." Otherwise, Jonas enjoyed the admiration and respect of the entire province.

This great vegetarian had renounced the use of language. When his brother and sister followers discussed things at the edge of his woods, he would sometimes sit on a branch over their heads, grinning with encouragement or laughing with disapproval, but he himself never uttered a word. Instead, he sought through gestures to indicate that his language was the infallible language of nature and would later become the world language of all vegetarians and nature people. His closest friends were with him every day, enjoyed his lessons in the art of chewing and cracking nuts, and watched in awe as he progressively perfected himself. Yet they were worried because he supposedly was going to withdraw into the native wilderness of the mountains to be at one with nature, and this was to happen soon.

Some of the fanatics wanted to bestow divine honors on this remarkable being who had completed the circle of life and found his way back to the beginning point of human development. But on the morning when they went looking for him in his woods to honor him and begin the establishment of their cult with a song, the celebrated Jonas appeared on his favorite large branch, swung his detached loincloth derisively in the air, and threw hard pine cones at the worshippers.

Deep in his timid soul, Dr. Knoegle felt nothing but repulsion for Jonas the Perfect One, the "gorilla." All that he had always held in the silent depths of his heart against the excesses of the vegetarian outlook and fanatical, crazy behavior was horrifyingly embodied in this character. Jonas seemed to crudely mock his own moderate vegetarianism, and Dr. Knoegle, the unassuming teacher, felt that in some way Jonas had insulted human dignity itself. In fact, Dr. Knoegle, who readily tolerated numerous people with different opinions from his, could not walk past the dwelling place of the Perfect One without feeling hate and rage. Likewise, the "gorilla," who had observed all kinds of followers, admirers, and critics from his branch with equanimity, felt an increasing bestial bitterness toward this man, whose hate he had instinctively scented. Whenever the doctor happened to come near the woods, he would glare at the tree-dweller with reproachful, insulting glances, which Jonas answered with teeth-baring and angry hissing.

Dr. Knoegle had already decided to leave the province the following month and to return home. But one night, when there was a full moon, he took a walk and was drawn almost against his will near the woods. With sadness he thought of former times when he had still been a meat-eater and normal human being in full health, living among his kind. As he was recalling those more tranquil years, he spontaneously whistled an old student song.

All of a sudden Jonas broke out of the bushes, making a loud cracking sound, for he had been wildly aroused by the song. He stood threateningly in front of the walker, swinging a monstrous club. So bitter and enraged was the surprised doctor, however, that he did not take to his heels. Rather, he felt that the time had arrived to settle accounts with his enemy. Laughing grimly, he bowed and said with as much mockery and affront as he could express, "Permit me to introduce myself. I am Dr. Knoegle."

Then the "gorilla" threw his club away with an angry cry, pounced on the weak doctor, and strangled him instantly with his

terrible hands. Dr. Knoegle was found the next day. Many people suspected what had happened, but nobody dared to take action against the ape Jonas, who cracked his nuts calmly in the branches of his tree. The few friends that the stranger had made during his stay in paradise buried him nearby and placed a simple stone on his grave with the inscription: "Dr. Knoegle, Mixed Vegetarian from Germany."

THE
BEAUTIFUL
DREAM

When Martin Haberland, a high school student, died at the age of seventeen from pneumonia, everyone talked about him and his untimely death. In particular, they regretted that he had not been able to make something out of his abundant talents and to experience success.

It is true that I, too, felt sorry about the death of the handsome, talented young man, and I thought, with a certain amount of sorrow, how much enormous talent there must be in the world for nature simply to toss it away so arbitrarily! But nature could not care less what we think about it, and as far as talent is concerned, there is such an excess that our artists will soon become their own audiences, and audiences made up of ordinary people will no longer exist.

As a result, I cannot mourn the young man's death the same

way I might if he had been harmed and cruelly robbed of the best and beautiful things in the world that had been destined for him. Whoever has happily reached the age of seventeen in good health and with nice parents has the best part of his life behind him in many respects. If his life ended too early and did not assume the form of a Beethoven symphony because he had not endured much suffering or many harsh experiences or gone through wild phases, it could still be considered a small Haydn chamber concerto, and you cannot say such a thing about many people's lives.

In the case of Martin Haberland, I am very certain of the circumstances. The young man did indeed experience the most beautiful things in life that it was possible for him to experience. He had absorbed the rhythms of such unearthly music that his death was necessary because his life could have ended only in discord after that. The fact that the student enjoyed his happiness only in a dream should not diminish it, for most people experience their dreams more intensely than their lives. So it was with Martin, who had the following dream on the second day of his sickness as his fever rose, three days before his death.

His father placed his hand on his shoulder and said, "I understand very well that you cannot learn much more here. You must become a great and good man and pursue a special kind of happiness that cannot be found in your nest at home. Pay attention: First you must climb the Mountain of Knowledge, then you must perform some deeds, and finally you must find love and become happy."

While his father spoke these words, his beard seemed longer, and his eyes larger. For a moment he looked like a wise king. Then he gave his son a kiss on his forehead and told him to depart. So Martin walked down wide beautiful stairs like those in a palace, and just as he was crossing the street and about to leave the small city, he encountered his mother, who called to him, "So, Martin, do you want to go away without even saying good-bye to me?"

He glanced at her with a startled look and was ashamed that he had thought her long since dead. But he could see her standing alive and well before him, more beautiful and younger than he had remembered. In fact, there was something girlish about her, so that when she kissed him, he blushed and did not dare return her kiss. She peered into his eyes with a bright clear look that radiated like a light within him, and she nodded to him as he hastily departed in confusion.

Outside the city he was not surprised to find a harbor instead of the valley and the country road lined with ash trees, and there was a large old-fashioned ship with brownish sails that rose into the golden sky, just like in his favorite painting by Claude Lorrain. Soon he was sailing toward the Mountain of Knowledge.

But then the ship and the golden sky vanished completely from sight. Now the young student Haberland found himself wandering down the country road, already far from home. He approached a mountain that glowed as red as the sunset in the distance and seemed not to come any closer as long as he continued to walk. Fortunately, Professor Siedler was accompanying him, and he said in a fatherly tone, "There is no construction to be used here other than the *ablativus absolutus*. Only by using it will you suddenly come *media in res*." Martin immediately followed this advice and recalled an *ablativus absolutus* that, to a certain extent, was his entire past. It included the world and made a clean sweep of every kind of past in such a thorough way that everything became bright and full of the present and the future. And suddenly he stood on the mountain, and Professor Siedler was also right next to him and all at once began talking to him in a familiar way. In turn, Martin spoke familiarly with the professor and confided in him as though he were his real father. Indeed, as the professor talked, he became more and more like his father. Soon Haberland's love for his father and his love for scholarship flowed together and merged in him, both stronger and more beautiful, and while he sat and thought, surrounded by nothing but foreboding wonder, his father whispered to him, "So, now look around you!"

He could see nothing but immense clarity all around him, and everything in the world was in the best of order and as clear as the sun. He understood completely why his mother had died and yet still lived. He understood deep in his heart why people were so different in looks, customs, and languages and yet came from *one* being and were close brothers. He fully grasped that want and suffering and nastiness were necessary and were desired or ordained by God so that they became beautiful and bright and spoke loudly about the order and joy of the world. And before he was completely certain that he had been on the Mountain of Knowledge and had become wise, he felt himself called upon to perform a deed, and although he had constantly thought about various professions for two years and had never decided on a particular one, he now knew for sure that he was an architect, and it was wonderful to know this and not to have the slightest doubt about it anymore.

All at once, white and gray stones lay on the ground. There were also long beams and machines. Many people stood around and did not know what to do. However, he gave instructions with his hands and explained and ordered. He held plans and needed only to gesticulate and point, and people ran about and were happy to do sensible jobs. They lifted stones and shoved carts, set up poles and chiseled logs. The architect's will was in all their hands and eyes. Soon the building was erected and became a palace that displayed a very evident, simple, joyous beauty with its gables and vestibules, its courtyards and bay windows. And it was clear that only a few such things needed to be built in order for suffering and want, dissatisfaction and discontent, to vanish from the earth.

With the completion of the building, Martin became sleepy and could no longer pay careful attention to everything. He heard something like music and festive sounds roaring around him and surrendered to a profound, beautiful fatigue with deep and rare contentment. Now after all these experiences, his consciousness began to rise for the first time, and then his mother stood before him again and took him by the hand. Immediately he knew that she wanted to go with him into the land of love, and he became quiet, full of expectation, and forgot everything that he had already experienced and done on this journey. At the same time, there was a splendid light that shone after him from the Mountain of Knowledge and his palace as well as from a conscience that had been thoroughly cleansed.

His mother smiled and took him by the hand. They went down the mountain into a nocturnal landscape. Her dress was blue, and as they walked, she vanished. What had been her blue dress became the blue of the deep distant valley, and as he recognized this and no longer knew whether his mother had really been with him, he was overcome by sadness. He sat down in the meadow and began to weep, without pain, as devoted and sincere as he had been before, when he had used his creative drives to build the palace and then had rested in exhaustion. In his tears he felt that he was now supposed to encounter the sweetest thing that a person could experience, and when he tried to ponder this, he knew quite well what love truly was, but he could not imagine it exactly and ended with the feeling that love is like death. It is fulfillment and an evening after which nothing more may follow.

He was still thinking about all this when everything became different once again. In the distance he could hear delightful music in the blue valley, and the daughter of the village mayor came walking down the meadow, and suddenly he knew that he loved her. She looked the same as ever, but wore a very simple, elegant dress like a Greek goddess. No sooner was she there than night fell, and it was impossible to see anything more except a sky filled with large bright stars.

The girl stood still in front of Martin and smiled. "So you're here?" she said in a friendly way, as though she had been waiting for him.

"Yes," he said. "My mother showed me the way. I'm now finished with everything, even with the large house that I had to build. You must live there."

She smiled and seemed very maternal, sovereign, and a little sad, like an adult.

"What should I do now?" Martin asked, and placed his hands on the girl's shoulders. She leaned over and gazed into his eyes so closely that he became a bit frightened, and he now saw nothing but large calm eyes and numerous stars above her in a mist of gold. His heart began to throb painfully.

The beautiful girl moved her lips to Martin's lips, and right away his soul melted and he lost his entire will. In the blue darkness the stars began to resound softly. Now Martin felt that he had tasted love and death and the sweetest thing that a person can experience. He heard the world around him move and ring like an exquisite recurring refrain, and without taking his lips from the mouth of the girl and without wanting or desiring anything more in the world, he felt that he, the girl, and everything else were being absorbed by the recurring refrain. He closed his eyes and rushed down an eternal predestined street resounding with music, and he felt somewhat dizzy. Now no knowledge, no deed, nor anything earthly waited for him at the end anymore.

THE
THREE LINDEN
TREES

More than three hundred years ago, three splendid, old linden trees stood on the green grass in the cemetery next to the Hospital of the Holy Spirit in Berlin. They were so huge that they formed an arch over the entire cemetery, like an enormous roof, for their branches and boughs had become intertwined and grown into a gigantic crown. The origin of these beautiful linden trees goes back another three hundred years, and it has often been recounted as follows.

Three brothers lived in Berlin and had developed a remarkably close friendship and loyalty to one another, of a sort that is very rarely seen in this world. Now it happened one evening that the youngest went out alone and did not tell his brothers anything about it, because he wanted to meet a young woman in another part of the city and take a walk with her. As he was sauntering toward their meeting place, engrossed in pleasant dreams, he heard soft moans and gasps coming from an alley between two houses where it was dark and desolate. Immediately he went over to the alley to see what was happening, because he thought an animal or perhaps even a child might have had an accident and was lying there waiting for help. As he entered the dark secluded place, he was horrified to see a man bathed in blood. When he bent over and asked him compassionately what had happened, he received as answer only a weak groan and gulp, for the injured man had a knife wound in his heart and, a few moments later, passed away in the arms of his helper.

The young man was completely at a loss as to what he should do, and since the murdered man showed no more signs of life, the young man returned, confused and dumbfounded, with vacillating steps, to the street. Right at that moment two sentries happened to come by, and while the young man was still contemplating whether he should call for help or leave the place without drawing attention, the sentries noticed how frightened he was and approached him. As soon as they saw the blood on his shoes and sleeves, they forcefully grabbed hold of him, paying little attention to his explanations and pleas. Indeed, once they found the dead body, which had already turned cold, they took the suspected murderer straight to jail, where he was put in irons and closely guarded.

The next day the judge interrogated him, and at one point the corpse was brought into the room. Now, in daylight, the young man recognized the dead man as a blacksmith's apprentice with whom he had had a fleeting friendship some time ago. However, right before this he had testified that he had not been acquainted with the murdered man and had not known the slightest thing about him. Consequently, he was suspected even more of stabbing the dead man, especially since witnesses who had known the dead man stated that the young man had been friends with the apprentice some time ago, but they had drifted apart because of a dispute over a girl. There was really not much truth to this, but there was enough of a kernel of truth that the innocent man even boldly acknowledged it, all the while maintaining his innocence and asking not for a pardon but for justice.

The judge had no doubts that he was the murderer and thought that he would soon find enough evidence to sentence him and hand him over to the hangman. The more the prisoner denied everything and insisted that he knew nothing about the murder, the more he was regarded as the guilty party.

In the meantime one of his brothers—the oldest was still traveling somewhere on business—had been waiting in vain for the youngest to come home and eventually set out to look for him. When he heard the news that his brother was in prison and had been accused of murder and was stubbornly denying it, he went straight to the judge.

"Your Honor," he said, "you've arrested an innocent man. You must set him free! You see, I'm the murderer, and I don't want an innocent man to be wrongly punished for my crime. The blacksmith and I were enemies, and I was lying in wait for him. Last night I saw him as he went into that alley to relieve himself, and I followed him and stabbed him in the heart with my knife."

Stunned, the judge listened to this confession, then ordered the brother to be placed in irons and kept under close watch until he cleared up this mystery. So now both brothers lay in irons in the same jail. However, the youngest had no inkling whatsoever that his brother was trying to save him and kept insisting passionately that he was innocent.

Two days passed without the judge being able to discover anything new, and he was now tending to believe that the brother who had confessed to the crime was the murderer. Then the oldest brother returned to Berlin from his business trip, found nobody at home, and learned from his neighbors what had happened to the youngest, and how the second brother had told the judge that he was the real murderer, not his brother.

That very same night, the oldest brother went to the judge, woke him, and knelt down before him. "Noble judge," he said, "you have two innocent men in irons, and both are suffering because of a crime that I committed. Neither my youngest brother nor the other killed the blacksmith's apprentice. In fact, I was the one who committed the murder. I can bear it no longer that others sit in prison for me when they are not at all to blame. I beg you with all my heart to let them go and to arrest me. I'm ready to pay for my crime with my life."

Now the judge was even more astounded and did not know what to do except to place the third brother under arrest.

Early the next morning, when the jailkeeper handed the youngest brother some bread through the door, he said to him, "I'd really like to know the truth. Which one of you three is truly the vile culprit?" When the youngest brother asked him what he meant by that, the jailkeeper refused to say anything more. However, the prisoner did manage to conclude from his words that his brothers had come to sacrifice their own lives for his. All at once, he broke down, began sobbing, and demanded vehemently to be brought before the judge. And when he stood in front of the judge in irons, he began weeping again and said, "Forgive me, sir, for having refused so long to admit my guilt. But I thought that nobody had seen my crime and nobody could prove my guilt. Now I realize that justice must be done. I can no longer resist it and want to confess that I was truly the one who killed the blacksmith's apprentice. I'm the one who must pay for the crime with my life."

The judge's eyes opened wide in surprise, and he thought he was dreaming. His astonishment was indescribable, and his heart shuddered because of this strange affair. He ordered the prisoner to be locked up once more and placed under guard, like the other two brothers, and sat steeped in thought for a long time. Indeed, he realized that only one of the brothers could be the murderer and that two of them were willing to be executed and to sacrifice their lives out of magnanimity and brotherly love.

The judge could not reach a conclusion, but he did realize that it would be impossible to make a decision with customary thinking. As a result, he had the prisoners placed under tight security, and the next day, he went to the prince and painted a vivid picture of this strange affair.

The prince listened and was most astonished. "This is a strange and rare case!" he commented at the end of the judge's story. "Deep in my heart I believe that none of them committed the crime, not even the youngest, whom your watchmen arrested. Rather, I think he spoke the truth. But since we are concerned with a capital crime involving murder, we cannot let the suspects go free just like that. Therefore, I am going to call upon God Himself to be the judge of these three loyal brothers and let Him decide their fate."

And that was what was done. It was springtime, and the three brothers were led to a green field on a bright warm day. Each one of

them was given a robust, young linden tree to plant. However, each had to place his linden tree so that its crown went into the ground and its roots faced up toward the sky. According to the prince's decree, whoever's tree perished or withered first would be considered the murderer and would be executed.

The brothers did as they were told, and each one planted his little tree with its branches into the ground with great care. It was not long, however, before the trees, all three of them, began taking root and forming new crowns, indicating that all three brothers were innocent. The linden trees continued to grow to a very large size and stood for many hundreds of years in the cemetery of the Hospital of the Holy Spirit in Berlin.

AUGUSTUS

~❦~

$\mathcal{A}$ young woman named Elizabeth, who lived on Mostack Street, had lost her husband due to an accident shortly after their marriage, and now she sat poor and desolate in her little room, about to give birth to a child who would have no father. Because she was so utterly alone, she kept thinking about the child she was expecting, and her thoughts turned into wishes and dreams about all the beautiful, splendid, and desirable things she wanted for the child. A stone house with plate-glass windows and a fountain in the garden seemed barely good enough for the young one, and as far as his future was concerned, he had to become at least a professor or a king.

Next to Elizabeth's house lived an old man who was seldom seen. He was a little fellow who wore a tasseled cap on his gray head and carried a green umbrella with whalebone ribs, as in the old days.

The children were afraid of him, and the grown-ups believed he probably had his reasons for living as secluded as he did. No one saw him very much for long periods of time, but sometimes in the evening strange music could be heard coming from his small dilapidated house, as though tiny, delicate instruments were being played. Then as the children walked by the house, they would ask their mothers whether angels or perhaps nixies were singing inside. Their mothers, however, knew nothing about it and would respond, "No, no, that must be a music box."

This little man, who was called Mr. Binsswanger by his neighbors, had a strange kind of friendship with Elizabeth. They never spoke to one another, and yet the little old man would greet her in the friendliest manner each time he passed her window, and she would nod gratefully to him in return, for she liked him very much. And each of them thought: If ever I am really desperate and need help, I'll certainly go to my neighbor for advice. When the days began to turn dark, Elizabeth sat at her window all by herself. She would mourn her dead husband, think about her small child, or slip into a reverie. Then Mr. Binsswanger would quietly open his casement window, and tranquil music would flow from his dark room, softly and silvery like moonlight through a crack in the clouds. In return, Elizabeth made a point of looking after Mr. Binsswanger's geranium plants at his back window, which he always forgot to water. They were always green and in full bloom and never wilted because Elizabeth carefully tended them early each morning.

Now one raw windy evening, when autumn was making its presence felt and no one could be seen on Mostack Street, the poor young woman realized that her time had come, and she was afraid because she was completely alone. At nightfall, however, an old woman, carrying a lantern in her hand, arrived at her door, entered the house, boiled water, and laid out the linens in the proper manner. She did everything that has to be done when a child is about to be born, and Elizabeth let her do it all without saying a word. Only when the baby was there and was enjoying its first slumber on earth, wrapped in new diapers, did she ask the old woman where she had come from.

"Mr. Binsswanger sent me," the old woman said, and then the tired Elizabeth fell asleep. The next morning when she awoke, she found that the milk had been boiled and was ready for her. Everything in the room had been cleaned and put away, and next to her lay her tiny son, who cried because he was hungry. But the old woman was gone. So now the mother drew her baby to her breast and was happy that he was so good looking and strong. She thought of his father, who had not lived long enough to see his son, and tears rose up in her eyes. Then she hugged the little child and was forced to smile as she and her son fell asleep once more. When she woke up, there was more milk. Some soup had been cooked, and the baby was wrapped in clean diapers.

Soon the mother was again healthy and strong enough to take care of herself and little Augustus. Gradually, it occurred to her that her son had to be baptized and that she had no godfather for him. So toward evening, when darkness was about to cover the streets and the sweet music sounded once again from the little house next door, she went to see Mr. Binsswanger and knocked timidly on the dark door.

"Come in," he called out in a friendly voice, and as he went toward her, the music suddenly stopped. Inside there was a small old table with a lamp and book on it, and everything was just as it was in other people's homes.

"I've come to thank you," Elizabeth said, "because you sent that good woman to me. I'd also like to pay her as soon as I begin working again and can earn some money. But right now I have something else on my mind. The boy must be baptized, and I want him to be named Augustus after his father. But I don't know anyone around here and don't have a godfather for him."

"Yes, I know, and I've also been thinking about this," the neighbor said, stroking his gray beard. "It would be good if he had a kind and rich godfather who could take care of him if ever things were not to go too well for you. But I am only a lonely old man, and I, too, have few friends in the neighborhood. Therefore, I can't recommend anyone to you, unless you want to accept me as the godfather."

The poor mother was relieved to hear this and thanked the little man, whom she did indeed choose as the godfather. On the following Sunday they carried the baby to the church and had him baptized. The old woman, too, appeared once more and gave the infant a taler as a present. When Elizabeth refused to accept it, the old woman said, "Please, take it. I'm old and have everything that I need. Perhaps the taler will bring him luck. It was a pleasure for me to do a favor for Mr. Binsswanger this time. We're old friends."

Then they went home together, and Elizabeth made coffee for her guests. Mr. Binsswanger had brought a cake, so they enjoyed a real baptismal feast. When they had finished eating and drinking everything and the baby had long since fallen asleep, Mr. Binsswanger said modestly, "Now that I'm little Augustus's godfather, I'd like to give him a present and provide him with a royal castle or a sackful of gold coins, but I don't have these things. I can only give him a taler, just as my good friend has already done. Meanwhile, I'll do whatever I can for him. Elizabeth, you've probably wished many beautiful and good things for your boy. Now, think about what you feel would be the very best thing for him, and I'll make sure that your wish comes true. You have one free wish for your child, whatever you want—but only one. Think about it carefully, and when you hear my music box playing tonight, you must whisper your wish into the left ear of your little one, and it will be fulfilled."

Thereupon, Mr. Binsswanger quickly left the room, and the old woman departed with him. Elizabeth remained alone, totally bewildered. If the two talers had not been lying in the cradle and the cake had not been on the table, she would have thought it all a dream. Then she sat down next to the cradle and rocked her child, while she meditated and thought up many beautiful wishes. At first she wanted Augustus to become rich or handsome or tremendously strong. Then she thought it might be best if he were clever and intelligent, but she constantly had misgivings. Finally she thought: "Oh, the little old man was only joking with me."

It had already become dark, and she would have fallen asleep in her chair beside the cradle, worn out from entertaining her guests and from her worries and thinking of so many wishes, if it had not been for the sounds of the fine soft music that drifted over from the house next door. The music was so delicate and exquisite that no other music box could have ever produced the same sounds. Upon hearing them, Elizabeth came quickly to her senses and remembered everything that had happened. Now she believed in her neighbor Binsswanger once more and in his godfather's gift. Yet the more she reflected and the more she wanted to make a wish for something, the more confused her thoughts became. As a result, she could not decide upon anything and became so distressed that she had tears in her eyes. Then the music sounded more softly and faintly, and she thought that if she did not make a wish right at that moment, it would all be too late and everything would be lost.

So she sighed, leaned over her boy, and whispered in his left ear, "My little son, I wish—I wish," and just as the beautiful music was about to fade completely away, she became frightened and said quickly, "I wish that everyone will have to love you."

Now the sounds of the music had entirely vanished, and it was deathly quiet in the dark room. However, she flung herself over the cradle and cried and was filled with fear and anxiety. "Oh!" she exclaimed. "Now that I've wished the best thing that I know for you, I feel that it was perhaps not the right thing. Even if everybody loves you, every single person, nobody can love you as much as your mother."

In the following years Augustus grew up like all other children do. He was a cute blond-haired boy with bright fiery eyes, and he was spoiled by his mother and well liked by everyone. Elizabeth soon realized that her baptismal wish for her son was being fulfilled. Indeed, no sooner was the little boy able to walk through the streets than everybody he encountered found him good looking, pert, and smart, an unusual child, and everybody shook his hand, peered into his eyes, and wanted to do him a favor. Young mothers smiled at him, and old women gave him apples, and if he did anything naughty, nobody believed that it had been he, or if it was obvious that he was the guilty one, people shrugged and said, "You really can't blame that nice little boy."

People who had been drawn to the handsome boy also started coming to see his mother. Up until this time, nobody had taken the time to get to know her, and she had received only a few sewing jobs.

Now, however, she was well known as the mother of Augustus and had more customers than she could have ever wished. Everything went well for her and for the young boy, too, and whenever they went out together, the neighbors were delighted and greeted them and followed the happy pair with their eyes.

Augustus himself had his best times next door with his god-father, who sometimes called him over to his house in the evening when it was dark. The only light in the room would be produced by small red flames burning in the black opening of the fireplace. The little old man would draw the child to him on a fur rug on the floor and look into the flames and tell him stories. But sometimes when a story had come to an end and the little one was very sleepy and looked over at the fire with drooping eyelids in the dark silence, a sweet polyphonic music would ring out of the darkness, and when the two of them listened to it for a long time, it often happened that the entire room would suddenly be filled with tiny glittering children, who flew back and forth in circles with bright golden wings, dancing gracefully around each other in pairs. They also sang, and it sounded as though a hundred voices were rejoicing with exuberance and serenity. It was the most beautiful thing that Augustus had ever heard or seen, and when he later thought about his childhood, it was the dark, comfortable room of his godfather and the red flames in the fireplace with the music and the festive golden magic flight of the angelic creatures that rose in his memory and made him homesick.

In the meantime the boy grew bigger, and now there were times when his mother was sad and compelled to think back to that baptismal night with regret. Augustus ran around carefree in the neighborhood and was welcome everywhere. People gave him nuts and pears, cookies and toys as gifts. They let him have things to eat

and drink, play on their knees, and pick flowers in their gardens. He often came home late in the evening and shoved his mother's soup aside, unwilling to eat. If she became upset and wept, he would find the entire scene boring and go to bed in a bad mood. And if she scolded and punished him, he would scream with all his might and complain that everyone was nice and kind to him except his mother. So she often had distressing times and would become seriously angry with her son. But afterward, when he lay sleeping with his head on his pillow and her candle would cast a ray of light on his innocent childish face, all the bitterness in her heart would vanish, and she would kiss him, taking care that he did not wake up. It was her own fault that everyone liked Augustus, and sometimes she thought with sorrow and also some dread that it might have been better if she had never made her wish.

One time she happened to be standing right by Mr. Binss-wanger's window of geraniums, cutting the wilted flowers from their stems with some shears, when suddenly she heard her son's voice in the courtyard behind the two houses, and she looked over to see what was happening. He was leaning against the wall with his handsome and arrogant face, and in front of him stood a girl who was bigger than he was. She looked at him imploringly and said, "Come now. Be nice and give me a kiss."

"I don't want to," Augustus said, and stuck his hands in his pockets.

"Please," she said again. "I'll give you something wonderful if you do."

"What?" asked the boy.

"I have two apples," she said shyly.

But he turned around and made a face.

"I don't like apples," he remarked with disdain, and was about to run away.

But the girl grabbed hold of his arm tightly and cajoled him further: "I also have a beautiful ring."

"Show me!" said Augustus.

She showed him the ring, and he examined it carefully. Then he took it off her finger, put it on his own, held it up to the light, and decided that he liked it.

"Well, you can have your kiss now," he said abruptly, and gave her a quick peck on her mouth.

"How about playing with me now?" she asked in a trusting way, and she put her arm through his.

But he pushed her away and shouted viciously, "Stop pestering me! Just leave me alone! I want to play with some other friends."

The girl began to cry and left the courtyard with slumped shoulders, while Augustus looked after her with a bored and irritated expression on his face. Then he turned the ring on his finger and studied it. Soon he began to whistle and slowly walked away from the place.

However, his mother, standing there with the shears in her hand, was horrified by the harshness and contempt with which her son had treated the girl's love. She left the flowers where they were, and as she shook her head, she kept repeating, "He's really evil. He has no heart at all!"

Later, when Augustus came home, she took him to task, but he merely laughed and looked at her with his blue eyes, showing no sign of guilt. Then he began to sing and flatter her, and he was so funny and nice and tender with her that she had to laugh and realized that you could not take everything so seriously with children.

Meanwhile the boy did not entirely escape punishment for his misconduct. His godfather Binsswanger was the only one whom Augustus respected, and when he went to the old man's room in the evening, the godfather said, "There's no fire burning tonight, and there is no music. The little angelic children are sad because you were so bad." Then Augustus went home without saying a word and flung himself on his bed and cried. Afterward, he tried hard for many days to be good and kind.

Nevertheless, the flames in the fireplace burned less and less, and the godfather could not be bribed with tears and hugs. By the time Augustus turned twelve years old, the magic angelic flight in his godfather's room had become more a distant dream than anything else. Once when he had a dream in his own room during the night, he was twice as wild and boisterous the next day, and like a military general he ordered his numerous playmates to do reckless things.

His mother had long since grown tired of hearing everyone praise her son and tell her how fine and charming he was. In fact, all she did was worry about him. One day, when his teacher came to her and told her that he knew someone who had offered to send her son to a boarding school for his education, she consulted with Mr. Binsswanger. Shortly thereafter, on a spring morning, a carriage drove up to the house, and Augustus, dressed in a fine new suit, climbed into it and said farewell to his mother, godfather, and neighbors because he was going to the capital to live and study. His mother had parted his blond hair neatly for the last time and gave him her blessing. Now the horses tugged, and Augustus was off on his journey into a new and unknown world.

After many years had passed and Augustus had become a college student and wore a red cap and moustache, he returned home because his godfather had written to him that his mother would not live much longer because of an illness. The young man arrived in the evening, and the neighbors watched with astonishment as he stepped out of the carriage, followed by the coachman, who carried a large leather suitcase into the house, where his mother lay dying in the old room with the low ceiling. When the handsome student saw her pale withered face on the white pillows and that she was barely able to greet him with silent eyes, he sank to the floor next to her bed and began to weep. He kissed his mother's limp hands and knelt by her side the entire night until her hands had become cold and her eyes, extinguished.

After his mother was buried, his godfather Binsswanger took him by the arm and went with him into his house, which seemed to the young man to have become even smaller and darker. When they had sat together for a long time and the small windows were glimmering dimly in the darkness, the little old man stroked his gray beard with his lean fingers and said to Augustus, "I want to make a fire in the fireplace. Then we won't need the lamp. I know that you must leave tomorrow, and now that your mother is dead, you won't be back again very soon."

As he said this, he lit a small fire in the fireplace and moved his easy chair closer to it. Augustus did the same. Once again, they sat for a long time and watched the glowing logs until the flames died down. Then the old man said softly, "Farewell, Augustus, I wish you well. You had a fine mother, who did more for you than you know. I would have liked to make music for you one more time and show you the small blessed creatures, but you know it won't work anymore. Nevertheless, you mustn't forget them, and you must remember that they are still singing and that you may even be able to hear them one more time if you ever feel a deep craving for them with a lonely and longing heart. Give me your hand, my boy. I'm old, and I must go to sleep."

Augustus shook hands with him and could not utter a word. He went sadly across the way into the desolate little house and lay down to sleep for the last time in his old home. But before he fell asleep, he thought he heard the sweet soft music of his childhood once again from far away. The next morning he departed, and nothing was heard about him for a long time.

Soon Augustus forgot even godfather Binsswanger and his angels. Swept away by a life of luxury, he rode its waves. No one could equal the manner in which he went through bustling streets, greeting the attentive girls with a contemptuous look. No one could dance as gracefully and charmingly as he did, drive in a coach as smoothly and elegantly, or carouse as loudly and boastfully in a garden during a summer night. In addition, Augustus became the lover of a rich widow who gave him money, clothes, horses, and everything he needed or wanted. He traveled with her to Paris and Rome and slept under her silken sheets. His true love, however, was the soft blond daughter of an upright citizen, and he risked his life by visiting her at night in her father's garden. Whenever he took a trip, she kept contact with him by writing long passionate letters.

But one time he did not return. He had found friends in Paris, and since he had tired of the rich widow and long since treated his studies as a nuisance, he remained far away in France and enjoyed the life of high society. He kept horses, dogs, and women. He won and lost money in large sums, and people everywhere pursued him, fit their lives to his needs, and were at his service. And he smiled and accepted it all, just as he had long ago accepted the girl's ring when he was a boy. The magic of the wish lay in his eyes and on his lips.

Women overwhelmed him with tenderness, and his friends raved about him, and nobody saw—he himself hardly noticed it—how empty and greedy his heart had become and how his soul was sick and languishing in pain. Sometimes he became tired of being loved by everyone and went by himself in disguise to foreign cities. Yet everywhere he went he found that the people were foolish and very easy to conquer. In fact, he found that love had become ridiculous as it continued to pursue him so zealously and yet was content with so little. He was often repulsed by women and men because they did not show more pride, and he spent whole days with his dogs hunting in beautiful regions of the mountains. If he stalked and shot a stag, it made him happier than courting a beautiful and spoiled woman.

One time, however, while he was on a sea voyage, he noticed the young wife of an ambassador, an austere, slender lady of Nordic nobility, standing amidst many other distinguished ladies and cosmopolitan men. She was clearly the most striking person among them, proud and quiet, without peer. While he was observing her, he noticed that her glance seemed to touch him too, fleetingly and indifferently. It was as though he now felt for the first time what love was, and he became determined to win her love. From then on, he was always near her and within sight of her, and because he himself was constantly surrounded by women and men who admired him and sought his company, he and the beautiful austere lady were always kept apart, at the center of attention of the other travelers, like a prince and princess. Even the husband of the blond lady treated him with deference and endeavored to please him.

It was practically impossible for Augustus to be alone with this remarkable woman until the ship sailed into the port of a southern city, and all the voyagers disembarked for a few hours to walk around the foreign city and feel some earth under their feet once again. Augustus did not budge from the side of his beloved and eventually succeeded in drawing her into a conversation amid the hustle and bustle of a lively marketplace. There were numerous small, dark alleys connected to the marketplace, and it was into one of these alleys that he led her, for she had no reason not to trust him. Yet when she suddenly found herself alone with him, without her companions, she became timid, while Augustus fervently took her reluctant hands into his and implored her to remain on land and to flee somewhere with him.

The young lady turned pale and kept her eyes fixed on the ground. "Oh, this is not very gentlemanlike," she said softly. "Allow me to forget what you've just said!"

"I'm not a gentleman!" exclaimed Augustus. "I'm a lover, and a lover knows nothing but his beloved and has no other thought than to be with her. You're such a beautiful woman! Come with me, and I'll make you happy."

She looked at him earnestly and reproachfully with her bright blue eyes. "How could you know that I love you?" she whispered dolefully. "I can't lie—I do love you and have often wished that you were my husband, for you are the first man whom I've loved with my heart. Oh, how can love go so far astray! I had never thought it possible for me to love a man who's not pure and good. But I prefer a thousand times to remain with my husband than to go off with you, even though I do not love him very much. You see, he is a gentleman and full of honor and chivalry, qualities that you lack. And now don't say one more word to me, but bring me back to the ship. Otherwise, I'll call some people to protect me from your intrusive behavior."

No matter how much Augustus begged and protested, she turned away from him, and she would have walked off alone if he had not run after her and accompanied her silently to the ship. Once he was there, he had his suitcases brought ashore and did not say good-bye to anyone.

From then on the fortunes of this well-beloved man declined. He came to hate virtue and honor and trampled them underfoot. He took pleasure in seducing virtuous women with all the magic wiles at his disposal, and he exploited unsuspecting men whom he quickly won as friends, only to discard them with contempt. He reduced women and girls to poverty, then denied having anything to do with their downfall, and he sought out young men from noble families, whom he led astray and corrupted. He tried out every sort of pleasure to the point of exhaustion, and there was no vice that he did not learn and then abandon. But there was no longer any joy in his heart, and nothing in his soul responded to the love that he attracted everywhere he went.

Cynical and morose, he lived in a beautiful country mansion by the sea, and he tormented the women and friends who visited him there with wild whims and malicious acts. He took pleasure in humiliating people and showing them how much he despised them. Satiated, he felt sick and tired of being sought, demanded, and given love, which did not interest him. He sensed the worthlessness of his dissipated and decadent life and of the way that he had always taken and never given anything. Sometimes he fasted for a while, just to be able to feel a voracious desire again and to satisfy his appetite.

News spread among his friends that he was sick and needed peace and quiet. Letters came, but he never read them, and people who were worried about him asked his servants how his health was. He sat alone, however, deeply troubled, in his mansion overlooking the sea. His life lay ravaged and empty behind him; it was barren and without a trace of love, like the gray, undulating water of the sea. He looked hideous as he sat hunched over in his easy chair at the high window and held himself to account. White gulls drifted in the wind on the beach. He followed the course of their flight with a vacuous look, devoid of joy and interest. Only his lips smiled harshly and maliciously as he finished his thoughts and rang for his servant, whom he ordered to send invitations to his friends to attend a party on a particular day. His intention was to horrify and mock them by confronting them on arrival with an empty house and his own corpse. Indeed, he had decided to end his life with poison before they came.

On the evening when the party was to take place, he sent all the servants from the house, so it became completely quiet in the large rooms. Then he went into his bedroom, mixed strong poison into a glass of Cyprus wine, and raised it to his lips. Just as he was about to drink it, there was a knock at the door. When he did not answer, the door opened, and a little old man entered. He went straight to Augustus, carefully took the glass out of his hands, and said with a very familiar voice, "Good evening, Augustus. How are you?"

Surprised, annoyed, and somewhat ashamed, Augustus smiled mockingly and said, "Why, Mr. Binsswanger, are you still alive? It's been a long time, and you truly do not seem to have grown any older. But you're disturbing me at this moment, my dear man. I'm tired, and I was just about to take a sleeping potion."

"So I see," his godfather responded calmly. "You want to take a sleeping potion, and you're right. It's the last sort of wine that can still help you. But before you drink it, let's have a little chat, my boy. And since I've traveled so far, you won't be angry at me if I refresh myself with a small drink."

Upon saying this, he took the glass and raised it to his lips, and before Augustus could prevent him, he lifted it high and drank it all in one quick gulp.

Augustus turned deathly pale. He rushed over to his godfather, shook him by the shoulders, and cried out in a shrill voice, "Old man, do you know what you have just drunk?"

Mr. Binsswanger nodded his wise gray head and smiled. "It's Cyprus wine, I see, and it's not bad. You don't seem to be suffering from a lack of good wine. But I have little time, and I don't want to keep you unnecessarily long if you'll just listen to me."

Confused, Augustus kept looking at his godfather with horror in his bright eyes, expecting him to collapse at any moment. Meanwhile, his godfather sat down comfortably in a chair and nodded kindly to his young friend.

"Are you worried that the drink of wine will harm me? Just relax! It's nice of you to worry about me—I would never have expected it. But now let's talk as we used to in the old days! It seems to me that you've had your fill of the easy life. I can understand that, and when I leave, you can refill your glass and drink it down. But before that, I must tell you something."

Augustus leaned against the wall and listened to the kind, pleasant voice of the ancient little man. The familiar voice from his childhood brought back to life shadows of the past that he could picture in his mind. Profound shame and sorrow gripped him, as if he were actually viewing his innocent childhood.

"I drank your poison," the old man continued, "because I'm the one responsible for your misery. You see, when you were baptized, your mother made a wish, and I fulfilled it even though it was a foolish wish. You don't need to know what it was. It has become a curse, as you yourself have realized. I'm sorry that it turned out this way, and it would make me happy if I could live to see you sitting with me at home by the fireplace once more and listening to the angels sing. It will not be easy, and at the moment it may seem impossible to you that your heart could ever become healthy and pure and cheerful again. But it is possible, and I want to ask you to try it. Your poor mother's wish cost you dearly, Augustus. How would it be now if I granted you another wish, any one you want? I don't think that you'll want money and possessions, nor power or the love of women. You've had enough of all this. Think about it carefully, and when you believe you know the right magic that will make your ruined life better and beautiful and that could also make you happy once more, then wish it for yourself."

Now Augustus sat deep in thought and did not respond. He was too tired and too much in despair, but after a while he said, "Thank you, godfather Binsswanger. However, I believe that my life is so tangled that there's no comb in the world that could ever smooth it out. It's better for me if I do what I intended to do when you came in. But I want to thank you nevertheless for coming."

"Yes," said the old man discreetly. "I can understand that it's not easy for you, Augustus. But perhaps you can still reconsider. Perhaps you can recall what you were missing most of all. Or perhaps you can remember the early days, when your mother was still alive and you occasionally came to me in the evening. Weren't you sometimes happy then?"

"Yes, but that was long ago." Augustus nodded, and the picture of his radiant youth came back to him from afar, a faint reflection, as though from an antique mirror. "But that can't return. I cannot wish to be a child again. Why, then everything would start all over again!"

"You're perfectly right. That would make no sense. But think once more about the time when we were all together at home and about the poor girl whom you used to visit as a student at night in her father's garden, and think about the beautiful blond lady with whom you once traveled on a ship, and think about all those moments when you've ever been happy, when life seemed to be good and precious. Perhaps you can recognize what made you happy during those times and can wish for it. Do it, my boy. Do it for me!"

Augustus closed his eyes and recalled his life as one looks back from a dark corridor to a distant point of light from where one has come, and he saw once again how everything had once been bright and beautiful around him and had gradually become darker and darker until he stood in pitch-blackness and could no longer be happy about anything. And the more he contemplated and remembered, the more beautiful and lovable and desirable the distant small spot of life seemed to glisten at him, and finally he recognized it, and tears burst from his eyes.

"I'll try it," he said to his godfather. "Take away the old magic. It hasn't helped me at all. In its place, give me the power to love people!"

Weeping, he knelt before his old friend, and as he sank to the ground, he could feel love for this old man burning within him, and he struggled to express it in forgotten words and gestures. But his godfather, that tiny man, took him gently into his arms and carried him to his bed. There he laid him down and stroked his hair from his feverish brow.

"Everything's all right," he whispered softly to Augustus. "Everything's all right, my child. Everything will turn out well."

Augustus felt totally worn out by fatigue, as if he had aged many years in one instant. He fell into a deep sleep, and the old man silently left the forsaken house.

The next day, Augustus was wakened by a wild tumult that resounded throughout the house, and when he got up and opened the bedroom door, he found the hall and all the rooms filled with his former friends, who had come to the party and found the house abandoned. They were angry and disappointed, and when he went toward them to cajole them as usual with a smile or a joke, he suddenly felt that he had lost the power to do so. No sooner did they see him than they all began simultaneously to yell at him, and when he smiled helplessly and stretched out his hands in self-defense, they fell upon him in rage.

"You crook!" one person cried. "Where's the money you owe me?" And another: "And the horse that I loaned you?" And a furious pretty woman: "The entire world knows my secrets now that you've blabbed about them. Oh, how I hate you, you monster!" And a hollow-eyed young man screamed with a distorted face: "Do you know what you've made of me? You're Satan, the corrupter of youth!"

And so it continued, each person heaping insults and curses on him, and each one was justified, and many hit him, and they left broken mirrors behind when they departed and took many precious articles. Augustus got up from the floor, beaten and dishonored. Then he went into his bedroom and looked into the mirror in order to wash himself, and he regarded his wrinkled and ugly face, the red eyes oozing with tears, and blood dripping from his forehead.

"I deserved it," he said to himself and washed the blood from his face. No sooner had he cleared his mind a bit than the tumult began once more in the house, and people came storming up the stairs: the moneylenders who held the mortgage on the house; a husband whose wife he had seduced; fathers whose sons he had enticed into a life of vice and misery; servants and maids whom he had dismissed; and policemen and lawyers. One hour later, he sat handcuffed in a patrol car and was being taken to jail. Behind the car people yelled and sang songs mocking him. Through the window of his cell, a guttersnipe threw a handful of dirt that landed on his face.

The city was full of reports of disgraceful crimes committed by this man, whom so many people had known and loved. He was accused of every possible sin, and he did not deny a single one. People whom he had long ago forgotten stood before the judges and made accusations about things that he had done many years ago. Servants, to whom he had given presents and who had stolen from him, revealed his secret vices. Every face was full of disgust and hate. Nobody came to speak in his behalf, praise him, or exonerate him. In fact, nobody recalled anything good about him.

He let everything happen, let himself be led into and out of the cell before the judges and witnesses. Confused and sad, he gazed with sick eyes into the many angry, disturbed, and spiteful faces, and in each one of them, he saw a hidden charm and a spark of affection that glimmered from beneath the hate and distortion. All these people had loved him at one time, and he had not loved any of them. Now he begged their forgiveness and sought to remember something good about each one of them.

In the end he was imprisoned, and nobody was allowed to visit him. So he talked in feverish dreams to his mother, his first lover, godfather Binsswanger, and the Nordic lady from the ship. And when he awoke and sat alone and lost during those terrible days, he suffered all the pains of yearning and abandonment, and he longed for the sight of people as he had never longed for any kind of pleasure in his life.

And when he was released from prison, he was sick and old, and nobody recognized him anymore. The world was still going its way. People drove and rode and walked in the streets. Fruit and flowers, toys and newspapers were sold all over. But nobody turned to speak to Augustus. Beautiful women whom he had once held in his arms while enjoying champagne and music drove by him in their carriages and left him behind in their dust.

Still, he no longer felt the terrible emptiness and loneliness that had stifled him when he had led a life of luxury. When he stopped for a moment at the gateway of a house in order to find some protection from the heat of the sun, or when he asked for a drink of water in the courtyard of some building, he was surprised to see how irritated and inhospitable the people were who had formerly responded to his proud and harsh words with gratitude and sparkling eyes. Nevertheless, the sight of each and every person delighted and touched him. He loved the children whom he saw playing and going to school, and he loved the old people sitting on benches in front of their little homes and warming their wrinkled hands in the sun. If he saw a young boy follow a girl with longing looks, or a worker taking his children in his arms when he returned home at the end of the day, or a fine smart doctor driving silently and quickly in his car and thinking about his sick patients, or a poor, simply dressed prostitute waiting by a lamppost in the evening at the edge of the city and even offering him, the outcast, her love—then all these people were his brothers and sisters. Each one of them carried the memory of a beloved mother and a better past, or a secret sign of a more beautiful and more noble destiny, and each person was dear to him and

remarkable and gave him something to think about. Indeed, he felt
that nobody was worse than he was himself.

Augustus decided to wander through the world and to search
for a place where it would be possible for him to be useful to people
in some way and to show them his love. He had become accustomed
to the fact that his appearance no longer made people happy. His
cheeks were caved in; his clothes and shoes were like those of a
beggar. Even his voice and gait had lost the charm that used to
delight people. Children were afraid of him because of the long
scraggly beard that hung down from his chin. Well-dressed people
kept their distance from him because they would feel anxious and
dirty if he were to come too close. Poor people were distrustful
because they regarded him as an intruder who might snap up some
bits of their food. Consequently, he found it difficult to be of service
to anyone, but he learned how to help and was not discouraged. One
time he saw a child stretching out his hand in vain to reach the
doorknob of a bakery, and he gave him a boost. Sometimes there were
people who were worse off than he, blind people or invalids, and he
would help them on their way and do some good deed for them. And
when he could not assist them, he cheerfully gave them what little he
had—a bright kind look and brotherly greeting, a gesture of understanding and sympathy. Along the way he learned to tell from
people's expressions what they expected of him and what would make
them happy. Some needed a loud spontaneous salutation, some a
silent look, while others wanted to be left alone, undisturbed. He was
amazed each day to see how much misery there was in the world and
yet how content people could be, and he found it splendid and
inspiring to experience over and over again how sorrow could soon be
followed by joyous laughter; a death knell, by the song of children;

every predicament and mean act, by simple kindness, a joke, a comforting word, or a smile.

People seemed to arrange their lives in remarkable ways. If he turned a corner and a group of schoolboys came rushing toward him, he marveled at their courage and zest for life and at the beauty of youth that glistened in all their eyes. If they teased and annoyed him a little, it was not so bad—he could even understand it. When he saw his reflection in a store window or the water of a fountain, he found that he looked shabby and wrinkled. No, for him it was no longer a question of pleasing people or wielding power. He had experienced enough of that. For him, it was now wonderful and edifying to see how other people struggled and groped their way along those paths that he had once taken in his life, and how everyone pursued goals with zeal, vigor, pride, and joy. For him, this was a wonderful drama.

In the meantime winter came and went, and now it was summer. Augustus lay ill for a long time in a charity hospital, and there he silently and gratefully enjoyed the pleasure of seeing poor downtrodden people clinging to life with all their might and passion and overcoming death. It was marvelous to see the patience of those who were terribly sick. Then there was the vigorous passion for life and brightness in the eyes of those people who were convalescing. And it was also beautiful to see the silent, dignified faces of the dead. Most of all, he admired the love and patience of the pretty, well-kempt nurses. But this period also came to an end. The autumn wind blew, and Augustus set about wandering again as winter approached. Now a strange impatience gripped him as he saw how endlessly slowly he proceeded. He still wanted to travel all over and meet many more people face to face. His hair had turned gray, and his eyes smiled shyly behind infected red lids, and gradually he began to lose his memory so that it seemed to him that he had never seen the world other than it was on that particular day. But he was satisfied and found the world most glorious and deserving of love.

At the onset of winter he arrived in a city, and the snow drifted through the dark streets. Though it was late, a few boys were still walking around, and they threw some snowballs at the wanderer. Otherwise, a veil of silence covered the city. Augustus was very tired. He came to a narrow street, which seemed very familiar to him, and then to another. Suddenly he was standing in front of his mother's house, and right next door was his godfather's dwelling. Both were small and old, covered by the cold snow. A light was burning in one of the windows of his godfather's house. It glimmered red and seemed peaceful in the winter night.

Augustus entered and knocked at the living-room door. The little man came toward him and led him into the room without saying a word. It was warm and quiet there, and a small bright fire burned in the fireplace.

"Are you hungry?" asked his godfather. But Augustus was not hungry. He only smiled and shook his head.

"But you're certainly tired." His godfather spoke again, and he spread his old fur rug on the floor. The two old men squatted next to one another and looked into the fire.

"You've come a long way," said his godfather.

"Oh, it was very beautiful, but I've become a little tired. May I sleep here? I'll move on tomorrow."

"Yes, you may. But how would you like to see the angels dance again?"

"The angels? Oh yes, I certainly would, if I become a child once more."

"We haven't seen each other for a long time," his godfather continued. "You're so handsome. Your eyes are kind and gentle again, as they were in the old days, when your mother was still alive. It's nice of you to visit me."

The wanderer, clad in torn clothes, was slouched over as he sat quietly next to his friend. He had never been so exhausted, and the pleasant warmth and glow of the fire made him so confused that he could no longer clearly distinguish between today and yesterday.

"Godfather Binsswanger," he said, "I've been naughty again, and Mother cried at home. You must talk to her and tell her that I'm going to be good again. Will you do that?"

"I will," responded his godfather. "Don't get upset. She loves you very much."

Now the fire dwindled, and Augustus stared into the dim glow with large sleepy eyes, just as he had done a long time ago in his childhood. His godfather placed Augustus's head on his lap, and some soft and blissful music sounded through the room. Then a thousand beaming spirits came floating through the air and circled gracefully around each other in pairs. And Augustus watched and listened with the keen sensitivity and openness of a child to the paradise regained.

It seemed to him at one point that he heard his mother calling him, but he was too tired to answer and his godfather had promised to talk to her. And when he fell asleep, his godfather folded his hands and listened to his heart until it stopped beating and the room was completely enveloped by the night.

THE POET

There is a story told about the Chinese poet Han Fook, who, as a young man, had been inspired by a wondrous urge to learn all he could and become perfect in everything that was in any way related to the art of poetry. At that time he was still living in his hometown on the Yellow River and by his own wish had become engaged to a young woman from a good family, with the help of his parents who loved him dearly. The wedding date was soon to be set on a day that promised to be auspicious. Han Fook was then about twenty years old. He was a handsome and modest young man, pleasant in his manners and well rounded in his education. In spite of his youth, he had already made a name for himself with many an excellent poem, and he was known in the literary circles of this region. Without being exactly rich, he could nevertheless expect to have enough money to lead a comfortable life, and this money would be increased through the dowry of his bride. Moreover, since this bride was very beautiful and virtuous, nothing whatsoever seemed to be missing to complete the young man's happiness. Nevertheless, he was not entirely content, for his heart's desire was to become a perfect poet.

One evening while the festival of lanterns was being celebrated on a bank of the river, Han Fook happened to be wandering alone on the other side. He leaned against the trunk of a tree that protruded over the water and looked at the thousand lights swimming and shimmering in the reflection in the river. He saw men and women and young girls on boats and barges greeting one another. They were dressed in festive costumes and beamed like beautiful flowers. He heard the faint murmuring of the glittering water, the melodies of the singers, the hum of the zither, and the sweet tones of the flute players. And high above all of this, he saw the blue night hover like the arch of a temple. The young man's heart pounded while he stood there as a lonely spectator, and he became enraptured by all this beauty. Yet as much as he longed to cross the river and become part of everything, to be near his bride and his friends and enjoy the festivities, he also desired just as passionately to absorb all of this as a keen observer and to capture it in a totally perfect poem: the blue of the night and the play of light on the water, as well as the enjoyment of the people and the yearning of the silent onlooker leaning against the trunk of the tree on the bank. He sensed that there would never be a festive occasion or any pleasure in the world that would make him feel entirely at ease and cheerful. Even in the midst of life he would remain solitary and, to a certain degree, a spectator and stranger. He felt, among other things, that his soul was formed in such a way that compelled him to feel both the beauty of earth and the strange longing of the outsider at the same time. He became sad about that, and as he pondered this matter, he came to the conclusion that true happiness and deep fulfillment could be his only if he were to succeed one time in capturing the world so perfectly in his poems that he would possess the world itself, purified and eternalized, in these images.

Han Fook hardly knew whether he was still awake or had fallen asleep when he heard a slight rustling and saw a stranger standing next to the trunk of the tree. The man was old and venerable and dressed in a violet robe. Han Fook stood up straight and greeted him with the respect due to wise and distinguished men. But the stranger only smiled and recited a few verses that expressed everything that the young man had just felt so perfectly and beautifully and in such exact accord with the rules of the great poets that the young man's heart stood still in amazement.

"Who are you?" he exclaimed with a deep bow. "You who can peer into my soul and recite such poems that are more beautiful than any I have ever heard from my teachers?"

Once again the stranger smiled the smile of a man of great accomplishment and said, "If you want to become a poet, come to me. You'll find my hut at the source of the Great River in the northwestern mountains. My name is Master of the Perfect Word."

Upon saying this, the old man stepped into the narrow shadow of the tree and disappeared. Han Fook searched for him, and when he could find not a single trace of the man, he became completely convinced that everything had been a dream caused by his fatigue. He rushed over to the boats on the other side of the river and joined in the festival, but between conversations and the sound of flutes, he continued to hear the mysterious voice of the stranger. Han Fook's

soul seemed to have abandoned him and gone away with the old man, for he sat there with dreamy eyes, cut off from the cheerful people who teased him for being in love.

A few days later, Han Fook's father prepared to summon his friends and relatives to set the date of the wedding. But the bridegroom opposed this and said, "Forgive me if I seem to neglect the duty that a son owes his father. But you know how great my desire is to distinguish myself in the art of poetry, and though some of my friends may praise my poems, I know quite well that I'm still a beginner and have a long way to go. Therefore I beg you to let me go off by myself for a while to devote myself to my studies. It seems to me that I'll be kept from doing such things when I am obliged to take charge of a wife and home. Right now I'm still young and without obligations, and I'd like to live awhile just for my poetry, from which I hope to gain pleasure and fame."

This speech astonished Han Fook's father, and he replied, "You must indeed love poetry more than anything else if you want to postpone your wedding for it. Or has something come between you and your bride? If so, tell me, so that I can help to reconcile you or provide you with another bride."

However, the son swore that he still loved his bride just as much as he had loved her before and would continue to love her in the future. They had not quarreled in the least. Then Han Fook told his father that a master had appeared to him through a dream on the day of the festival of lamps, and his greatest wish in the world was to become his student.

"Very well," said his father. "I shall grant you one year. During this time you may follow your dream, which was perhaps sent to you by a god."

"It might even take two years," Han Fook replied hesitantly. "Who can know?"

Though saddened by all this, his father let him go. In the meantime the young man wrote a letter to his bride, said farewell, and departed.

After he had wandered for a very long time, he reached the source of the river and found a bamboo hut in an isolated spot. In front of the hut sat an old man on a woven mat. It was the same old man whom he had seen by the trunk of the tree on the riverbank. He was sitting and playing a lute, and when he saw the guest approach with reverence, he did not stand up; nor did he greet the young man. Rather, he only smiled and let his agile fingers run across the strings, so that a magical music floated like a silver cloud through the valley. The young man stood there bedazzled and forgot everything else in sweet astonishment until the Master of the Perfect Word set his small lute aside and entered the hut. Han Fook followed him in awe and stayed with him as his servant and student.

One month passed, and Han Fook came to despise all the songs that he had previously composed, and he erased them from his memory. And again, a few months later, he erased the songs that he had learned from his teachers at home. The Master rarely spoke to him. He taught Han Fook the art of lute playing in silence until the student was completely saturated by music, to the very core of his existence. One time, Han Fook composed a small poem describing the flight of two birds on a fall evening, and he was pleased with it. He did not dare to show it to the Master, but he did sing it one evening by the side of the hut. The Master clearly heard it, but he did not say a word about it. He merely played softly on his lute, and the air soon became cool, and dusk rapidly descended. A sharp wind arose, although it was the middle of summer, and two herons, tremendously intent on migrating, flew through the sky, which had just become gray. All this was so much more beautiful and perfect than the verses of the student that Han Fook became sad and silent and felt worthless. Each time Han Fook wrote a poem, the old man did the exact same thing. After a year had passed, Han Fook learned to play the lute almost perfectly, although he continued to regard the art of poetry as more difficult and sublime.

Two years later, the young man felt an intense longing to see his parents, his bride, and his native land, and he asked the Master for permission to travel home.

The Master smiled and nodded. "You are free," he said, "and you can go wherever you want. You may come back, and you may stay away, just as you like."

So the student set out on his journey and traveled without resting until one morning he stood and watched the sunrise on the bank of the familiar river and looked across the arched bridge at his native city. He snuck unnoticed into the garden of his father, who was still sleeping, and he heard his father's breathing through the window of the bedroom. Then he stole into the orchard near the house of his bride. After he climbed to the top of a pear tree, he saw her standing in her room and combing her hair. When he compared all that he was now seeing with the picture that he had painted of it in his homesickness, he realized that he was very much destined to become a poet, and he saw that the dreams of a poet contain a beauty and charm that are sought in vain in the real things of the world. And he climbed down from the tree and fled from the garden across the bridge and out of his native city. When he returned to the high mountain valley, the old Master sat just as he had before, in front of the hut on his modest mat, and played the lute with his fingers. Instead of greeting Han Fook, the Master recited two verses about the blessings of art, and the student's eyes filled with tears upon hearing such profundity and harmony.

Once more, Han Fook remained with the Master of the Perfect Word, who now gave him zither lessons since he had mastered the lute, and the months melted away like snow before the west wind. Two more times Han Fook was overcome by homesickness. One time he left the mountains secretly at night, but before he reached the last bend in the valley, the nocturnal wind blew across the zither hanging near the door of the hut, and the tones flew after him and called him back in such a way that he could not resist. The other time he dreamed that he was planting a young tree in his garden. His wife stood nearby, and his children were watering the tree with wine and milk. When he awoke, the moon was shining into his room, and he got up in an agitated state and looked at the Master slumbering next to him with his gray beard softly trembling. At first Han Fook was overcome by bitter hatred toward this man who, so it seemed, had destroyed his life and had robbed him of his future. He was about to pounce on the Master and murder him, but the wise old man opened his eyes and instantly smiled with a sad and fine gentleness that disarmed the student.

"Remember, Han Fook," the old man said softly, "you are free to do whatever you please. You may return to your home and plant trees. You may hate and kill me. It doesn't matter."

"Oh, how could I hate you!" exclaimed the poet, tremendously moved. "It would be like hating heaven itself."

And he remained and learned to play the zither, followed by the flute, and later he began to write poems under the Master's guidance. Slowly he grasped that mysterious art and learned how to say seemingly plain and simple things in such a way that they stirred the soul of the listener like the wind on the surface of the water. He described the coming of the sun as it hesitates on the edge of the mountains, and the soundless darting of fish when they flee like shadows underwater, and the swaying of a young willow in the spring wind. And when people heard his words, it was not only the sun, the play of fish, or the whispering of the willow that they depicted. It seemed that heaven and earth chimed together for one moment in perfect harmony, and the listeners would think with pleasure or pain about something that they loved or hated—the boy about his games, the young man about his lover, and the old man about death.

Han Fook lost track of the years that he spent with the Master at the source of the Great River. It often seemed to him as though it had been only yesterday that he had entered the valley and been received by the old man playing the lute. It also seemed as if all the times and ages of humankind had faded and become unreal.

Then one morning he awoke alone in the hut, and no matter where he searched and called, he could not find the Master. Autumn seemed to have arrived overnight, and a rough wind shook the old hut. Great flocks of migratory birds flew over the ridge of the mountains even though it was not their time to do so.

Han Fook took the little lute with him and traveled to his native land. Wherever he met people, they addressed him with the proper greeting for old and distinguished men. When he came to his home city, he learned that his father, his bride, and his relatives had died, and other people were living in their houses. That evening the festival of lanterns was celebrated on the bank of the river, and the poet Han Fook stood across the water on the darker bank, leaning on the trunk of the old tree, and when he began to play the lute, the women sighed and looked into the night, delighted and anxious, and the young girls called out to the lute player, whom they could not find anywhere. None of them had ever heard such sounds from a lute before, they exclaimed loudly. Meanwhile, Han Fook smiled. He looked into the river where the reflections of the thousand lanterns were floating, and just as he could no longer distinguish between the reflections and the real lanterns, so he found in his soul no difference between this festival and the first one, when he had stood there as a young man and had first heard the words of the strange Master.

FLUTE DREAM

"*H*ere," my father said, and he gave me a small ivory flute. "Take this, and don't forget your old father when you entertain people in distant countries with your music. It's high time you saw the world and learned something. I had this flute made for you because you don't like to do any other kind of work and just want to sing all the time. But I want you to remember to sing mostly songs that are pretty and pleasant. Otherwise, it would be a shame for the God-given gift that you have."

My dear father understood very little about music. He was a scholar. He thought I had only to blow into the pretty little flute, and everything would be fine. Since I didn't want to contradict him, I thanked him, put the flute into my pocket, and said farewell.

I knew our valley up to the large court mill. Beyond that, the world began for me, and I liked it very much. A bee that was tired of flying settled on my sleeve, and I carried it with me, so that I would later have a messenger who could carry my regards back home from my first resting place.

Woods and meadows accompanied me on my way, and the river ran briskly along. I realized that the world was not much different from my home. The trees and flowers, the ears of corn and hazelnut bushes spoke to me. I sang their songs along with them, and they understood me, just as they did at home.

All at once a young girl came out of the woods. She carried a basket on her arm and was wearing a broad, shady straw hat on her blond head.

"Good day," I said to her. "Where are you going?"

"I must bring the harvesters their food," she said, and walked alongside me. "And where are you going today?"

"I'm going to see the world. My father sent me away. He thinks I should play the flute for people. But I can't really do it yet. I've got to learn first."

"Well, well. But what can you actually do? You must be able to do something."

"Nothing special. I can sing songs."

"What kind of songs?"

"All kinds of songs, you know. I can sing songs for morning and evening and for all the trees and animals and flowers. For example, right now I could sing a pretty song about a young girl who comes out of the woods and brings food to the harvesters."

"Can you really do that? Well, then sing it for me."

"All right, but first tell me your name."

"Brigitte."

Then I sang the song about pretty Brigitte with the straw hat, and what she had in her basket, and how the flowers looked after her, and how the blue bind-weed from the garden fence reached for her, and I put everything that fit the scene into my song. She paid close attention and said my song was good. And when I told her that I was hungry, she opened the lid of the basket and took out a piece of bread for me. As I took a bite and kept walking at a fast pace, she said, "You shouldn't eat while walking. You should only do one thing at a time." And so we sat down in the grass, and I ate my bread, and she wrapped her tan hands around her knees and looked at me.

"Do you want to sing something for me again?" she asked when I was finished eating.

"Certainly. What should I sing?"

"Sing about a girl whose sweetheart has run away, and she is sad."

"No, I can't do that. I don't know what that's like, and I don't like sad things. My father said I should sing only nice and pleasant songs all the time. So I'll sing you something about the cuckoo or the butterfly."

"And you know nothing at all about love?"

"About love? Oh yes, it's the most beautiful thing there is."

Immediately I began singing about the sunbeam that loved the red poppy flowers and how he played with them and was full of joy. And about the little female finch who waited for the male finch, and when he came, she flew away and pretended to be scared. And I continued to sing about the girl with the brown eyes, and about the young man who came and sang and sang and received a piece of bread for his singing. But now he didn't want bread anymore. He wanted a kiss from the maiden and wanted to peer into her brown eyes, and he continued to sing for a long time and didn't stop singing until she smiled and closed his mouth with her lips.

Then Brigitte leaned over and closed my mouth with her lips and closed her eyes and opened them again, and I looked at the golden-brown stars and saw myself and several meadow flowers reflected in them.

"The world is very beautiful," I said. "My father was right. Now I'll help you carry the food to your people."

I took her basket, and we continued to walk. Her step sounded in stride with mine, and her good humor matched mine as well. The forest talked to us softly and coolly from the mountaintop. I had never wandered with so much delight, and I sang cheerfully for quite some time until I almost burst with exhilaration. There were just too many things rushing together from valley and mountain, from grass, leaves, river, and bushes, and they all told stories.

Right then I had to think: If I could understand and sing all these thousands of songs of the world at the same time, about the grass and flowers and people and clouds and everything, about the jungles and pine forests and also about the animals, and in addition all the songs about the distant seas and mountains and stars and moons, and when all that could resound and sing at the same time within me, then I would be the dear Lord Himself, and every new song would have to glow like a star in heaven.

But just as I was thinking all this, I grew very quiet and felt strange because none of this had ever occurred to me before. Meanwhile, Brigitte stood still and held my hand tightly on the handle of the basket.

"Now I must go over that hill," she said. "Our people are over there in the field. And you? Where are you going? Do you want to come with me?"

"No, I can't come with you. I must see the world. Thanks very much for the bread, Brigitte, and for the kiss. I'll think of you often."

She took the basket of food, and her eyes tilted toward me over the basket in the brown shadow, and her lips hung on mine, and her kiss was so good and tender that I almost became sad because I felt so good. But I quickly said farewell and marched down the road.

The girl climbed the hill slowly, and she stood under the leaves hanging from a birch tree on the edge of the woods and looked after me. As I waved to her and tilted my hat on top of my head, she nodded to me one more time and disappeared silently like a picture into the shadows of the birch trees.

So I calmly went my way and was steeped in thought until the road led me around a corner, where a mill stood, and next to the mill was a boat on water, and a man was sitting in the boat, and he seemed to be waiting for me, for when I took off my hat and climbed into the boat, it began to sail at once and headed down the river. I sat in the middle of the boat, and the man sat behind at the helm, and when I asked him where we were going, he looked up and regarded me with veiled gray eyes.

"Wherever you would like," he said with a subdued voice. "Down the river and into the sea, or to the large cities. You have the choice. It all belongs to me."

"It all belongs to you? Then you're the king."

"Perhaps," he said. "And you're a poet, it seems to me. So sing me a song about sailing."

I collected myself. I was somewhat afraid of the solemn man, and our boat sped silently down the river. I sang about the river that carried the ships and reflected the sun and rushed against the rocky banks with force, and then joyfully completed its journey.

The man's face did not change, and when I stopped, he nodded like a dreamer. And suddenly, to my astonishment, he himself began to sing, and he too sang about the river and the river's journey through the valleys, but his song was more beautiful and more powerful than mine, and it all sounded very different. The way he sang, the river rushed from the mountains as a staggering destroyer, sinister and wild. The gnashing current felt itself harnessed by the mills and covered by bridges. It hated each boat that it had to carry, and it smiled as it cradled and rocked the white corpses of drowned people in its waves and long green water plants.

None of this pleased me, and yet the sound was so beautiful and mysterious that I became completely confused and said nothing out of fear. If everything that this old, fine, and smart singer sang with his subdued voice was true, then all my songs were only foolishness and mere boyish games. The world was not basically good and bright like God's heart, but rather was dark and ailing, evil and sinister, and when the woods murmured, it was not out of pleasure but due to torture.

We continued sailing, and the shadows grew long, and each time I began to sing, it sounded less bright, and my voice became softer, and each time the strange singer responded with a song that made the world even more enigmatic and painful, and I became more disconcerted and sad.

My soul hurt, and I regretted that I had not remained on land with the flowers and the beautiful Brigitte. To console myself in the

growing dusk, I sang again about Brigitte and her kisses, in a loud voice through the nocturnal glimmer.

As it grew darker, I became silent, and the man at the helm began singing. He, too, sang about love and the pleasure of love, about brown eyes and blue eyes, about red moist lips. It was beautiful and gripping how he sang, full of grief and sorrow about the river growing dark. But in his song love had also become dark, anxious, and a deadly mystery that caused people to grope around and become confused, until in their hurt, need, and yearning, they tormented and killed one another.

I listened and became tired and despondent, as if I had been traveling for years and had waded through nothing but distress and misery. I felt the stranger constantly infecting me with a gentle, cool stream of sadness and spiritual anxiety that crept into my heart.

"So life is actually not the most sublime and beautiful thing in the world," I finally cried with bitterness. "It's death. Well, then I beg you, sad king, sing me a song about death."

The man at the helm sang about death, and he sang more beautifully than I had ever heard anyone sing. Nevertheless, not even death was the most beautiful and sublime thing in the world, nor did he consider it consolation. Death was life, and life was death, and they were entwined in an eternal furious struggle of love, and this was the ultimate word and the meaning of the world. From there came a glimmer that exalted all misery, and from there came a shadow that cast a gloom on all pleasure and beauty and covered it with darkness. But pleasure burned out of the darkness more intensely and more beautifully, and love glowed more deeply during this night.

I listened and became very quiet. I had no will other than that of the strange man. His glance settled on me. It was silent and possessed a certain sad kindness, and his gray eyes were full of the hurt and beauty in the world. He smiled at me, and then I took courage and implored, "Can't we turn around? I'm scared here in the night. I want to turn around and go where I can find Brigitte or return home to my father."

The man stood up and pointed into the night, and his lantern shone bright on his lean firm face.

"There is no way back," he said in a sincere and friendly way. "You must always move forward if you want to fathom the world. You've already had the best and most beautiful from the girl with brown eyes, and the farther you are from her, the more beautiful and better it will become. So continue to travel where you like. I'm going to give you my place at the helm."

I was deeply despondent, and yet I realized that he was right. Full of nostalgia, I thought about Brigitte, home, and everything that had been close and dear to me and everything that I had lost. But now I wanted to take the stranger's place and be at the helm. This is the way it had to be. Consequently, I stood up in silence and went to the helm, and the man came toward me in silence. When we were right next to each other, he looked straight into my eyes and gave me his lantern.

Then when I took my place at the helm with the lantern by my side, I realized with fright that the man had disappeared. But I was not horrified. I had sensed it. It seemed as if my beautiful day of wandering and Brigitte and my father and home had only been a dream, and that I was old and sad and had been sailing forever on this nocturnal river.

I realized that I was not allowed to call the man, and as soon as

I understood this, I felt chilled to the bone and wanted to know if what I had already sensed was true. So I leaned over the water and lifted the lantern and saw a sharp and serious face with gray eyes reflected in the dark water—an old, knowing face—and it was me.

And since there was no way back, I continued my voyage through the night.

A
Dream
About the
Gods

I walked alone and helplessly and saw that everything around me was becoming dark and shapeless. So I began searching and running to find what had happened to all the light. All at once I saw a new building with glistening windows and a light as bright as day shining above the doors, and I went through a gate and entered a brightly lit hall. Many people had gathered there and sat quietly, full of attention, for they had come to be consoled and enlightened by the priests of science.

In front of the people on a raised platform stood a priest of science, a somber man dressed in black with intelligent, tired eyes, and he spoke with a clear, mild, and convincing voice to the numerous people in the audience. There were bright charts in front of him with many pictures of gods. He stepped up to the god of war and told the listeners how this god originated long ago in the olden days, out of the needs and wishes of the people of that time, who had not yet recognized the unity of all the world's forces. No, they had always seen just the single and momentary thing, those primitive people, and so they needed and created for each thing a special god—a god for the sea and the land, for hunting and war, for rain and sun. And thus the god of war was called into being. The lecturer who served wisdom told the audience politely and clearly where this god's first statues had been erected and when the first sacrifices had been made to him, until this god had later become superfluous due to the triumph of knowledge.

As he moved his hand to extinguish the light shining on this chart, the god of war faded and was gone. In its place appeared a picture of the god of sleep. This picture was explained much too quickly, for I would have liked to hear much more about this noble god. Soon after his picture faded away, others appeared—the god of drink and the god of joyful love and the goddesses of farming, hunting, and home. Each one of these divinities radiated their unique form and beauty as a greeting and reflection from the remote early stage of civilization. They were all explained, with reasons given for why they had long since become superfluous. One image after the next was extinguished by the lecturer and then vanished, and each time a small refined triumph of the mind registered in us, along with mild sympathy and regret in our hearts.

But some people laughed throughout and clapped their hands and shouted, "Get them away!" even before the words of the learned man came to an end and the pictures were extinguished.

As we listened attentively, we learned that not even birth and death needed special symbols any longer, nor did love, envy, hate, or anger, for humankind had recently tired of all these gods and realized that individual forces and qualities did not exist in the souls of human beings or in the depths of the earth and sea. Rather, there was only a primordial force, and the next great task of the human mind was to explore this essence.

Meanwhile, the hall had become dimmer and darker, and I was not certain whether it was due to the extinguishing of the pictures or to other reasons unknown to me. Whatever the cause was, I realized that the pure and eternal source of all things would not be illuminated in this temple, and I decided to flee this house in search of brighter places.

But before I was able to act on my decision, I saw the twilight in the hall become even more dismal, and the people grew restless and began to shout and push by each other as sheep do when a storm suddenly erupts and scares them. Nobody desired to listen to the words of the wise man anymore. The crowd was overcome by a terrible fear and became frantic. I heard sighs and cries and saw people forcing their way to the gates. The air became full of dust and as thick as brimstone. It was completely gloomy, but behind the high windows one could see a turbulent glow and a dim red flicker as in a fire.

I lost consciousness. I lay on the ground. Numerous people fled and stepped on me.

When I woke up and straightened myself out with my bloodied hands, I was completely alone in an empty and destroyed building, whose walls were falling and splitting apart and threatening to collapse on me. In the distance I heard noise and thunder and random sounds roaring faintly. The air that beamed through the broken walls vibrated from fires as if from a painful bleeding visage. But the suffocating gloom had vanished.

As I crawled out of the ruined temple of knowledge, I saw half the city standing in flames and the dark sky fluttering through fiery columns and trails of smoke. Dead people lay here and there in the rubble of the buildings. It was quiet all around me, although I could detect the crackling and the whispering of the distant sea of flames. And beyond it I heard a wild and dreadful howling that came from very far away, as if all the people of the earth had raised their voices in an endless cry or sob.

The world was sinking, and I was hardly surprised. It was as if I had been waiting for this a long time.

Now I saw a boy coming out of the middle of the flames and the collapsing city. He had his hands in his pockets and skipped and danced from one foot to the next. He seemed resilient and full of life. Suddenly he stood still and whistled in a particular way. It was our friendship whistle from my high school days, and the boy was my friend Gustav, who later shot himself as a university student. All of a sudden, I was like him and once again a boy of twelve, and the burning city and distant thunder and roaring and howling storm from all the corners of the world sounded wonderfully delightful to our alert ears. Oh, now everything was good, and the dark nightmare in which I had been living for so many desperate years went away and sank out of sight.

With a laugh, Gustav pointed to a castle and a high tower that had just collapsed against each other. May that junk collapse! It was no real loss. One could build new and more beautiful things. Thank God that Gustav was there again! Now life had meaning once more.

Just then, an enormous figure freed itself from a gigantic cloud that had arisen over the collapse of the majestic building. Full of expectation, we both stared at it in silence. Slowly the head of a god, along with gigantic arms, stretched itself up into the air, and the figure stepped triumphantly into the smoke-filled world. It was the god of war, exactly as I had seen him depicted in the temple of knowledge. But he was alive and enormously large, and his flaming, illuminated face smiled proudly, like a boy who was in good spirits. Right away, without saying a word, we agreed to follow him, and we pursued him as if we were on wings, flying rapidly and tempestuously above the burning city in the wide fluttering stormy night as our hearts pounded in excitement.

The god of war stopped on the peak of the mountain. He was jubilant and shook his round shield—and behold, in the distance large holy figures raised themselves from all edges of the circle of the earth and came toward him. They were tremendous and glorious, those gods and goddesses, demons and demigods. The god of love came floating, and the god of sleep came tumbling, and the goddess of hunting was slender and severe. They kept coming, with no end in sight. And since I was blinded by their noble figures, I lowered my eyes, and soon I realized that I was no longer alone with my dear friend. All around us stood a new kind of people, and together we bowed on our knees before the gods who were returning home.

STRANGE NEWS
FROM
ANOTHER
PLANET

*I*n one of the southern provinces of our beautiful planet there was a horrible catastrophe. An earthquake, accompanied by terrible thunderstorms and floods, caused great destruction to three large villages and all their gardens, fields, forests, and farms. Many people and animals were killed, and saddest of all, the villagers lacked enough flowers to make wreaths for the dead and adorn their graves in the appropriate way.

Of course, the people took care of everything else that had to be done. Immediately after the horrible event, messengers rushed through the neighboring regions carrying pleas for aid and charity, and from all the towers of the entire province, chanters could be heard singing those stirring and deeply touching verses known for ages as the "Salutation to the Goddess of Compassion." It was impossible for anyone listening to these chants to resist them. Large groups of rescuers and helpers came right away from all the towns and cities, and those unfortunate people who had lost the roofs over their heads were overwhelmed by kind invitations and took refuge in the dwellings of relatives, friends, and strangers. Food and clothes, wagons and horses, tools, stones, and wood, and many other useful things were brought from all over. The old men, women, and children were comforted, consoled, and led away to shelters by kindly hands. The injured were carefully washed and bandaged. And while some people were still searching for victims of the quake under the ruins, others had already begun to clear away the fallen roofs, to prop up the wobbly walls with beams, and to prepare everything necessary for the quick reconstruction of the villages. Still, a cloud of horror from the accident hung in the air, and the dead were a reminder to everyone that this was a time of mourning and austere silence. Yet a joyful readiness and a certain vibrant festive mood could also be detected in all the faces and voices of the people, for they were inspired by their common action and zeal and the certainty that they were all doing something unusual and necessary, something beautiful and deserving of thanks. Initially people had worked in silence and awe, but cheerful voices and the soft sounds of singing could soon be heard here and there. As one might well imagine, two ancient proverbs were among the favorites that were sung: "Blessed are those who bring help to those who have recently been overcome by need. Don't they drink the good deed as a parched garden drinks the first rainfall, and shouldn't they respond with flowers of gratitude?" and "The serenity of God flows from common action."

However, it was just then that they discovered they did not have enough flowers for the burials. To be sure, the first dead bodies to be found had been buried and adorned with flowers and branches gathered from the destroyed gardens. Then the people began fetching all the flowers in the vicinity. But as luck would have it, they were in a special dilemma because the three destroyed villages had been the ones with the largest and most beautiful gardens of flowers during this time of year. It was here that visitors came each year to see the narcissus and crocuses because they could not be found anywhere else in such immense quantities. Moreover, they were always cultivated with great care in remarkably different colors. Yet all this had now been devastated and ruined. So the people were in a quandary—they did not know how to follow the customary rites regarding the burial of the dead. Tradition required that before burial each human being and each animal be adorned lavishly with flowers of the season, and that the burial ritual be all the richer and more resplendent, the more sudden and more sorrowful that death had struck.

The Chief Elder of the province, who was one of the first to appear with help in his wagon, soon found himself so overwhelmed by questions, requests, and complaints that he had difficulty keeping his composure. But he took heart. His eyes remained bright and friendly; his voice was clear and polite; and under his white beard his lips never lost the silent, kind smile for one moment—something that suited him as a wise councilor.

"My friends," he said, "a calamity has struck that was most likely sent by the gods to test us. Of course, whatever has been destroyed here, we shall be able to rebuild for our brothers and give it all back to them, and I thank the gods that I've been able to experience in my old age how you all stopped whatever you were doing and came here to help. But where are we going to find the flowers to adorn all these dead people and celebrate their transformation in a beautiful and reverent manner? As long as we are alive and well, we must make sure that not a single one of these weary pilgrims be buried without their rightful floral tribute. Don't you all agree?"

"Yes," they cried. "We all agree."

"I knew it," said the Elder in his fatherly voice. "Now I want to tell you, my friends, what we must do. We must carry all the remains that cannot be buried today to the large summer temple high in the mountains, where snow is still on the ground. They will be safe there and will not decompose before we can fetch flowers for them. Only one person can really help us obtain so many flowers at this time of the year, and that is the King. Therefore one of us must be sent to the King to request his assistance."

And again the people all nodded and cried out, "Yes, yes, to the King!"

"So be it," the Elder continued, and everyone was pleased to see his pleasant smile glistening from beneath his white beard. "But whom shall we send to the King? He must be young and robust because he shall travel far on our best horse. Furthermore, he must be handsome and kind and have sparkling eyes, so that the King's heart will not be able to resist him. He needn't say much, but his eyes must be able to speak. Clearly, it would be best if we sent a child, the handsomest child in the community. But how could he possibly undertake such a journey? You must help me, my friends, and if there is anyone here who wants to volunteer to be the messenger, or if you know somebody suitable for this task, please tell me."

The Elder stopped and looked around with his bright eyes, but nobody stepped forward. Not a single voice could be heard. When he repeated his question a second and then a third time, a young man suddenly emerged from the crowd. He was sixteen years old, practically still a boy, and he fixed his eyes on the ground and blushed as he greeted the Elder.

As soon as the Elder looked at him, he realized that the young man was the perfect messenger. So he smiled and said, "It's wonderful that you want to be our messenger. But why is it that, among all those people, you should be the one to volunteer?"

The young man raised his eyes to the old man and said, "If there is no one else here who wants to go, then I should be the one to go."

Someone from the crowd shouted, "Send him, Elder. We know him. He comes from our village, and the earthquake destroyed his flower garden, which was the most beautiful in the region."

The Elder gave the young man a friendly look and asked, "Are you sad about what happened to your flowers?"

The young man responded very softly, "Yes, I'm sorry, but that is not why I've volunteered. I had a dear friend and also a splendid young horse, my favorite, and both were killed by the earthquake. Now they are lying in our hall, and we must have flowers so that they can be buried."

The Elder blessed the young man by placing his hands on his head, and the best horse was soon brought out for him. Immediately the young man sprang onto the horse's back, slapped it on the neck, and nodded farewell to the people. Then he dashed out of the village and headed straight across the wet and ravaged fields.

The young man rode the entire day, and in order to reach the distant capital and see the King as soon as he could, he took the path over the mountains. In the evening, as it began to turn dark, he led his horse by the reins up a steep path through the forest and rocks.

A large dark bird, a kind that the young man had never seen

before, flew ahead of him, and he followed it until the bird landed on the roof of a small open temple. The young man left his horse and walked through wooden pillars into the simple sanctuary. There he found a sacrificial altar, but it was only a solid block made of a black stone not usually found in that region. On it was an obscure symbol of a deity that the messenger did not recognize—a heart that was being devoured by a wild bird.

He paid tribute to the deity by offering a bluebell flower that he had plucked at the foot of the mountain and stuck in the lapel of his coat. Thereafter he lay down in a corner of the temple, for he was very tired and wanted to sleep.

However, he could not fall asleep as easily as he was accustomed to at home each evening. Perhaps it was the bluebell on the stone, or the black stone itself, or something else, but whatever it was, something odd disturbed him by exuding a penetrating and scintillating aroma. Furthermore, the eerie symbol of the god glimmered like a ghost in the dark hall, and the strange bird sat on the roof and vigorously flapped its gigantic wings from time to time so that it seemed as if a storm were brewing.

Eventually the young man got up in the middle of the night, went outside the temple, and looked up at the bird, which raised and lowered its wings.

"Why aren't you sleeping?" asked the bird.

"I don't know," the young man replied. "Perhaps it's because I've suffered."

"What exactly have you suffered?"

"My friend and my favorite horse were both killed."

"Is dying so bad?" the bird asked disdainfully.

"Oh, no, great bird, it's not so bad. It's only a farewell. But that's not the reason why I'm sad. The bad thing is that we cannot bury my friend and my splendid horse because we no longer have any flowers."

"There are worse things than that," said the bird, ruffling its feathers indignantly.

"No, bird, there is certainly nothing worse than this. Whoever is buried without a floral tribute cannot be reborn the way his heart desires. And whoever buries his dead people without celebrating the floral tribute will continue to see their shadows in his dreams. You see, I already cannot sleep anymore because my dead people are still without flowers."

The bird rasped and screeched with its bent beak, "Young boy, you know nothing about suffering if this is all that you've experienced. Haven't you ever heard about the great evils? About hatred, murder, and jealousy?"

As he listened to these words, the young man thought he was dreaming. Then he collected himself and said discreetly, "Yes, bird, I can remember. These things are written in the old stories and tales. But they have nothing to do with reality, or perhaps it was that way once upon a time in the world before there were flowers and gods that are good. Who in the world still thinks about such things as that now?"

The bird laughed softly with its raspy voice. Then it stretched itself taller and said to the boy, "And now you want to go to the King, and I'm to show you the way?"

"Oh, you already know!" the young man joyfully exclaimed. "Yes, I'd appreciate it if you'd lead me there."

Then the great bird floated silently to the ground, spread out its wings without making a sound, and ordered the young man to leave his horse behind and fly with him to the King. In response,

the messenger sat down on the bird's back and prepared himself for the ride.

"Shut your eyes," the bird commanded, and the young man did as he was told, and they flew through the darkness of the sky silently and softly like the flight of an owl. The messenger could hear only the cold wind roaring in his ears, and they flew and flew the entire night.

When it was early morning, they came to a stop, and the bird cried out, "Open your eyes!" The young man opened his eyes and saw that he was standing at the edge of a forest. Beneath him was a plain that glistened so brightly in the early hours that its light blinded him.

"You'll find me here in the forest again," the bird announced, whereupon he shot into the sky like an arrow and soon disappeared into the blue.

A strange feeling came over the young messenger as he began wandering from the forest into the broad plain. Everything around him was so different and changed that he did not know whether he was awake or dreaming. Meadows and trees were just as they were at home. The sun shone, and the wind played in the fresh grass. But there were no people or animals, no houses or gardens to be seen. Rather, it appeared that an earthquake had taken its toll here just as in the young man's home country, for ruins of buildings, broken branches, uprooted trees, wrecked fences, and lost farm equipment were spread all over the ground. Suddenly he saw a dead man lying in the middle of a field. He had not been buried and was horribly decomposed. The young man felt a deep revulsion at the sight of the dead body, and nausea swelled up within him, for he had never seen anything like it. The dead man's face was not even covered and seemed to have already been ravaged by the birds in its decayed condition. So the young man plucked some green leaves and flowers, and with his face turned away, he covered the visage of the dead man with them.

An inexpressible, disgusting, and stifling smell hung in the tepid air and seemed glued to the entire plain. Again the young man saw a corpse lying in the grass, with ravens circling overhead. There was also a horse without its head, and bones from humans and animals, and they all lay abandoned in the sun. There seemed to have been no thought of a floral tribute and burial. The young man feared that an incredible catastrophe had caused the death of every single person in this country, and that there were so many dead that he would never be able to pick enough flowers to cover their faces. Full of dread, with half-closed eyes, he wandered farther. The stench of carrion and blood swept toward him from all sides, and an even stronger wave of unspeakable misery and suffering rose from a thousand different piles of corpses and rubble. The messenger thought that he was caught in an awful dream. Perhaps it was a warning from the divine powers, he thought, because his own dead were still without their floral tribute and burial. Then he recalled what the mysterious bird had said to him the night before on the temple roof, and he thought he heard its sharp voice once more claiming, "There are much worse things."

Now he realized that the bird had carried him to another planet and that everything he saw was real and true. He remembered the feeling he had experienced when he had occasionally listened to ghastly tales of primeval times. It was this same exact feeling that he had now—a horrid chill, and behind the chill a quiet, pleasant feeling of comfort, for all this was infinitely far away from him and had long since passed. Everything here was like a horror story. This whole strange world of atrocity, corpses, and vultures seemed to have no meaning or order. In fact, it seemed subject to incomprehensible laws, insane laws, according to which bad, foolish, and nasty things occurred instead of beautiful and good things.

In the meantime he noticed a live human being walking across the field, a farmer or hired hand, and he ran quickly toward him, calling out. When the young man approached, he was horrified, and his heart was overcome by compassion, for this farmer was terribly ugly and no longer resembled anything like a child of the sun. He seemed more like a man accustomed to thinking only about himself and to seeing only false, ugly, and horrible things happen everywhere, like a man who lived constantly in ghastly nightmares. There was not a trace of serenity or kindness in his eyes and in his entire face and being, no gratitude or trust. This unfortunate creature seemed to be without the least bit of virtue.

But the young man pulled himself together and approached the man with great friendliness, as though the man had been marked by misfortune. He greeted him in brotherly fashion and spoke to him with a smile. The ugly man stood as though paralyzed, looking bewildered with his large, bleary eyes. His voice was rough and without music, like the growl of a primitive creature. But it was impossible for him to resist the young man's cheerful and trustworthy look. And after he had stared at the stranger for a while, the farmer expressed a kind of smile or grin on his rugged and crude face—ugly enough, but gentle and astonished, like the first little smile of a reborn soul that has just risen from the lowest region of the earth.

"What do you want from me?" the man asked the young stranger.

The young man responded according to the custom of his native country: "I thank you, friend, and I beg you to tell me whether I can be of service to you."

When the farmer did not reply but only stared and smiled with embarrassment, the messenger said to him, "Tell me, friend, what is going on here? What are all these horrible and terrible things?" And he pointed all around him.

The farmer had difficulty understanding him, and when the messenger repeated his question, the farmer said, "Haven't you ever seen this before? This is war. This is a battlefield." He pointed to a dark pile of ruins and cried, "That was my house." And when the stranger looked into his murky eyes with deep sympathy, the farmer lowered them and looked down at the ground.

"Don't you have a king?" the young man asked, and when the farmer said yes, he asked further, "Where is he?"

The man pointed to a small, barely visible encampment in the distance. The messenger said farewell by placing his hand on the man's forehead, then departed. In response, the farmer felt his forehead with both hands, shook his heavy head with concern, and stared after the stranger for a long time.

The messenger walked and walked over rubble and past horrifying sights until he arrived at the encampment. Armed men were standing here and there or scurrying about. Nobody seemed to notice him, and he walked between the people and the tents until he found the largest and most beautiful tent, which belonged to the King. Once there, he entered.

The King was sitting on a simple low cot inside the tent. Next to him lay his coat, and behind him in deep shadow crouched his servant, who had fallen asleep. The King himself sat bent over in deep thought. His face was handsome and sad; a crop of gray hair hung over his tan forehead. His sword lay before him on the ground.

The young man greeted the King silently with sincere respect, just as he would have greeted his own King, and he remained standing with his arms folded across his chest until the King glanced at him.

"Who are you?" he asked severely, drawing his dark eyebrows together, but his glance focused on the pure and serene features of the stranger, and the young man regarded him with such trust and friendliness that the King's voice grew milder.

"I've seen you once before," he said, trying to recall. "You resemble somebody I knew in my childhood."

"I'm a stranger," said the messenger.

"Then it was a dream," remarked the King softly. "You remind me of my mother. Say something to me. Tell me why you are here."

The young man began: "A bird brought me here. There was an earthquake in my country. We want to bury our dead, but there are no flowers."

"No flowers?" said the King.

"No, no more flowers at all. And it's terrible, isn't it, when people want to bury their dead and the floral tribute cannot be celebrated? After all, it's important for people to experience their transformation in glory and joy."

Suddenly it occurred to the messenger that there were many dead people on the horrible field who had not yet been buried, and he held his breath while the King regarded him, nodded, and sighed deeply.

"I wanted to seek out our King and request that he send us many flowers," the messenger continued. "But as I was in the temple on the mountain, a great bird came and said he wanted to bring me to the King, and he carried me through the skies to you. Oh, dear King, it was the temple of an unknown deity on whose roof the bird sat, and this god had a most peculiar symbol on his altar—a heart that was being devoured by a wild bird. During the night, however, I had a conversation with that great bird, and it is only now that I understand its words, for it said that there is much more suffering and many more terrible things in the world than I knew. And now I am here and have crossed the large field and have seen endless suffering and misfortune during this short time—oh, much more than there is in our most horrible tales. So now I've come to you, oh King, and I would like to ask you if I can be of any service to you."

The King, who listened attentively, tried to smile, but his handsome face was so serious and bitter and sad that he could not.

"I thank you," he said. "You've already been of service to me. You've reminded me of my mother. I thank you for this."

The young man was disturbed because the King could not smile. "You're so sad," he said. "Is it because of this war?"

"Yes," said the King.

The young man had the feeling that the King was a noble man who was deeply depressed, and he could not refrain from breaking a rule of courtesy and asking him a straightforward question: "But tell me, please, why are you waging such wars on your planet? Who's to blame for all this? Are you yourself responsible?"

The King stared at the messenger for a long time. He seemed indignant and angry at the audacity of this question. However, he was not able to maintain his gloomy look as he peered into the bright and innocent eyes of the stranger.

"You're a child," said the King, "and there are things that you can't understand. The war is nobody's fault. It occurs by itself, like thunder and lightning. All of us who must fight wars are not the perpetrators. We are only their victims."

"Then you must all die very easily?" the young man asked. "In my country death is not at all feared, and most people go willingly to their death. Many approach their transformation with joy. But nobody would ever dare to kill another human being. It must be different on your planet."

"People are indeed killed here," said the King, shaking his head. "But we consider it the worst of crimes. Only in war are people permitted to kill because nobody kills for his own advantage. Nobody kills out of hate or envy. Rather, they do what society demands of them. Still, you'd be mistaken if you believed that my people die easily. You just have to look into the faces of our dead, and you can see that they have difficulty dying. They die hard and unwillingly."

The young man listened to all this and was astounded by the sadness and gravity in the lives of the people on this planet. He would have liked to ask many more questions, but he had a clear sense that he would never grasp the complex nature of all these obscure and terrible things. Indeed, he felt no great desire now to understand them. Either these sorrowful people were creatures of an inferior order, or they had not been blessed by the light of the gods and were still ruled by demons. Or perhaps a singular mishap was determining the course of life on this planet. It seemed to him much too painful and cruel to keep questioning the King, compelling him to provide answers and make confessions that could only be bitter and humiliating for him. He was sorry for these people—people who lived in gloom and dread of death and nevertheless killed each other in droves. These people, whose faces took on ignoble, crude countenances like that of the farmer, or who had expressions of deep and terrible sorrow like that of the King. They seemed to him to be rather peculiar—and almost ridiculous, to be ridiculous and foolish in a disturbing and shameful way.

There was one more question, however, that the young man could not repress. Even if these poor creatures were backward, children behind the times, sons of a latter-day planet without peace; even if their lives ran their course as a convulsive cramp and ended in desperate slaughter; even if they let their dead lie on the fields and perhaps even ate them—for horror tales were told about such things occurring in primeval times—they must still have a presentiment of the future, a dream of the gods, some spark of soul in them. Otherwise this entire unpleasant world would be only a meaningless mistake.

"Forgive me, King," the young man said with a flattering voice. "Forgive me if I ask you one more question before I leave your strange country."

"Go ahead," replied the King, who was perplexed by this stranger, for the young man seemed to have a sensitive, mature, and insightful mind in many ways, but in others he seemed to be a small child whom one had to protect and was not to be taken seriously.

"My foreign King," spoke the messenger, "you've made me sad. You see, I've come from another country, and the great bird on the temple roof was right. There is infinitely more misery here than I could have imagined. Your life seems to be a dreadful nightmare, and I don't know whether you are ruled by gods or demons. You see, King, we have a legend—I used to believe that it was all fairy-tale rubbish and empty smoke. It is a legend about how such things as war and death and despair were common in our country at one time.

These terrible words, which we have long since stopped using in our language, can be read in collections of our old tales, and they sound awful to us and even a little ridiculous. Today I've learned that these tales are all true, and I see you and your people dying and suffering what I've known only from the terrible legends of primeval times. But now tell me, don't you have in your soul a sort of intimation that you're not doing the right thing? Don't you have a yearning for bright, serene gods, for sensible and cheerful leaders and mentors? Don't you ever dream in your sleep about another, more beautiful life where nobody is envious of others, where reason and order prevail, where people treat other people only with cheerfulness and consideration? Have you never thought that the world might be a totality, and that it might be beneficial and salutary to honor this unity of all things? Don't you know anything about what we at home call music and divine worship and blessedness?"

As he listened to these words, the King's head sank, and when he raised it again, his face had been transformed, and it glowed radiantly with a smile, even though there were tears in his eyes.

"Beautiful boy," said the King, "I don't know for certain whether you're a child, a sage, or perhaps a god. But I can tell you that we sense all this and cradle it in our souls, all that you have mentioned. We have intimations of happiness, freedom, and gods. Indeed, we have a legend about a wise man who lived long ago and who perceived the unity of the worlds as harmonious music of the heavenly spheres. Does this answer suffice? You may be, you see, a blessed creature from another world, or you may even be God Himself. Whatever the case may be, you have no happiness in your heart, no power, no will that does not live as a presentiment, a reflection, a distant shadow in our hearts, too."

Suddenly the King stood up, and the young man was surprised, for the King's face was soaked in a bright, clear smile for a moment like the first rays of the sun.

"Go now," he cried to the messenger. "Go, and let us fight and murder! You've made my heart soft. You've reminded me of my mother. Enough, enough of this, you dear handsome boy. Go now, and flee before the next battle begins! I'll think of you when the blood flows and the cities burn, and I'll think of the world as a whole, and how our folly and fury and ruthlessness cannot separate us from it. Farewell, and give my regards to your planet, and give my regards to your deity, whose symbol is a heart being devoured by a wild bird. I know this heart, and I know the bird very well. And don't forget, my handsome friend from a distant land: When you think of your friend, the poor King in war, do not think of him as he sat on the cot plunged in deep sorrow. Think of him with tears in his eyes and blood on his hands and how he smiled!"

The King raised the flap of the tent with his own hand so as not to wake the servant, and he let the stranger out. The young man crossed the plain again steeped in thought, and as he went, he saw a large city blazing in flames on the horizon in the evening light. He climbed over dead people and the decayed carcasses of horses until it grew dark and he reached the edge of the forest.

Suddenly the great bird swooped down from the clouds and took the young man on its wings, and they flew through the night silently and softly like the flight of the owl.

When the young man awoke from a restless sleep, he lay in the small temple in the mountains, and his horse stood before the temple in the wet grass, greeting the day with a neigh. However, the messenger recalled nothing of the great bird and his flight to a foreign planet, nothing of the King and the battlefield. All this remained only as a shadow in his soul, a tiny, obscure pain, as if from a sharp thorn. It hurt, just as sympathy hurts when nothing can be done, just as a little unfulfilled wish can torment us in dreams until we finally encounter the person we have secretly loved, with whom we want to share our joy and whose smile we wish to see.

The messenger mounted his horse and rode the entire day until he came to the capital, where he was admitted to the King. And he proved to be the right messenger, for the King received him with a greeting of grace by touching his forehead and remarking, "Your request was fulfilled before I even heard it."

Soon thereafter the messenger received a charter from the King that placed all the flowers of the whole country at his command. Companions and messengers went with him to the villages to pick them up. Joined by wagons and horses, they took a few days to go around the mountain on the flat country road that led back to his province and community. The young man led the wagons and carts, horses and donkeys, all loaded with the most beautiful flowers from gardens and greenhouses that were plentiful in the north. There were enough flowers to place wreaths on the bodies of the dead and to adorn their graves lavishly, as well as enough to plant a memorial flower, a bush, and a young tree for each dead person, as custom demanded. And the pain caused by the death of his friend and his favorite horse subsided in the young man and turned into silent, serene memories after he adorned and buried them and planted two flowers, two bushes, and two fruit trees over their graves.

Now that he had done what he had desired and fulfilled his obligations, the memory of that journey through the night began to stir in his soul, and he asked his friends and relatives to permit him to spend a day all alone. So he sat under the Tree of Contemplation one whole day and night. There he unfolded, clean and unwrinkled in his memory, the images of all that he had seen on the foreign planet. One day later on, he went to the Elder, requested a private talk with him, and told him all that had happened.

The Elder sat and pondered everything as he listened. Then he asked, "Did you see all this with your eyes, my friend, or was it a dream?"

"I don't know," said the young man. "I believe that it may have been a dream. However, with your permission, may I say that it seems to me there is hardly a difference whether I actually experienced everything in reality. A shadow of sadness has remained within me, and a cool wind from that other planet continues to blow upon me, right into the midst of the happiness of my life. That is why I am asking you, my honorable Elder, what to do about this."

"Return to the mountains tomorrow," the Elder said, "and go up to the place where you found the temple. The symbol of that god seems odd to me, for I've never heard of it before. It may well be that he is a god from another planet. Or perhaps the temple and its god are so old that they belong to the epoch of our earliest ancestors, to those days when there are supposed to have been weapons, fear, and dread of death among us. Go to that temple, my dear boy, and bring flowers, honey, and song."

The young man thanked the Elder and followed his advice. He took a bowl of honey, such as was customarily presented to honored guests at the first festival of the bees in early summer, and carried his lute with him. In the mountains he found the place where he had once picked the bluebell, and he found the steep rocky path in the forest that led up the mountain, where he had recently gone on foot leading his horse. However, he could not find the place of the temple or the temple itself, the black sacrificial stone, the wooden pillars, the roof, or the great bird on the roof. He could not find them on that day, nor on the next, and nobody he asked knew anything about the kind of temple that he described. So he returned to his home, and when he walked by the Shrine of Lovely Memories, he went inside and offered the honey, played the lute and sang, and told the god of lovely memories all about his dream, the temple and the bird, the poor farmer, and the dead bodies on the battlefield. And most of all, he told about the King in his war tent. Afterward he returned to his dwelling with a light heart, hung the symbol of the unity of the world in his bedroom, and recuperated from the events of the past few days in deep sleep. The next morning he helped his neighbors remove the last traces of the earthquake from the gardens and fields, singing as they worked.

FALDUM

Faldum

$\mathcal{T}$he road leading to the city of Faldum ran right through some hills, and here and there along the way it was lined with woods, large green pastures, and wheat fields. The closer it came to the city, the more it passed barns, dairy farms, gardens, and country houses. The sea was too far away to be seen, and the world seemed to consist of nothing but small hills, pretty valleys, meadows, woods, farmlands, and orchards. It was a country that had plenty of fruit and wood, milk and meat, apples and nuts. The villages were very attractive and clean, and the people were on the whole upright and diligent and did not like to undertake dangerous or disturbing projects. They felt satisfied if they could keep up with their neighbors and if their neighbors kept up with them. That was how life was in Faldum, and most countries in the world are the same, as long as unusual things do not happen.

On this morning, the pretty road that led to Faldum (the surrounding country had the same name) had become extremely lively since the cock first crowed. It bustled with people and wagons and carriages just as it did once each year, for the city held its great fair that day. Indeed, every single farmer and farmer's wife, every single master, apprentice, and farmhand, every single maiden and lad within twenty miles of the city had been thinking of the great fair for weeks and dreaming of visiting it. Of course, not everyone could go. Someone had to stay behind and look after the animals and small children, the sick and the old, and once lots were drawn, the person who lost had to remain at home and take care of house and farm. For those people, it seemed that almost a year of their lives had been futile, and everything was spoiled for them, including the beautiful sun, which stood warm and jubilant in the blue sky of late summer starting early that morning.

The women and young girls carried small baskets on their arms as they walked, and the young men with clean-shaven cheeks had pink carnations and asters in their lapels. Everyone was clad in neat Sunday clothes, and the schoolgirls had carefully braided their hair, which was still wet and sparkling in the sunshine. Those people riding in carriages wore flowers or had little red ribbons tied to the handle of the whips, and whoever could afford it had decorated the harness of his horses with brightly polished brass disks that hung along the wide decorative leather down to their legs. Rack wagons came by, whose green roofs of beech branches were bent in arches over the seats, and beneath the roofs people sat crowded together with children or baskets on their laps, most of them singing loudly in a chorus. Every now and then a wagon appeared among the others that was especially colorful, decorated with flags and paper flowers, red and blue and white, mixed in with the green leaves of the beech branches. Village music resounded bombastically from this wagon, and through the branches one could see the gold horns and trumpets gleaming softly and exquisitely in the half shadows. Little children who had been obliged to walk since sunrise began to weep from exhaustion and were comforted by their perspiring mothers. Many of them were given lifts by kind and generous drivers. An old woman was pushing twins in a carriage, both asleep, and between the sleeping children's heads lay two dolls, beautifully dressed and combed with cheeks just as round and red as those of the babies.

Those people who lived along the way but were not going to the fair this day had an entertaining morning because there was so much to see. Yet only a very few did stay at home. A ten-year-old boy sitting on the garden stairs wept because he had to remain with his grandmother. But after he sat and cried for what he thought was a sufficient amount of time, he leaped onto the road and joined some village boys as they came marching by.

Not far from there lived an old bachelor who wanted nothing to do with the fair because he did not like to spend his money. He intended to spend the day trimming the high hawthorn hedge around his garden while everyone was away celebrating, for it needed cutting. As soon as the morning dew began to evaporate, he went cheerfully about his work with his big hedge shears. But after working just about an hour, he stopped and retreated angrily into his house, for each and every boy who had come by, either on foot or on horseback, had gazed in astonishment at the man cutting the hedge and made some sort of joke about his untimely zeal, while the girls had joined in with laughter. When the old man threatened them with his long shears, they had all swung their hats, waved, and mocked him. Now he sat inside behind locked shutters; yet he peered through the cracks with envy, and when his anger gradually subsided and he saw the last few people dashing to the fair as though their lives depended on it, he put on his boots, stuck a taler into his pouch, took a cane, and got set to go. Suddenly it occurred to him that a taler was indeed a lot of money. So he pulled it out of the leather pouch, replaced it with half a taler, and tied the pouch with a string. Then he put it into his pocket, locked the house and garden gate, and ran so fast that he passed many pedestrians and even two wagons on his way to the city.

Once he was gone and his house and garden stood empty, the dust settled gently on the road. The sounds of trotting horses and brass bands floated and faded away. The sparrows began to come out of the fields of stubble. Bathed in the white dust, they inspected what was left over from the tumult. The road was empty and dead and hot. From the remote distance shouts of joy and sounds of music still drifted from time to time, faint and lost.

Just then a man emerged from the forest. The broad brim of his hat sloped over his eyes, and he meandered casually all by himself along the deserted country road. He was a large man and had the firm, calm stride of a wanderer who has traveled a great deal on foot. His clothes were plain and gray, and his eyes peered out from the shadow of his hat, carefully and serenely leaving the impression of a man who desires nothing from the world but observes everything with great attention. Indeed, nothing escaped his view. He saw the countless tangled wagon tracks running ahead of him. He saw the hoof marks of a horse that limped on its left hind foot. He saw the tiny glimmering roofs of Faldum rise on the hill in the distance. He saw a little woman, anxious and desperate, wandering about a garden as if lost and calling for someone who did not answer. He saw a small piece of metal flash on the edge of the road, and he bent over and picked up a bright round brass disk that a horse had lost from its collar. He put it into his pocket. And then he saw an old hawthorn hedge that had just been partially trimmed. The first part of the work was precise and clean and seemed to have been done with pleasure. Yet as he went along the hedge, he saw that less and less care had been taken, so that there were deep cuts, and neglected branches stuck out with sharp bristles and thorns.

Farther on the stranger found a child's doll lying on the road. A wagon wheel must have run over its head. He saw a piece of rye bread still gleaming with melted butter. Finally, he found a sturdy leather pouch with a half taler inside it. He leaned the doll against a curbstone at the edge of the road, crumbled the bread and fed the pieces to the sparrows, and stuck the pouch with the half taler into his pocket.

It was incredibly silent on the abandoned road. The turf on both sides was thick with dust and parched by the sun. Chickens ran around a nearby farmyard, and nobody could be seen far and wide as the chickens clucked and stuttered dreamily in the warm sun. But then he saw an old woman leaning over a bluish cabbage patch and pulling weeds from the dry ground. The wanderer called out and asked her how far it was to the city. She was deaf, however, and when he called again louder, she only looked at him helplessly and shook her gray head.

As the stranger walked on, he heard the sounds of music rise and fall from the city. They became more frequent and longer the closer he came to the city, until they flowed continually like a distant waterfall, music and the murmur of voices, as if all the people had gathered together and were enjoying themselves there. Now a stream flowed next to the road, wide and quiet. There were ducks on it, and brown-green water weeds beneath the blue surface. When the road began to climb, the stream curved to the side, and a stone bridge traversed it. A thin man, who looked like a tailor, was asleep atop the low wall of the bridge, with his head slumped over. His hat had fallen down into the dust, and sitting next to him, a small cute dog kept guard over him. The stranger wanted to wake the tailor because he could easily fall over the wall of the bridge while sleeping. However, once he looked over the wall, the stranger realized that it was not very high, and the water was shallow. So he let the tailor continue sleeping.

After walking up a steep footpath, the stranger came at last to the city gate of Faldum. It was wide open, and not a person was to be seen. The man strode through the gate, and suddenly his footsteps echoed loudly on a paved street, where a row of empty, unharnessed wagons and carriages were stationed alongside the houses. Some signs of life and noise sounded from other streets, but not a single soul could be found here. The little street was filled with shadows, and only the upper windows of the houses reflected the golden day. The wanderer rested here for a short time, sitting on the shaft of a rack wagon. Before he set off again, he placed the brass disk of the harness that he had found alongside the road on the driver's seat.

He had walked no farther than a block before he was engulfed by the noise and tumult of the fair. There were a hundred booths, and dealers were shouting loudly and trying to sell their goods. Children blew silver-tinseled horns. Butchers fished strings of wet sausages from large boiling kettles. A medicine man posing as a doctor stood high on a platform and peered eagerly through his thick horn-rimmed glasses. He had set up a chart that pictured all sorts of human diseases and maladies. A man with long black hair passed by his booth leading a camel by a rope. With its long neck, the camel looked arrogantly down at the crowd of people, moved its split lips back and forth, and made signs of chewing.

The man from the woods scanned everything with great interest. He let himself be pushed and shoved by the crowd. He glanced into the booth of a man who sold colored prints. At another booth he read the sayings and mottos on sugar-coated gingerbread cookies. He did not stay at any one place very long, however, and seemed to be looking for something that he had not yet found. So he moved forward slowly until he came to the large central square where a bird dealer was setting up a cage on the corner. There he listened for a while to the voices that came from the many small cages, and he answered them by whistling softly to the linnet, the quail, the canary, and the warbler.

Suddenly he was attracted by something nearby, something bright and dazzling, as if all the sunshine were concentrated on this one spot, and when he headed in that direction, he came upon a mirror hanging in a booth. Next to it were other mirrors, hundreds of them, big and small, square, round, and oval, mirrors to be hung on walls and to stand up. There were also hand mirrors and small, thin pocket mirrors that you could take anywhere, so that you would not forget your own face. The dealer stood there, caught the sun in a bright mirror, then let the sparkling reflection dance over his booth. Meanwhile, he shouted incessantly, "Mirrors, ladies and gentlemen, buy your mirrors here! The best mirrors! The cheapest mirrors in Faldum! Mirrors, ladies, splendid mirrors! Just take a look. Everything's genuine. The very best crystal!"

The stranger stopped at the booth of mirrors and appeared to find what he was looking for. Among the people examining the mirrors were three young girls from the countryside. He moved to a spot close by and watched them. They were lively and robust peasant girls, neither beautiful nor ugly, wearing thick-soled shoes and white stockings. Their blond braids had been somewhat bleached by the sun, and they had bright young eyes. Each girl had taken an inexpensive mirror in her hand, and as all three hesitated and deliberated whether they should buy, while also enjoying the sweet torment of choosing, each looked forlornly and dreamily into the translucent depths of the mirror and regarded her reflection, her mouth and eyes, the small jewel of her necklace, the freckles around her nose, the smooth part in her hair, and the rosy ear. Then they became silent and serious. The stranger, who stood right behind the girls, saw their large, almost jubilant eyes and reflections gazing at him from the mirrors.

"Oh," he heard the first girl say, "I wish I had long hair, shiny red hair, that hung down to my knees!"

Upon hearing her friend's wish, the second girl sighed softly and looked deep into her mirror. Then she, too, divulged her heart's dream with a blush and said shyly, "If I could wish, I'd like to have the most beautiful hands, totally white and delicate, with long slender fingers and rosy fingernails." As she said this, she looked at her hand holding the oval mirror. The hand was not ugly, but the fingers were a bit short and thick and had become coarse and hardened from work.

The third girl, the smallest and most vivacious of the three, laughed at all this and cried merrily, "That's not a bad wish! But you know, hands aren't all that important. What I'd prefer most of all would be to become the best and most nimble dancer in the whole country of Faldum from this moment on."

All of a sudden the girl jumped in fright and turned around. A strange face with black glaring eyes had been looking out at her in the mirror from behind her own face. It was the face of the stranger, who had stepped behind her, and until then the three girls had not noticed him. Now they stared into his face with amazement, while he nodded to them and said, "You've made three beautiful wishes, my girls. Do you really mean what you've said?"

The small girl put down the mirror and hid her hands behind her back. She wanted to pay the man back for frightening her and was thinking of a sharp word or two to say to him. But when she looked into his face, she saw so much power in his eyes that she became timid.

"Does it matter to you what I wish?" she said simply, and turned red.

But the other girl, who had wished for the elegant hands, felt that she could trust him. There was something fatherly and distinguished about him.

"Yes," she said. "We are serious about what we said. Can one wish for anything more beautiful?"

The mirror dealer had joined them, and now other people, too, were listening. The stranger had turned up the brim of his hat so that everyone could see his smooth, high forehead and imperious eyes. Now he nodded to the three girls in a friendly way, smiled, and announced, "Look, you already have what you wished for!"

The girls gazed at one another and then looked into their mirrors. Suddenly all three of them turned pale out of astonishment and joy. The first girl's hair had turned into thick golden-red locks that hung down to her knees. The second was holding her mirror in the slenderest and whitest hands, just like those of a princess, and the third was suddenly wearing red leather dancing shoes, standing with ankles as slim as those of a deer. None of the girls could grasp what had happened, but the girl with the elegant hands burst into tears of joy. She leaned on her friend's shoulder and wept blissfully into her long golden-red hair.

Now the story of the miracle spread by word of mouth and through loud cries all around the booth. A young journeyman who had watched everything stood and stared at the stranger with wide-open eyes, as though he were paralyzed.

"Would you like to wish for something?" the stranger asked him all at once.

The journeyman was frightened and completely confused. He looked around helplessly to spot something to wish for. Then he saw an enormous string of thick red sausages hanging in front of the pork butcher's stand, and he stammered as he pointed to it.

"I'd like to have a string of sausages like that."

No sooner did he say this than a wreath of sausages hung around his neck, and everyone present began to laugh and shout. People tried to move closer, and everyone wanted to make a wish. And they were all allowed to do so. The very next man was bolder and wished for new Sunday clothes from top to bottom. All at once he was wearing a fine, brand-new suit more elegant than that of the mayor. Then a country woman came up and, after summoning her courage, demanded ten talers on the spot. Immediately the talers were jingling in her pocket.

Now the people saw that real miracles were actually happening, and the news spread like wildfire throughout the marketplace and the city. People gathered rapidly in large crowds all around the booth of the mirror dealer. Many laughed and joked; others did not believe a thing and voiced their doubts. But many had already been infected by the wish-fever and came running with glowing eyes and hot faces distorted by greed and need, for they all feared that the source of the wishes might dry up before they could dip into it. Little boys wished for cookies, crossbows, bags of nuts, books, and bowling games. Little girls went away happy with new clothes, ribbons, gloves, and umbrellas. A little ten-year-old boy, who had run away from his grandmother and was excited by all the glories and splendor of the fair, wished in a clear voice for a live pony, but it had to be black. All at once a black colt neighed behind him and rubbed its head warmly on his shoulder.

An old bachelor with a walking stick in his hand forced his way through the crowd, which was totally intoxicated by the magic, and stepped forward trembling. He could barely speak a word because he was so excited.

"I wish," he said, stuttering, "I wi-wi-wish two hundred times—"

The stranger looked at him closely, then pulled a leather pouch out of his pocket and held it before the eyes of the excited little man.

"Wait a second!" said the stranger. "Didn't you lose this money pouch? There's half a taler inside."

"Yes, I did!" exclaimed the bachelor. "It's mine."

"Do you wish to have it back?"

"Yes, give it to me."

So he recovered his pouch, but at the same time he wasted his wish, and when he realized this, full of anger he lifted his cane against the stranger and tried to hit him, but he missed and smashed a mirror. The pieces of glass were still clinking as the dealer came over and demanded money, and the bachelor had to pay.

Now a stout house-owner approached and made a splendid wish. To be precise, he wished for a new roof for his house, and within seconds it glistened from his street with brand-new tiles and a chimney as white as chalk. Then everyone was stirred up once more and began to wish for bigger and better things. Soon one man was not embarrassed to wish for a new four-story house on the marketplace, and a quarter of an hour later he was leaning over his own windowsill and observing the fair from there.

Actually there was no longer a fair since everyone and everything in the city was flowing like a river from a source—the spot by the booth of mirrors, where the stranger stood and allowed each person to make a wish. Cries of astonishment, envy, or laughter followed each wish, and when a hungry little boy wished for nothing more than a hatful of plums, his hat was refilled with taler coins by one of the people whose wish had been less modest. The fat wife of a grocer received great applause and cheers when she wished away a heavy goiter. But then the people were given an example of what anger and resentment can do. Her own husband, who was unhappily married to her and had just had a bad argument with her, used his wish, which could have made him rich, to restore the goiter to the same place where it had been before. Nevertheless, the better precedent had already been set, and a group of feeble and sick people were brought to the booth. The crowd became delirious again when the lame people began to dance and the blind greeted the light with blessed new eyes.

In the meantime the young people had already run all over the city announcing the miraculous events. They told everyone, including a loyal old cook who was standing at the hearth and roasting a goose for the family in the house where she worked. When she heard the news about the wishes through the window, she, too, could not resist running to the marketplace to wish herself rich and happy for the rest of her life. Yet the more she pushed her way through the crowd, the more perceptibly her conscience began to bother her, and when it was her turn to wish, she gave up everything and desired only that the goose not burn before she was back home tending it.

The tumult did not end. Nursemaids rushed out of houses dragging children by their arms. Excited invalids jumped out of their beds and ran out onto the streets in their nightgowns. A little woman, very confused and desperate, arrived from the countryside, and when she heard about the wishes, she sobbed and begged that she might find her lost grandson safe and sound. Within seconds, the boy came riding up on a small black pony and fell laughing into her arms.

In the end, the entire city gathered and became ecstatic. Couples in love whose wishes had been fulfilled wandered arm in arm. Poor families drove around in carriages, still wearing their old patched clothes from that morning. Many people who regretted making a foolish wish either departed sadly or were drinking themselves into forgetfulness at the old fountain in the marketplace that a jokester had filled with the very best wine through his wish.

Eventually there were only two people in the entire city of Faldum who did not know anything about the miracle and had not made wishes for themselves. They were two young men, and they were up high in the attic of an old house at the edge of the city, behind closed windows. One of them stood in the middle of the room, held a violin under his chin, and played with all his soul and passion. The other sat in a corner, held his head between his hands, and was completely absorbed in listening. The sun shone obliquely through the small windowpanes and cast a bright hue, illuminating a bouquet of flowers standing on the table, and its rays played on the torn wallpaper. The room was completely filled with warm light and the glowing tones of the violin, like a small secret treasure chamber glistening with the luster of precious stones. The violinist had closed his eyes and now swayed back and forth as he played. The listener stared quietly at the floor and was lost in the music as if there were no life in him.

Then loud footsteps pounded outside on the street. The door of the house burst open, and the steps came rumbling up the stairs all the way to the attic room. It was the landlord, and he ripped the door open and barged into the room with yells and laughter. The violin music broke off at once, and the silent listener leaped into the air, distraught. The violinist was angry at being interrupted, and he glared reproachfully at the landlord's laughing face. But the man paid no attention to this. Instead, he waved his arms like a drunkard and screamed, "You fools! You sit here and play the violin, and outside the entire world is being changed. Wake up and run so that you won't be too late! There's a man at the marketplace granting wishes to everyone and making them come true. If you hurry, you won't have to live in this tiny attic anymore and owe me the measly rent. Get up and go before it's too late! Even I've become a rich man today!"

The violinist listened with astonishment, and since the man would not leave him in peace, he set the violin down and put his hat on his head. His friend followed without saying a word. No sooner did they leave the house than they saw that half the city had already changed in the most remarkable way, and they walked past the houses somewhat uneasily, as if in a dream. Yesterday these houses had been gray and crooked, humble dwellings. Now, however, they stood tall and elegant like palaces. People whom they had known as beggars were driving around in four-horse carriages, or they were now proud and affluent and looking out of the windows of their beautiful houses. A haggard-looking man who resembled a tailor, followed by a tiny dog, plodded along, tired and sweaty, dragging a large heavy sack, and gold coins trickled through a small hole onto the pavement.

Almost automatically, the two young men arrived at the marketplace and found themselves before the booth with mirrors. The stranger standing there said to them, "You're not in much of a hurry to make your wishes. I was just about to leave. Well, tell me what you want, and feel free to make any wish you desire."

The violinist shook his head and said, "Oh, if only you had left me in peace! I don't need anything."

"Are you sure? Think about it!" cried the stranger. "You may wish for anything that comes to your mind. Anything."

Then the violinist closed his eyes and contemplated for a while. Finally he spoke in a soft voice and said, "I wish I could have a violin and play it in such a wonderful way that nothing in the whole world would be able to disturb me with its noise anymore."

Within seconds he held a beautiful violin and bow in his hands. He tucked the violin beneath his chin and began to play. The music sounded sweet and rhapsodic like the song of paradise. Whoever heard it stopped still and listened with somber eyes. As the violinist played more and more intensely and magnificently, however, he was lifted up by invisible forces and disappeared into thin air. His music continued to resound from a distance with a soft radiance like the red glow of the sunset.

"And you? What do you wish?" the man asked the other young man.

"You've taken the violinist away from me!" complained the young man. "Now the only thing I want from life is to be able to listen and observe, and I want only to think about things immortal. So I wish I were a mountain as large as the country of Faldum, so tall that my peak would tower above the clouds."

All at once there was a rumbling beneath the earth, and everything began to sway. The glass clattered and broke. The mirrors fell one by one in splinters onto the pavement. The marketplace rose up as a sheet rises when a cat that has fallen asleep underneath awakes and arches its back up high. The people were overwhelmed by terror. Thousands screamed and began fleeing the city into the fields. Those who remained at the marketplace watched a mighty mountain climb behind the city into the evening clouds. Beneath it they saw the quiet stream transformed into a white and wild mountain torrent that rushed from the top of the mountain with many falls and rapids down into the valley below.

Only a moment had passed, and yet the entire countryside of Faldum had turned into a gigantic mountain. At its foot was the city, and far away in the distance the ocean could be seen. Nobody had even been harmed in the process.

An old man who had been standing beside the booth of mirrors and had witnessed everything said to his neighbor, "The world's gone mad. I'm happy that I don't have much longer to live. I'm only sorry about the violinist. I'd like to hear him just one more time."

"Yes, indeed," said the other. "But tell me, where's the stranger gone to?"

They looked around, but he had vanished. When they gazed

up at the new mountain, however, they saw the stranger up high, walking away with his cape fluttering in the wind. He stood for a moment, a gigantic figure against the evening sky, then disappeared around the corner of a cliff.

The Mountain

*E*verything passes away in time, and everything new grows old. The annual fair had long ago become history, and many people who wished themselves rich on that occasion had become poor again. The girl with the long golden-red hair had married and had children, who also went to the fair in the city in the late summer of each year. The girl with the nimble dancing feet had become the wife of a guild master in the city, and she could still dance splendidly, much better than many young people. Though her husband had wished for a lot of money, it seemed as though the merry couple would run through all of it before the end of their lives. However, the third girl with the beautiful hands still thought about the stranger at the mirror booth more than anyone else. Though this girl had never married and had not become rich, she still had her delicate hands, and because of her hands she had stopped doing farm work and instead looked after the children in her village wherever she was needed and told them fairy tales and stories. Indeed, it was from her that all the children learned about the miraculous fair, and how the poor had become rich and how the country of Faldum had become a mountain. Whenever she told this story, she would look at her slender princess hands, smile, and become so moved and full of love that one was apt to believe that nobody had received a better fortune at the booth of mirrors than she had, even though she was poor and without a husband and had to tell beautiful stories to children who were not her own.

Everyone who had been young at that time was now old, and those who had been old were now dead. Only the mountain stood unchanged and ageless, and when the snow on his peak glistened, he seemed to smile and be happy that he was no longer a human being and no longer had to calculate according to standards of human time. The cliffs of the mountain beamed high above the city and the countryside. His tremendous shadow wandered every day over the land. His streams and rivers announced in advance the change of the seasons. The mountain had become the protector and father of all. He generated forests and meadows with waving grass and flowers. He produced springs, snow, ice, and stones. Colorful grass grew on the stones, and forget-me-nots alongside the streams. Deep down in the mountain were caves where water dripped like silver threads year after year from stone to stone in eternal rhythm, and in his chasms were secret chambers where crystals grew with a thousand-year patience. Nobody had ever reached the peak of the mountain. But many people claimed to know that there was a small round lake way up on the top, and that nothing but the sun, moon, clouds, and stars had ever been reflected in it. Neither human nor animal had ever looked into this basin of water that the mountain held up toward the heavens, for not even the eagles could fly that high.

The people of Faldum lived on cheerfully in the city and in the numerous valleys. They baptized their children. They were active in trading and in the crafts. They carried one another to their graves. Their knowledge of and dreams about the mountain were passed on from grandparents to grandchildren and lived on. Shepherds and

chamois hunters, naturalists and botanists, cowherds and travelers increased the treasured lore of the mountain, and ballad singers and storytellers passed it on. They knew all about the endless dark caves, about waterfalls without light in hidden chasms, about glaciers that split the land in two. They became familiar with the paths of the avalanches, and the unpredictable shifts in the weather, and what the country might expect in the way of heat and frost, water and growth, weather and wind—all this came from the mountain.

Nobody knew anything more about the earlier times. Of course, there was the beautiful legend about the miraculous annual fair, at which every single soul in Faldum had been allowed to wish for whatever he or she wanted. But nobody wanted to believe anymore that the mountain himself had arisen on that day. They were certain that the mountain had stood in his place from the very beginning of time and would continue to stand there for all eternity. The mountain was home. The mountain was Faldum. More than anything the people loved to hear the stories about the three girls and about the violinist. Sometimes a young boy would abandon himself while playing the violin behind a closed door and dream of disappearing in beautiful music like the violinist who had drifted into the sky.

The mountain lived on silently in his greatness. Every day he watched the sun, far away and red, climb from the ocean and circle around his peak from east to west, and every night he watched the stars take the same silent path. Each winter the mountain would be wrapped in a coat of snow and ice, and each year the avalanches would rumble at a given time down his sides, and at the edge of the remains of the snow, the bright-eyed summer flowers, blue and yellow, laughed in the sun, and the streams swelled and bounced, and the lakes sparkled with more blue and more warmth in the sunlight. Lost water thundered faintly in invisible chasms, and the small round lake high upon the peak lay covered with heavy ice and waited the entire year to open its bright eyes during the brief period of high summer when for a few days it could reflect the sun and for a few nights the stars. The water in the dark caves caused the stones to chime in eternal dripping, and in secret gorges the thousand-year crystals grew steadfastly toward perfection.

At the foot of the mountain, a little higher than the city, there was a valley through which a wide brook with a smooth surface flowed between alders and meadows. The young people who were in love went there and learned about the wonders of the seasons from the mountain and trees. In another valley the men held their training exercises with horses and weapons, and each year during the eve of solstice, an enormous fire burned on one of the high steep knolls.

Time flew by, and the mountain protected the valley of love and the training ground. He provided space to the cowherds, wood-cutters, hunters, and craftsmen. He gave stones for building and iron for smelting. He watched calmly and let the summer fire blaze on the knoll and watched the fire return a hundred times and another hundred times. He saw the city below reach out with small stumpy arms and grow beyond its old walls. He saw hunters discard their crossbows and turn to firearms to shoot. The centuries passed like the seasons of the year and the years like hours.

He did not care that one time over the years the solstitial fire had stopped burning on the rocky plateau and from then on re-mained forgotten. He was not troubled when, after many years passed, the training grounds became deserted, and plantain and thistle ran all over the fields. And as the centuries marched on, he did not prevent a landslide from altering his shape and causing half the city of Faldum to lie in ruins under the rocks that rolled down upon it. Indeed, he rarely glanced down and thus did not even notice that the city remained in ruins and was not rebuilt.

He did not care about any of this. But something else began to be of concern. The times raced by, and behold—the mountain grew old. When he saw the sun rise and wander and depart, he was not the same way he had once been, and when he saw the stars reflected in pale glaciers, he no longer felt himself their equal. The sun and stars were now no longer particularly important to him. What was important now was what was happening to himself and within himself, for he felt a strange hand working deep beneath his rocks and caves. He felt the hard primitive stone becoming brittle and crumbling away into layers of slate, the brooks and waterfalls causing corrosion inside. The glaciers had disappeared and lakes had grown. Forests were transformed into fields of stone, and meadows into black moors. The hollow patches of his moraines and gravel spread endlessly into the country with forked tongues, and the landscape below had become strangely different, strangely rocky, strangely scorched and quiet. The mountain withdrew more and more into himself. He felt certain that he was no longer the equal of the sun and stars. His equals were the wind and snow, the water and ice. His equals were the things that seemed to shine eternally and yet also disappeared slowly, the things that perished slowly.

He began to guide his streams down the valley more fervently, rolled his avalanches more carefully, and offered his meadows of flowers to the sun more tenderly. And it happened that in his old age he also began remembering about human beings again. Not that he now regarded people as his equal, but he began to look about for them. He began to feel abandoned. He began to think about the past. But the city was no longer there, and there was no song in the valley of love, and no more huts on the meadows. There were no more people there. Even they were gone. It had become silent. Everything had turned languid. A shadow hung in the air.

The mountain quivered when he felt all of that which had perished. And as he quivered, his peak sank to a side and collapsed. Pieces of rock rolled down into the valley of love, long since filled with stones, and down into the sea.

Yes, the times had changed. But what was it that caused him to remember and think about people so constantly now? Hadn't it once been wonderful when they burned the solstitial fire on the knoll and when young couples walked in the valley of love? Oh, and how sweet and warm their songs had often sounded!

The gray mountain became entirely steeped in memory. He barely felt the centuries flowing by. Nor did he pay much attention to how his caves were softly rumbling and collapsing here and there, or to how he shifted himself. When he thought about the people, he felt the pain of a faint echo from past ages of the world. It was as if something had moved and love had not been understood, a dark, floating dream, as if he had also once been human or similar to a human, had sung and had listened to singing, as if the thought of mortality had once ignited his heart when he was very young.

Epochs rushed by. The dying mountain clung to his dreams as he sank and was surrounded by a crude wasteland of stone. How had everything been at one time? Wasn't there still a sound, a delicate silver thread that linked him to a bygone world? He burrowed with great effort into the night of moldy memories, groped relentlessly for the torn threads, bent constantly far over the abyss of the past.

Hadn't he had a community, a love that glowed for him at one time? Hadn't a mother sung to him at one time at the beginning of the world?

He thought and thought, and his eyes, the blue lakes, became murky and heavy and turned into moors and swamps, while stone boulders rippled over the grassy strips of land and small patches of flowers. He continued to think, and he heard chimes from an invisible distance, felt notes of music floating, a song, a human song, and he began trembling in the painful pleasure of recognition. He heard the music, and he saw a man, a youth, completely wrapped in music, swaying through the air in the sunny sky, and a hundred buried memories were stirred and began to quiver and roll. He saw the face of a human with dark eyes, and the eyes asked him with a twinkle,

"Don't you want to make a wish?"

And he made a wish, a silent wish, and as he did so, he was released from the torment of having to think about all those remote and forgotten things, and everything that had been hurting him ceased. The mountain and the country collapsed together, and where Faldum had once stood, the endless sea now surged and roared far and wide, and the sun and stars took turns appearing high above it all.

A
DREAM
SEQUENCE

It seemed to me that I was spending a great deal of useless and stuffy time in the mysterious salon, whose north window offered a view of a false lake with artificial fjords. Nothing there held my attention and attracted me but the presence of the beautiful, suspicious lady, whom I took to be a sinner. I sought in vain to see her face as it really was, just once, that face that swayed imperceptibly among loose dark hair and consisted solely of pallor. Otherwise, there was nothing. Her eyes were perhaps dark brown. I felt inner reasons to expect something like that. But then her eyes would not match the face that my look wanted to read from the indeterminable pallor, whose shape I knew rested deeply in inaccessible layers of my memory.

Finally something happened. The two young men entered. They greeted the lady with exquisite manners and were introduced to me. *Monkeys,* I thought, and became angry at myself because one of them had a reddish-brown jacket tailored in a nice and stylish fit, and it put me to shame and made me feel jealous. It's terrible to feel such envy toward irreproachable people, toward free and easy, smiling people! "Control yourself!" I exclaimed softly to myself. The two young men shook my extended hand with indifference—why had I even offered it?—and with sneers on their faces.

It was then that I sensed something was wrong about me, and I felt an irritating chill begin to rise up my legs. As I looked down, I turned pale when I saw that I was standing only in my stocking feet without shoes. Once again those dreary, deplorable, paltry obstacles and restraints! Nobody else ever had experiences like appearing naked or half naked in a salon before people of irreproachable and correct manners! Pathetically, I tried at least to cover my left foot with my right. In the process I glanced through the window and saw the steep, wild, blue banks of the lake, threatening in false and gloomy tones and seeking to become demonic. Distressed and in need of help, I looked at the strangers, full of hatred toward these people and full of greater hatred toward myself—I was a nothing, and nothing ever turned out right for me. And why did I feel responsible for that dumb lake? Indeed, if I felt that way, then I was responsible, too. Imploringly I looked at the man dressed in the reddish-brown jacket. His cheeks glowed and revealed how healthy and well groomed he was, and I knew full well that I was placing myself at his mercy to no avail and that he could not be moved.

Just at that moment he noticed my feet in the coarse dark-green socks—oh, at least I could still feel grateful that there were no holes in them—and made a nasty smile. He nudged his friend and pointed to my feet. Then the other one also grinned, full of derision.

"Just look at the lake!" I cried, and pointed toward the window. The man dressed in the reddish-brown jacket shrugged. It did not occur to him in the least to turn toward the window, and he said something to the other man that I only half understood, but it was aimed at me and had to do with fellows in socks whom one should not really tolerate in such a salon. When I heard the word *salon*, it smacked of beautiful and somewhat false elegance and worldliness, as it had during my childhood.

Close to tears, I bent over to see if there was anything I could do to improve my feet and saw that they had slipped out of large house shoes. At least, a very large, soft, dark-red slipper lay behind me on the floor. I picked it up, not knowing what I should do with it, and I held it in my hand and was still on the verge of tears. Then it slipped out of my hand, but I caught it as it was falling—it had become even larger in the meantime—and now I lifted it by the toe.

As all this happened, I suddenly felt emotionally relieved and realized the profound value of the slipper, which was flapping a little in my hand, weighed down by the heavy heel. It was glorious to have such a red limp shoe, so soft and heavy! As an experiment, I swung it several times through the air. This was delightful, and joy flowed through my entire body to the roots of my hair. A club or a rubber tube was nothing in comparison to my large shoe. I called it *calziglione* in Italian.

When I gave the man in the reddish-brown jacket the first playful blow on the head with the *calziglione*, the irreproachable young man tumbled onto the couch, and the rest of the people, the room, and the terrible lake lost all their power over me. I was big and strong. I was free, and with the second blow to the head of the man in the reddish-brown jacket, the fight had all but ended, and I could let loose and not worry about self-defense. Instead there was pure rejoicing on my part, and I felt myself the lord of my own whims. But I did not hate my defeated foe in the least. He was interesting to me. He was precious and dear. I was now his master and creator. With each good blow of my strange shoelike club, I shaped his unripe and apelike head, forged it, built it, composed it. With each blow that formed it, his head became more pleasant, more handsome, and finer. He became my creature and work, something that satisfied me and that I loved. With one last tender forging blow, I drove his sharp head down so that it was sufficiently flat on top. He was finished. He thanked me. He stroked my hand.

"That's all right." I waved with my hand.

He crossed his hands over his heart and said shyly, "My name is Paul."

Wonderfully strong and happy feelings swelled within my breast and gave me some space. The room—forget calling it a salon!—retreated with shame and crawled away until it became nothing. I stood by the dark-blue lake. Steel clouds pressed on the somber mountains. In the fjords the turbid water boiled with foam. Sultry spring storms strayed compulsively and anxiously in circles. I looked above and stretched my hand out to signal that the storm could begin. A bolt of lightning exploded clear and cold out of the hard blue sky. A warm typhoon howled straight down to the ground. In the sky, gray forms blew apart and branched out into veins of marble. Enormous round waves rose terrifyingly out of the whipped-up lake. The storm ripped the tips of the foam and the clapping bits of water from the backs of the waves and threw them into my face. The black petrified mountains tore open their eyes full of horror. Their cowering and silence sounded like a plea.

In the middle of the glorious storm, hunting on gigantic horses, I could hear a timid voice nearby. Oh, I had not forgotten her, my pale lady with long black hair. I bowed over her. She spoke to me childishly—"The lake is coming." It was impossible to stay there. I kept looking at the gentle sinner. Her face was nothing but a silent pallor in the wide dusk of her hair. Then the breaking waves were already beating my knees and my breast, and the sinner floated helplessly and silently on the rising swells. I laughed a little and placed my arm under her knees and lifted her up to me. This, too, was beautiful and liberating. The woman was unusually light and small, full of fresh warmth, and her eyes were affectionate, trusting, and horrified, and I saw that she was not a sinner at all and not a distant enigmatic lady. No sins, no mystery. She was simply a child.

I carried her out of the waves and over rocks and through the royally dismal park made dark by rain to a place that the storm could not reach. Nothing but soft beauty spoke from the bowed crowns of old trees, nothing but poems and symphonies, a world of noble presentiments and charming cultivated pleasures, lovely painted trees by Corot and noble rustic woodwind music by Schubert that mildly enticed me with a fleeting upsurge of nostalgia to the beloved temple. However, it was in vain. The world has many voices, and the soul has its hours and moments for everything.

God knows how the sinner, the pale lady, the child, took her leave and vanished. There was an outside stairway made out of stone. There was a house gate. There were servants present, everything dim and murky, as if behind an opaque glass, and other things, much less substantial, much dimmer, figures blown there by the wind. A note of reproach and reprimand directed against me made me angry at that storm of shadows. Nothing remained of it except the figure of Paul, my friend and son Paul, and in his features an infinitely well-known face revealed itself and concealed itself and still could not be named, the face of a schoolmate, the face of a legendary nursemaid from ancient times, nurtured from the good, nourishing memories of the fabulous early years.

Good ardent darkness, warm cradle of the soul, and lost homeland—all this opened up. All this opened into the time of existence unformed and the first indecisive undulation on top of the ground of all things, beneath which the primordial time of the ancestors sleeps with dreams of the primeval forest. Just feel your way, soul, just wander about, burrow blindly into the full bath of innocent twilight drives! I know you, scared soul, nothing is necessary to you. Nothing is so much food, drink, and sleep for you as the return to your beginnings. The wave roars around you, and you are wave; the forest rustles, and you are forest. There is no more outside and inside. You fly, a bird in the air; you swim, a fish in the sea; you absorb light, and you are light; you taste darkness and are darkness. We wander, soul, we swim and fly, and smile and tie the torn threads again with ghostly fingers and blissfully drown out the destroyed pinions. We no longer seek God. We are God. We are the world. We kill and die along with others. We create and are resurrected with our dreams. Our most beautiful dream is the blue sky; our most beautiful dream is the sea; our most beautiful dream is the bright starry night, and is the fish, and is the clear happy noise and the clear happy light—everything is our dream. Each one is our most beautiful dream. We have just died and become earth. We have just invented laughter. We have just arranged a constellation.

Voices resound, and each one is the voice of our mother. Trees rustle, and each one rustles above our cradle. Roads divide in the form of a star, and each road is the way home.

He who called himself Paul, my creature and friend, was there again and had become as old as I. He resembled a friend of my youth. But I did not know which one, and therefore, I was somewhat uneasy with him and kept a polite distance. He drew power from this. The world no longer obeyed me, it obeyed him. Consequently, all previous things had disappeared and had collapsed in meek improbability, shamed by him who now ruled.

We were at a square. The place was called Paris, and in front of me was an iron beam standing straight up high. It was a ladder and had narrow iron rungs on both sides. You could hold on to them with your hands and climb on them with your hands. Since Paul wanted to climb, I began, and he was next to me on a similar ladder. When we had climbed as high as a house or a very high tree, I began to feel frightened. I looked over at Paul, who did not feel afraid, but he perceived that I was scared and smiled.

For one split second, while he smiled and I stared, I came close to recognizing him and recalling his name. A gap in the past was ripped open and kept splitting until it receded to my early school years when I was twelve years old, the most wonderful time of life, everything full of fragrance, everything ingenious, everything with an edible aroma of fresh bread and with an intoxicating shimmer of adventure and gilded heroism—Jesus was twelve years old when he shamed the scholars in the temple. By twelve, we have all shamed our scholars and teachers, have shown that we are smarter than they. Memories and images stormed in convulsions upon me: forgotten school notebooks, detention during the noon hour, a bird killed with a slingshot, a jacket pocket filled with sticky stolen plums, boys splashing wildly in a swimming hole, torn Sunday pants and a very bad conscience, fervent evening prayer about earthly cares, wonderful heroic feelings of splendor while reading poetry by Schiller.

It took only a second, a flash of lightning, an avid rushing sequence of images without a focus. The very next moment, Paul's face looked at me again, tormentingly somewhat familiar. I was no longer certain of my age. Perhaps we were boys. Farther and farther below the narrow rungs of our ladders were the masses of streets called Paris. When we were higher than any tower, our iron poles came to an end, and each ladder was crowned with a horizontal board, a tiny platform. It seemed impossible to climb upon them, but Paul did it with ease, and I had to do it, too.

Once on top I laid myself down flat on the board and looked down over the edge as though I were on a small high cloud. My gaze fell like a stone and did not hit a target. Then my friend pointed somewhere with his hand, and my eyes became glued to a marvelous sight that hovered in midair. All of a sudden I saw a strange-looking group of people in the air suspended over a wide street at the same level of the highest roofs but still very far beneath us. They seemed to be tightrope dancers, and indeed, one of the figures walked back and forth on a rope or a pole. Then I discovered that there were many, and most of them were young girls. They seemed to me to be gypsies or nomadic folk. They walked, lay, sat, moved at the height of the roofs on an airy scaffold made out of the thinnest planks and poles similar to an arbor. They lived there and were at home in this region. Beneath them one could sense the street. A fine whirling cloud extended from the ground until it almost reached their feet.

Paul made a remark about this.

"Yes," I answered. "It is touching—all those girls."

Of course, I was much higher than they were, and I clung fearfully to my post while they floated lightly and fearlessly, and I saw I was too high. I was at the wrong place. They were at the right height, not on the ground and yet not as hellishly high and remote as I was; not among the people and yet not so entirely isolated. Besides, there were many of them. I saw clearly they represented a bliss that I had not yet attained.

But I knew that I would have to climb down sooner or later from my gigantic ladder, and the thought of it was so oppressing that I felt nauseous and could not bear being up there one second longer. Full of desperation and shaking from dizziness, I felt beneath me for the rungs of the ladder with my feet—I couldn't see them from the plank—and I hung for some horrifying minutes at that terrible height suffering from convulsions. No one helped me. Paul was gone.

In profound dread I made some dangerous stabs with my feet and hands, and I felt myself enveloped by something like a fog. I felt that it was not the high ladder or the dizziness that I had to experience and endure. In fact, I lost perspective and could not determine the shape of things. Everything was foggy and uncertain. At one time, I was still hanging on the rungs of the ladder feeling dizzy, and then the next thing I knew, I was crawling, small and fearful, through dreadfully narrow underground shafts and corridors. Then I was hopelessly wading through swamp and dirt and felt the filthy slime rise up to my mouth. Darkness and obstacles were everywhere. Terrible tasks with serious yet concealed meaning. Fear and sweat, paralysis and cold. Hard dying, hard being born.

How much night surrounds us! How many dreadful, awful paths of torment we take! Go deep into the shaft of our run-down soul, eternal poor hero, eternal Odysseus! But we go on, we go on. We bow and wade. We swim and wade. We swim and suffocate in the slime. We crawl along the smooth treacherous walls. We weep and despair. We moan fearfully and sob loudly in pain. But we move on and bite our way through.

Once again images arose from the turbid vapors of hell. Again a small stretch of the dark path was illuminated and formed by a modest light of memories, and my soul pushed its way out of the primeval world into the familiar sphere of time.

Where was this? Familiar things confronted me. I recognized the air that I breathed. A large room in half darkness, an oil lamp on the table, my own lamp, a large round table somewhat like a piano. My sister was there and my brother-in-law. Perhaps they were visiting me, or perhaps I was at their place. They were quiet and worried, full of concern about me. And I stood in the large dismal room, walked back and forth, stood still, and walked again in a cloud of sadness, in a flood of bitter, suffocating sadness. And now I began searching for something, nothing important, a book or scissors or something like that, and I could not find it. I took the lamp in my hand. It was heavy, and I was terribly tired. I soon put it down and then picked it up again. I wanted to search, search, although I knew that it was in vain. I would find nothing. I would only confuse everything even more. The lamp would fall out of my hands. It was so heavy, so painfully heavy, and so I would continue to grope and search and wander through the room for the rest of my miserable life.

My brother-in-law looked at me anxiously and somewhat reproachfully. They realized that I was going mad. I thought quickly and picked up the lamp again. My sister came over to me, quietly, with pleading eyes, so full of fear and love that I thought my heart would break. I could say nothing. I could only stretch out my hand

and wave her away, to ward her off, and I thought: *Just leave me alone! Just leave me alone! You certainly can't know how I feel, how much everything hurts, how terribly much it hurts.* And again: *Just leave me alone! Just leave me alone!*

The reddish light of the lamp flowed dimly through the large room. Outside the trees sighed in the wind. For a moment I believed I felt and saw the night outside deep within me. Wind and wetness, autumn, bitter smell of foliage, scattered leaves of the elm tree. Autumn! Autumn! And once more, for a moment, I was not myself but saw myself like a picture: I was a pale, lean musician with flickering eyes, and my name was Hugo Wolf, and on this evening I was on the verge of going insane.

Meanwhile I had to continue searching, hopelessly searching and lifting the heavy lamp on the round table onto the chair, onto the heap of books. And I had to protect myself with imploring gestures when my sister looked at me again sadly and considerately, sought to console me, to be near me, and to help me. The sadness in me grew and filled me to the point of bursting, and the images all around me were impressive and eloquent in their clarity, much clearer than reality is otherwise. A few autumn flowers in a glass of water, a dark red-brown dahlia among them, glowed in such painful, beautiful loneliness, each thing, even the shining brass base of the lamp, was enchantingly beautiful and infused with a fateful loneliness, as in the pictures by the great painters.

I sensed my fate clearly. Yet another shadow in this sadness, another look from my sister, another look from the flowers, from the beautiful spiritual flowers—then it would overflow, and I would sink into madness. *Leave me alone! You certainly don't know!* On the polished side of the piano a ray of sunlight was reflected in the black wood, so beautiful, so mysterious, so filled with melancholy!

Now my sister stood up again and went over to the piano. I wanted to beg, ward her off with all my might, but I couldn't. No power whatsoever emanated from my loneliness that was sufficient to reach her. Oh, I knew what had to happen now. I knew the melody that now had to express itself and had to say everything and destroy everything. Enormous tension compressed my heart, and while the first hot tears sprang from my eyes, I threw my head and hands across the table and listened and felt with all my senses and with new senses as well, the text and melody at the same time, Wolf's melody and the verses.

What do you know, dark tops of trees
About the beautiful olden days?
Home lies beyond mountain peaks,
How far it lies, how far away!

With this song, the world glided apart before me and within me, sank away in tears and tones. Impossible to say how it all poured out, how it flowed, how good and painful it was! Oh tears, oh sweet collapse, blissful melting away! All the books of the world full of thoughts and poems are nothing in comparison to a minute of sobbing, when feeling surges in waves, the soul feels itself profoundly and finds itself. Tears are the melting ice of snow. All angels are close to the crying person.

Forgetting all causes and reasons, I wept my way down from the heights of unbearable tension into the mild twilight of everyday feelings, without thoughts, without witnesses. In between images fluttered: a coffin in which a person was lying, someone very dear and important to me, but I did not know who it was. *Perhaps it's you yourself,* I thought. Then another image came to me from a far pale distance. Hadn't I at one time, many years ago or in an earlier life, glimpsed a wonderful sight? A group of girls living in the air, nebulous and weightless, beautiful and blissful, swaying as light as air and as melodious as string music.

Years flew between, pushing me gently and firmly away from the picture. Oh, perhaps the meaning of my entire life had only been to see these noble floating girls, to approach them, to become like them! But now they vanished in the distance, unreachable, uncomprehended, unredeemed, tired, and surrounded by the fluttering of despairing nostalgia.

Years fell to the ground like snowflakes, and the world changed. Distressed, I wandered toward a small house. I was feeling very miserable, and a dreadful sensation in my mouth seized hold of me. Anxiously I touched a loose tooth with my tongue. Immediately it moved sideways and fell out. Then the next one fell out as well! A very young doctor was there. I complained to him. I held the tooth up to him imploringly with my fingers! He laughed cheerfully, waved me off with a deadly professional gesture, and shook his young head—it's nothing, quite harmless, happens every day. *Dear God,* I thought. But he continued and pointed to my left knee: That's the problem. That's something else and not a joking matter. I grabbed my knee terribly fast—there it was. There was a hole into which I could thrust my finger, and instead of skin and flesh, there was nothing to touch but an insensitive, soft loose mass, light and stringy like a wilted plant. Oh, my God, this was decay, this was death and putrefaction! "There's nothing more you can do?" I asked, trying to be friendly.

"Nothing more," the young doctor said, and he was gone.

Exhausted, I walked toward the little house, but I was not as desperate as I should have been. Indeed, I was almost indifferent. I had to go into the little house where my mother was expecting me—hadn't I already heard her voice? Seen her face? Steps led up to the house, crazy steps, high and smooth without railings, each one a mountain, a peak, a glacier. It was certainly too late—she had perhaps left already, perhaps she was already dead? Hadn't I just heard her call again? Silently I coped with the steep mountain of steps, falling and crushed, wild and sobbing, I climbed and pushed onward, supporting myself on my breaking arms and knees, and was on top, was at the gate, and the steps were again small and pretty and lined by box trees. Each one of my steps was sticky and heavy as though I were going through slime and glue, barely moving forward. The gate stood open, and inside my mother was walking about in a gray dress, a little basket on her arm, silent and steeped in thought. Oh, her dark, slightly gray hair in a little net! And her gait, the small figure! And the dress, the gray dress! Had I completely lost her image all these many, many years, not really thought about her at all? There she was. There she stood and walked. She could be seen only from behind, exactly as she was, completely clear and beautiful, pure love, pure thoughts of love!

Feeling lame, I furiously waded through the sticky air. Weeds wrapped themselves around me more and more like thin strong ropes. Hostile obstacles everywhere. There was no moving forward! "Mother," I called—but I had no voice. . . . There was no sound. There was glass between her and me.

My mother walked on slowly, without looking back, quietly absorbed in beautiful caring thoughts. She brushed an invisible thread from the dress with her hand that I knew so well. She bent over her little basket of sewing material. Oh, the little basket! She had hidden Easter eggs in it one time. I screamed in despair, unable to make a sound. I ran and could not leave the spot! Tenderness and rage tugged at me.

And she kept walking slowly through the garden house. She stood at the open back door and stepped outside. She sunk her head a little to one side, softly and attentively, deep in her thoughts. She lifted and set down the little basket. I noticed a note that I had found in her sewing basket one time when I was a boy. She had lightly written her plans for the day on it, what she wanted to remember: "Hermann's pants frayed—put away laundry—borrow book by Dickens—Hermann did not say his prayers yesterday." Streams of memory, cargoes of love!

Bound and chained, I stood at the gate, and beyond it the woman in the gray dress walked slowly away, into the garden, and was gone.

THE FOREST
DWELLER

❦

$\mathcal{A}$t the dawn of civilization, quite some time before human creatures began wandering over the face of the earth, there were forest
dwellers. They lived close together fearfully in the dark tropical
forests, constantly fighting with their relatives, the apes, and the only
divine law that governed their actions was—the forest. The forest
was their home, refuge, cradle, nest, and grave, and they could not
imagine life outside it. They avoided coming too close to its edges,
and whoever, through unusual circumstances while hunting or fleeing
something, made his way to the edges would tremble with dread later
when reporting about the white emptiness outside, where the terrifying nothingness glistened in the deadly fire of the sun.

There was an old forest dweller who decades before had been
pursued by wild animals and had fled across the farthest edge of the

forest. He had immediately become blind and was now considered a kind of priest and saint with the name Mata Dalam, or "he who has an interior eye." He had composed the holy forest song chanted during the great storms, and the forest dwellers always listened to what he had to say. His fame and mystery rested on the fact that he had seen the sun with his eyes and lived to tell about it.

The forest dwellers were small, brown, and very hairy. They walked with a stoop, and they had furtive, wild eyes. They could move both like human beings and like apes and felt just as safe in the branches of the forest as they did on the ground. They had not yet learned about houses and huts. Nevertheless, they knew how to fabricate many kinds of weapons and tools, as well as jewelry. They made bows, arrows, lances, and clubs out of wood and necklaces out of the fiber of trees that were strung with dried beets or nuts. They wore precious objects around their necks or in their hair: a wild boar's tooth, a tiger's claw, a parrot's feathers, shells from mussels. A large river flowed through the endless forest, but the forest dwellers did not dare tread on its banks except in the dark of night, and many had never seen it. Sometimes the more courageous ones crept out of the thickets at night, fearful and on the lookout. Then, in the faint glimmer of dusk, they would watch the elephants bathing and look through the treetops above them and observe the glittering stars with dread as they appeared to hang in the manifold interlaced branches of the mangrove trees. They never saw the sun, and it was considered extremely dangerous to see its reflection in the summer.

A young man by the name of Kubu belonged to the tribe of forest dwellers headed by the blind Mata Dalam, and he was the leader and spokesman for the dissatisfied young people. In fact, ever since Mata Dalam had grown older and become more tyrannical, the malcontents had made their voices heard in the tribe. Until then, it had been the blind man's uncontested right to be provided with food by the other members of the tribe. In addition, they came to him for advice and sang his forest song. Gradually, however, he had introduced all sorts of new and burdensome customs that were revealed to him, so he said, in a dream by the divine spirit of the forest. But several skeptical young men asserted that the old man was a swindler and was concerned only with advancing his own interests.

The most recent custom Mata Dalam had introduced was a new moon celebration in which he sat in the middle of a circle and beat a drum made of leather. Meanwhile the other forest dwellers had to dance in the circle and sing the song "Gulo Elah" until they were exhausted and collapsed on their knees. Then all the men had to pierce their left ears with a thorn, and the young women were led to the priest, who pierced each of their ears with a thorn.

Kubu and some other young men had shunned this ritual, and they endeavored to convince the young women to resist as well. One time it appeared that they had a good chance to triumph over the priest and break his power. It was when the old man was conducting the new moon ceremony and piercing the left ear of a woman. A bold young man let out a terrible scream while this was happening, and the blind man chanced to stick the thorn into the woman's eye, which fell out of its socket. Now the young woman screamed in such despair that everyone ran over to her, and when they saw what had happened, they were stunned and speechless. Immediately the young men intervened with triumphant smiles on their faces, and when Kubu dared to grab the priest by his shoulders, the old man stood up in front of his drum and uttered such a horrible curse, in such a squealing scornful voice, that everyone retreated in terror. Even the young man was petrified. Though nobody could understand the exact meaning of the old priest's words, his curse had a wild and awful tone and reminded everyone of the dreadful holy words of the religious ceremonies. Mata Dalam cursed the young man's eyes, which he granted to the vultures as food, and he cursed his intestines, which he prophesied would roast in the sun one day on the open fields. Then the priest, who at this moment had more power than ever before, ordered the young woman to be brought to him again, and he stuck out her other eye with the thorn. Everyone looked on with horror, and no one dared to breathe.

"You will die outside!" the old man cursed Kubu, and from the moment of this pronouncement, the other forest dwellers avoided the young man as hopeless. "Outside"—that meant outside the homeland, outside the dusky forest. "Outside"—that meant horror, sunburn, and glowing deadly emptiness.

Terrified, Kubu fled, and when he saw that everyone retreated from him, he hid himself far away in a hollow tree trunk and gave himself up for lost. Days and nights he lay there, wavering between mortal terror and spite, uncertain whether the people of his tribe would come to kill him or whether the sun itself would break through the forest, besiege him, flush him out, and slay him. But the arrows and lances did not come; nor did the sun or lightning. Nothing came except great languishment and the growling voice of hunger.

So Kubu stood up once again and crawled out of the tree, sober and with a feeling almost of disappointment. *The priest's curse was nothing*, he thought in surprise, and then he looked for food. When he had eaten and felt life circulating through his limbs once more, pride and hate surged up in his soul. He did not want to return to his

people anymore. All he wanted now was to be solitary and remain
expelled. He wanted to be known as the one who had been hated and
had resisted the feeble curses of the priest, that blind cow. He wanted
to be alone and remain alone, but he also wanted to take revenge.

So he walked around the forest and pondered his situation. He
reflected about everything that had ever aroused his doubts and
seemed questionable, especially the priest's drum and his rituals. And
the more he thought and the longer he was alone, the clearer he could
see. Yes, it was all deceit. Everything had been nothing but lies and
deceit. And since he had already come so far in his thinking, he began
drawing conclusions. Quick to distrust, he examined everything that
was considered true and holy. For instance, he questioned whether
there was a divine spirit in the forest or a holy forest song. Oh, all that
too was nothing. It too was a swindle. And as he managed to
overcome his awful horror, he sang the forest song in a scornful voice
and distorted all the words. And he called out the name of the divine
spirit of the forest, whom nobody had been allowed to name on the
pain of death—and everything remained quiet. No storm exploded.
No lightning struck him down!

Isolated, Kubu wandered for many days and weeks with a
furrowed brow and a piercing look. He went to the banks of the river
at full moon, something that nobody had ever dared to do. There he
looked long and bravely, first at the moon's reflection and then at the
full moon itself and all the stars, right in their eyes, and nothing
happened to him. He sat on the riverbank for entire moonlit nights,
reveling in the forbidden delirium of light, and nursed his thoughts.
Many bold and terrible plans arose in his mind. *The moon is my friend,*
he thought, *and the star is my friend, but the blind old man is my enemy.
Therefore, the "outside" is perhaps better than our inside, and perhaps the entire*

holiness of the forest is also just talk! And one night, generations before any other human being, Kubu conceived the daring and fabulous plan of binding some branches together with fiber, placing himself on the branches, and floating down the river. His eyes glistened, and his heart pounded with all its might. But this plan came to naught, for the river was full of crocodiles.

Consequently, there was no way into the future but to leave the forest by way of its edge—if there even was an edge to the forest at all—and to entrust himself to the glowing emptiness, the evil "outside." That monster, the sun, had to be sought out and endured, for—who knew?—in the end maybe even the ancient lore about the terror of the sun was just a lie!

This thought, the last in a bold, feverishly wild chain of reflections, made Kubu tremble. Never in the whole of history had a forest dweller dared to leave the forest of his own free will and expose himself to the horrible sun. And once more he walked around for days carrying these thoughts with him until he finally summoned his courage. Trembling, on a bright day at noon, he crept toward the river, cautiously approached the glittering bank, and anxiously looked for the image of the sun in the water. The glare was extremely painful to his dazzled eyes, and he quickly shut them. But after a while he dared to open them once more and then again and again, until he succeeded in keeping them open. It was possible. It was endurable. And it even made him happy and courageous. Kubu had learned to trust the sun. He loved it, even if it was supposed to kill him, and he hated the old, dark, lazy forest, where the priest croaked and where the young courageous man had been outlawed and expelled.

Now he made his decision, and he picked his deed like a piece of ripe sweet fruit. He made a full hammer out of ironwood and gave it a very thin and light handle. Then, early the next morning, he went looking for Mata Dalam. After discovering his footprints, he found him, hit him on the head with the hammer, and watched the old man's soul depart through his crooked mouth. Kubu placed his weapon on the priest's chest so that the people would know who had killed him, and using a mussel shell, he carved a sign on the flat surface of the hammer. It was a circle with many straight rays—the image of the sun.

Bravely he now began his trip to the distant "outside." He walked straight ahead from morning till night. He slept nights in the branches of trees and continued his wandering early each morning over brooks and black swamps and eventually over hills and moss-covered banks of stone that he had never seen before. As they became steeper, he was slowed down because of the gorges, but he managed to climb the mountains on his way through the infinite forest, so that he ultimately became doubtful and sad and worried that perhaps some god had prohibited the creatures of the forest from leaving their homeland.

And then one evening, after he had been climbing for a long time and had reached some higher altitude where the air was much drier and lighter, he came to the edge without realizing it. The forest stopped—but with it the ground stopped, too. The forest plunged down into the emptiness of the air as if the world had broken in two at this spot. There was nothing to see but a distant, faint red glow and above, some stars, for the night had already commenced.

Kubu sat down at the edge of the world and tied himself tightly to some climbing plants so that he would not fall over. He spent the night cowering in dread and was so wildly aroused that he could not shut his eyes. At the first hint of dawn, he jumped impatiently to his feet, bent over the emptiness, and waited for the day to appear.

Yellow stripes of beautiful light glimmered in the distance, and the sky seemed to tremble in anticipation, just as Kubu trembled, for he had never seen the beginning of the day in the wide space of air. Yellow bundles of light flamed up, and suddenly the sun emerged in the sky beyond the immense cleft of the world, large and red. It sprang up from an endless gray nothingness that soon became blue and black—the sea.

And the "outside" appeared before the trembling forest dweller. Before his feet the mountain plunged down into the indiscernible smoking depths, and across from him some rose-tinted cliffs glistened like jewels. To the side lay the dark sea, immense and vast, and around it the coast ran white and foamy, with small nodding trees. And above all of this, above these thousand new, strange mighty forms, the sun was rising, casting a glowing stream of light over the world that burst into flames of laughing colors.

Kubu was unable to look the sun in its face. But he saw its light stream in colorful floods over the mountains and rocks and coasts and distant blue islands, and he sank to the ground and bent his face to the earth before the gods of this radiant world. Ah, who was he, Kubu? He was a small dirty animal who had spent his entire dull life in the misty swamp hole of the dense forest, fearful, morose, and submitting to the rule of the vile, crooked gods. But here was the world, and its highest god was the sun, and the long, disgraceful dream of his forest life lay behind him and was already being extinguished in his soul, just as the image of the dead priest was fading. Kubu climbed down the steep abyss on his hands and

feet and moved toward the light and the sea. And over his soul in fleeting waves of happiness, the dreamlike presentiment of a bright earth ruled by the sun began to flicker, an earth on which bright, liberated creatures lived in lightness and were subservient to no one except the sun.

THE
DIFFICULT
PATH

When I reached the rocky entrance to the gorge, I stood still and hesitated, and then I turned to look back.

The sun was shining in that pleasant green world. The blossoms of cattails flickered and waved above the meadows. It was good there. Everything was warm and comfortable. You could hear the soul humming deeply and contentedly like a woolly bumblebee enjoying the full fragrance of the air and the sunlight. Perhaps I was a fool to want to leave all this and climb up into the mountains.

The guide touched me gently on my arm, and I tore my eyes away from the beloved landscape, as though forcing myself to spring out of a warm bath. Now I saw the gorge in darkness without the light of the day. A little black brook crept out of the crevice. Pale grass grew in small tufts on its banks. At the bottom of the brook lay stones that had been deposited there over time. They were of different colors, dead and pale like the bones of creatures that had once been alive.

"Let's rest," I said to the guide.

He smiled patiently, and we sat down. It was cool, and a mild stream of dark stone-cold air flowed from the rocky entrance.

It was horrible, really horrible to go this way. Horrible to torture ourselves by going through the cheerless rugged entrance, to cross this frigid brook, to climb up into this narrow and rugged crevice in the darkness.

"The path looks terrible," I said timidly. There was still a strong, incredulous, unreasonable hope that we could turn back, and this hope flickered within me like the dying light of a candle. Perhaps the guide might even let himself be persuaded, and we could spare ourselves all this. Yes, why not? Wasn't the spot that we had just left a thousand times more beautiful? Didn't life flow there richer, warmer, and lovelier? And wasn't I human, a childlike and mortal creature, with a right to a little happiness, to a little place in the sun, to a spot where I could view blue skies and flowers?

No, I wanted to remain there. I had no desire to play the hero and the martyr! I would be satisfied my entire life if I were allowed to stay in the valley and in the sun.

I had already begun to shiver. It was impossible to stand still very long.

"You're freezing," said the guide. "It's best that we move on."

After saying this, he stood up, stretched himself to his full height for a moment, and regarded me with a smile. There was neither mockery nor sympathy in his smile, neither harshness nor consideration. There was nothing there but understanding, nothing but knowledge. That smile said, "I know you. I know the fear that you're feeling, and I've not at all forgotten your boasting of yesterday and the day before. I know and am familiar with each desperate hop and jump that your heart takes like a scared rabbit, and with each flirt with the lovely sunshine out there, even before you feel it."

This was the smile with which my guide regarded me, as he took the first step into the dark rocky valley ahead of us, and I hated and loved him, just as a condemned man hates and loves the ax above his neck. Most of all, however, I hated and despised his knowledge, his leadership and coolness, his lack of likable weaknesses, and I hated everything in myself that acknowledged how right he was, that approved of him, that wanted to be like him and follow him.

He had already gone ahead, stepping on stones through the black brook, and was just on the point of disappearing from sight around the first rocky bend.

"Stop!" I called, so full of fear that I was forced to think at the same time that if this were a dream, my terror would explode it all this second, and I would wake up. "Stop," I called. "I can't go on. I'm not ready yet."

The guide stood still and looked at me in silence without a single reproach but with his dreadful understanding, with his unbearable knowledge, his intuition, his smug assurance that he knew what would happen in advance.

"Do you think it would be better if we turned around?" he asked, and he had not even finished uttering his last word when I already knew, full of repugnance, that I would say no, would have to say no. And at the same time all the old, habitual, lovely, and familiar things cried out reproachfully within me: "Say yes, say yes," as if the entire world and home were wrapped around my feet like a ball and chain.

I wanted to cry out yes, even though I knew for sure that I would not be able to do it.

Then the guide pointed back into the valley with his outstretched hand, and I turned once again to look at the region that I loved so much. But now I was faced with the most painful thing that I could possibly see: My beloved valleys and fields were lying pale and dull under a white, impoverished sun. The colors clashed in a false and shrill way. The shadows were rusty black and without magic, and the heart had been cut out of everything, the charm and fragrance depleted, so that it all smelled and tasted like things that one had eaten to the point of nausea. Oh, I had known it all the time! How I feared and hated my guide's terrible way of degrading things that were dear and pleasant to me! How I hated his way of letting the juice and spirit run out of it, falsifying the fragrances, and poisoning the colors with a light touch! Oh, I had known it! Yesterday's wine had become today's vinegar. And the vinegar would never again turn back to wine. Never again.

I kept quiet and sadly followed the guide. He was absolutely right, now as always. It was good that he at least remained with me and kept within sight, instead of—as he often had—suddenly disappearing at the moment a decision had to be made and leaving me alone, alone with that alien voice inside my breast into which he, at the time, would transform himself.

I kept quiet, but my heart cried fervently, "Just stay—I'll certainly follow!"

The stones in the brook were terribly slippery. It was tiring and made me dizzy to walk like this, step by step on narrow wet stones that shrank under my feet and eluded me. At the same time the path in the brook rose sharply, and the dark walls of the cliffs drew closer together. They swelled with gloom, and each corner revealed its nefarious intention of squeezing us and cutting off our retreat forever. A sheet of water ran over warty yellow rocks, all so slimy and sticky. No more sky, not even a cloud or some blue above us.

I walked and walked, following the guide, and often closed my eyes out of fear and repulsion. All at once there was a dark flower along the way, black velvet with a touch of sadness. It was beautiful and spoke familiarly to me, but the guide rushed on, and I felt that if I stayed a single moment longer, if I were to cast just one more glance at that sad velvet eye, then the distress and hopeless melancholy would become all too heavy and unbearable for me, and my spirit would remain banished forever in that sneering region of meaninglessness and madness.

Wet and dirty, I trudged onward, and as the damp walls pressed closer together above us, the guide began to sing his old song of comfort. With each step he took, he kept the beat with his clear, strong, young voice: "I will, I will, I will!" I knew quite well that he wanted to encourage me, to spur me on. He wanted to delude me and make me forget the horrible hardship and despair of this hellish journey. I knew he waited for me to chime in with his sing-song. But I refused to do it. I did not want to grant him this victory. Didn't I feel like singing? Wasn't I merely human, just a poor simple guy who had been drawn into doing things against my feelings that not even God would demand of me? Wasn't each carnation and each forget-me-not allowed to stay alongside the brook where it was growing, to bloom and wither in its own way?

"I will, I will, I will!" the guide sang staunchly. Oh, if only I could have turned around! But I had long since been climbing over walls and precipices thanks to the marvelous help of the guide, and there was no return, none whatsoever. I suppressed my tears and felt them strangling me, but I didn't dare weep, not in the least. And so I joined in the song of the guide, defiant and loud, in the same rhythm and tone. However, I did not sing his words. Instead, I kept repeating, "I must, I must, I must!" But it was not easy to sing while climbing. Soon I began gasping for breath and was forced to keep quiet. However, he kept singing tirelessly, "I will, I will, I will," and in time he compelled me as well to sing his words. Now the climbing went better, and I no longer felt under duress. Indeed, I wanted to climb onward, and I no longer felt the slightest trace of fatigue from the singing.

Everything became brighter inside me, and as it did, the smooth cliff also receded, became drier and more pleasant. It also offered help to my slipping foot, and the bright blue sky revealed itself above more and more like a small blue brook between the banks of stone, and then like a small blue lake that grew and became more expansive.

I tried to exert my will more ardently and firmly, and the lake in the sky grew wider, and the path became more accessible. In fact, I sometimes ran an entire stretch with ease, without complaining, next to the guide. Then unexpectedly, I saw the peak close by, right above us, steep and glistening in the glowing air of the sun.

When we were somewhat beneath the peak, we crawled out of a narrow crevice. The sun pierced my eyes and blinded me momentarily, and when I opened them again, my knees shook with dread, for I saw that I was standing free and without support on a steep ridge.

All around me was the infinite space of the sky and scary blue depths. Only the narrow peak towered above us like a ladder. But the sky and sun were there once again, and so we climbed up the last frightening steep path, step by step, with lips pressed together and our brows furrowed. And finally we stood on top, slender figures on glowing rock in sharp, biting, thin air.

It was a strange mountain and a strange peak! We had reached this peak by climbing over endless bare stone walls. A tree grew out of the stone, a small sturdy tree with some short, strong branches. There it stood, incredibly lonely and odd, hard and stiff in the rock, the cool blue of the sky between its branches. And at the very top of the tree sat a black bird that sang a harsh song.

Silent dream of a brief rest high above the world: The sun was ablaze; the rock glowed; the air stiffened; the bird sang harshly. And its harsh song meant, Eternity, eternity! The black bird sang, and its blank hard eye gazed at us like a black crystal. It was hard to bear its gaze. It was hard to bear its song, and most dreadful of all was the loneliness and emptiness of this place—the staggering expanse of the arid sky. To die was inconceivable joy. To stay here was unspeakable pain. Something had to happen, immediately, right away. Otherwise we and the world would turn to stone out of dread. I felt the event rise and blow toward us like a gust of wind before a storm. I felt it flicker like a burning fever over my body and soul. It threatened. It came. It was there.

All of a sudden the bird whirled from the branch and plunged into space.

Then my guide took a running leap into the blue and fell into the palpitating sky and flew away.

Now the wave of destiny had peaked. Now it ripped out my heart which broke quietly apart.

And already I was falling. I jumped, plunged. I flew. Tied up in the cold vortex, I shot blissfully through the air and felt ecstatic pain as I soared downward, quivering through infinity to the mother's breast.

*I*F THE
*W*AR
*C*ONTINUES

*E*ver since I was young, I used to disappear from time to time to re-invigorate myself, and I would lose myself in other worlds. People would search for me, and when they could not find me, they would report me as missing. Then after I returned, it was always a pleasure for me to hear the conclusions that so-called scientists would invent to explain who I was and the conditions of my absence or twilight existence. While I did nothing but what came naturally to me and what most people will be able to do sooner or later, I was regarded as a kind of phenomenon by these peculiar men—as a possessed person by one of them, and as a blessed person with miraculous powers by others.

To be brief, I had been away again for a while. After two years of war, the present had lost much of its charm for me, and I disappeared for a while in order to breathe some other air. In my customary way I left the realm in which we live and was a guest in distant parts for a long time, speeding through people and eras, and I became unhappy because I saw nothing but the usual tribulations, trade, progress, and improvements on the earth. Then I withdrew into the cosmic spheres for some time.

When I returned, it was 1920, and I was disappointed to find that people were still at war with each other all over the globe, and that there was still the same senselessness and obstinance. Some of the borders of countries had shifted; some select regions with ancient high cultures had been carefully destroyed, but all in all nothing much had changed on the surface of things.

Of course, great progress had indeed been made in the cause of equality in the world. At least in Europe, so I heard, the prospects were the same for everyone in all countries. Even the differences between the belligerent nations and the neutral ones had almost completely vanished. Ever since they began shooting the civilian population mechanically from air balloons that were fifteen to twenty thousand meters high in the sky and let their shots fall as they moved, ever since this time the borders of countries, although sharply guarded as before, had become somewhat illusory. The scattering of these random shots from the air was so great that the dispatchers of these balloons were satisfied if they could just keep the bombs from hitting their own territory. They no longer cared how many of their bombs fell on neutral countries or ultimately even on the territory of their allies.

This was actually the only progress that the institution of war itself had made. To a certain degree, the meaning of the war had finally been given its clearest expression by this random bombing. The world had been divided into two parts that sought to annihilate each other because they both desired the same thing, namely the liberation of the oppressed, the elimination of violence, and the establishment of permanent peace. Everyone was prejudiced against a peace that could not possibly last eternally—if eternal peace could not be obtained, then one certainly preferred eternal war, and the negligent manner in which the balloons with explosives let their blessings fall on just and unjust people from enormous heights fit the meaning of this war exactly. Aside from this, the war continued to be waged in the old way with significant but inadequate means. The limited imagination of the generals and the technicians had led to the invention of a few more weapons of annihilation. However, the visionary who had conceived the mechanical balloon that sprayed bombs had been the last of his kind. Since then, the intellectuals, the visionaries, the poets, and the dreamers had gradually lost interest in the war. The war was left up to the generals and the technicians and thus made little progress. The armies were to be found everywhere and confronted each other with tremendous perseverance, and although the lack of materials had long since led to awarding military medals that were made only out of paper, there was no sign anywhere that the bravery of the soldiers had abated.

I found my apartment partially destroyed by bombs from some planes, but I was able to sleep there even though it was cold and uncomfortable. Later the rubble on the floor and the damp mold on the walls disturbed me, and I left to take a walk.

I went through some streets of the city that had changed a great deal from the way they were before. I was struck most by the fact that there were no shops to be seen. The streets were without life. I had walked but a short time when I met a man with a tin number on his hat, and he asked me what I was doing. I told him I was taking a walk.

His response: "Do you have permission?"

I did not understand him. We exchanged words, and he demanded that I follow him to the nearest precinct.

We came to a street lined with buildings that all had white door plates hanging on them, designating the offices with numbers and letters.

"Unemployed Civilians" was stamped on a door plate, and the number 2487B4. That was where we entered. The usual offices, waiting rooms, and corridors smelled of paper, damp clothes, and stuffy air. After some questioning, I was taken to room 72D and interrogated there.

An official stood before me and examined me. "Can't you stand straight?" he asked severely. I said no. He asked: "Why not?" "I never learned how to do it," I responded coyly.

"So then, you were arrested as you were taking a walk without a certificate of permission. Do you admit this?"

"Yes," I said. "That's correct. I didn't know it was necessary. You see, I had been sick for a long time—"

He waved his hand. "You must be punished, and for the next three days you'll be prohibited from walking in shoes. Take off your shoes!"

I took off my shoes.

"My God!" the official exclaimed with horror. "My God, you're wearing leather shoes! Where did you get them? Are you completely crazy?"

"Perhaps I'm not absolutely normal. I'm not exactly the best judge of this. I bought the shoes some time ago."

"You know that the wearing of leather in any form whatsoever by civilians is strictly forbidden. Your shoes will stay here. They will be confiscated. Now show me your identification papers!"

Dear Lord, I didn't have any.

"I've not experienced anything like this for at least a year!" The official sighed and called for a policeman. "Bring this man into office 194, room 8."

I was forced to walk barefoot through some streets. Then we entered another administration building and went through corridors, breathing the smell of paper and hopelessness. I was pushed into a room and was interrogated by another official, who was wearing a uniform.

"You were found on the street without identification papers, so I must fine you two thousand guilders. I'll write the receipt for you right away."

"Forgive me," I said timidly. "I don't have that much with me. Couldn't you lock me up for a while instead of fining me?"

He laughed loudly.

"Lock you up? My dear man, how can you think something like that? Do you think that we'd like to feed you, in addition to all this? No, my good man, if you cannot pay this small amount, you will be given the hardest punishment of all. I'll have to demand the provisional deprivation of your license to exist. Please give me your license-to-exist card!"

I had none.

Now the official was completely speechless. He called for two colleagues, whispered to them for a long time, and pointed to me frequently. They all regarded me with fear and great astonishment. Then he had me taken to a jail until my case could be fully discussed.

Many people were standing and sitting there. A soldier stood on guard in front of the door. It struck me that, despite my lack of shoes, I was by far the best-dressed person in the cell, and the others were somewhat in awe of me. So they made room to let me sit down, and immediately a small, shy man pressed up next to me, leaned over carefully, and whispered into my ear, "Listen, I'll make you a fabulous deal. I have a sugar beet at home! A perfectly good sugar beet! It weighs almost six pounds. You can have it. But what will you offer me in return?"

He leaned over and put his ear close to my lips, and I whispered, "Make me an offer yourself! How much do you want to have?"

"Let's say a hundred and fifteen guilders!" he answered.

I shook my head and became absorbed in my thoughts.

I saw I had been away too long. It was difficult to accustom myself to this life again. I would have given a great deal for a pair of shoes or socks, for my bare feet were terribly cold, and I had been forced to walk through wet streets. But there was nobody in the room who was not barefoot.

After some hours had passed, they came for me. I was led into office number 285, room 19F. This time the policeman remained with me. He positioned himself between me and his superior, who seemed to me to be a very high official.

"You've managed to get yourself into quite a bad predicament," he began. "You're here in this city and living without a license to exist. I'm sure you know that this calls for the most severe punishment."

I made a slight bow.

"If you'll permit me," I said, "I have just one request to make of you. I completely agree that I can't handle this situation, and that my predicament is bound to become worse. So would it be possible for you to sentence me to death? I'd appreciate that very much!"

The high official gave me a mild look.

"I understand why you're saying this," he said gently. "But if I granted it, then everyone could eventually come with such a request. In any event, you'd have to buy a death card. Do you have the money for it? It costs four thousand guilders."

"No, I don't have that much. But I'd give all that I have. I have a great longing to die."

He smiled strangely.

"I believe you. You're not the only one. But it's not so easy to die. You're a citizen of a state and are obligated to this state with body and soul. I'm sure you know this. By the way—I see that you've registered yourself as Emil Sinclair. Are you the writer Sinclair?"

"Yes, I am."

"Oh, I'm very pleased. I hope I can be of service to you. Officer, you may leave now."

The policeman left, and the official offered me his hand.

"I've read your books with great interest," he said courteously, "and I'll try to help you as much as I possibly can. But tell me, dear God, how did you manage to get yourself into this terrible predicament?"

"Well, I was away for a long time. I had taken flight into the cosmos for a while. It may have been two or three years, and quite frankly I had hoped that the war would come to an end in the meantime, more or less. But tell me, can't you obtain a death card for me? I'd be extremely grateful."

"Perhaps I can manage it. But before I can arrange anything, you must have a license to live. Without it, any step I took would be hopeless. I'll give you a letter of recommendation for office 127.

With my guarantee you'll at least be able to obtain a provisional license to live. Of course it's only valid for two days."

"Oh, that's more than enough time!"

"Very well! After you have it, come back to me."

I shook hands with him.

"One more thing," I said quietly. "May I ask you another question? You can imagine how badly informed I am about current events."

"Please, please."

"Well then, I'd be interested most of all in knowing how it is possible that life can go on at all under these circumstances. How can the people put up with all of this?"

"Well now," he responded, "you're in a particularly bad situation as a civilian and entirely without papers! There are very few civilians left. Whoever is not a soldier is a civil servant. This makes life more bearable for most people. Many are even very happy. And they have gradually become accustomed to the deprivation. When we gradually had to give up potatoes and become accustomed to wood pulp—it's lightly charred, which makes it rather tasty—everyone thought that we would never be able to bear this. And now it's worked out well. And that's the way it is with everything."

"I understand," I said. "It's actually no longer astonishing. But there is something I don't entirely understand. Tell me, why is the whole world actually exerting such tremendous energy this way? These deprivations, these laws, these offices and officials—what is it actually that people are protecting and maintaining with all of this?"

The gentleman looked at me with astonishment.

"That is some question!" he exclaimed, and shook his head. "You know, don't you, that there is a war, war all over the world! And that's what we are maintaining. It is war. Without these enormous efforts and accomplishments, the armies could not remain in the battlefields one week more. They would starve—they would not be able to endure."

"Yes," I said, "that's certainly food for thought! So war is the good thing that is being maintained by all these sacrifices! Yes, but— permit me to ask a strange question—why do you place such high value on war? Is it really worth all this? Is war really a good thing at all?"

The official shrugged sympathetically. He saw that I did not understand him.

"My dear Mr. Sinclair," he said, "you've become very ignorant of the ways of the world. But please, just go through one street. Speak with the people. Just make a little effort to think and ask yourself: What else is left? What is it that constitutes our life? Then you will immediately have to say: War is the only thing that we still have! Pleasure and personal gain, social ambition, greed, love, intellectual work—all this no longer exists. War is the one and only activity for which we are grateful. It still gives us something like order, law, thought, and spirit in the world. Can you grasp this?"

Yes, now I understood, and I thanked the gentleman very much.

Then I left his room and mechanically stuck the letter of recommendation for office 127 into my pocket. I did not intend to make use of it. Nothing now was so important that I had to bother another one of those officials. And before I could be noticed again and taken to task, I spoke to the tiny blessed star within me, shut off my heartbeat, made my body disappear into the shadow of a bush, and continued my previous voyage without thinking about returning home ever again.

THE

EUROPEAN

˜∽✳✆˜

*F*inally, the Lord our God showed His consideration and brought
about an end to the bloody world war on earth by sending the great
flood. These tides of water mercifully cleansed the aging planet of
everything that had desecrated it—the bloody fields of snow and the
motionless mountains decked with cannons. They also cleared away
the rotting corpses, along with those people who wept for them; the
enraged and bloodthirsty individuals, along with the impoverished;
the hungry, along with the mentally deranged.

The blue skies of the world now cast a friendly look at the
brightly shining planet.

By the way, European technology had held its own splendidly
until the very end. For weeks Europe had taken precautions and
tenaciously resisted the gradually rising waters. First, it was through

gigantic dams that millions of prisoners of war had built, then through artificial structures that were erected with astonishing rapidity. At the beginning they had looked like gigantic terraces, but they culminated more and more into towers. The human sense of the heroic emanated from these towers, and they stood the test with touching steadfastness until the end. While Europe and the rest of the world were swamped, the spotlights still glistened from the last of the projecting towers, dazzling and unperturbed through the damp dusk of the sinking earth, and shells soared out of the cannons, back and forth, forming elegant arches. Two days before the end, the leaders of the middle powers decided to make a peace offer to their enemies through signals of light. However, their enemies demanded the immediate evacuation of the fortified towers that were still standing, and not even the most resolute friends of peace could declare themselves ready to do that. Therefore both sides kept shooting heroically to the very last hour.

Then the entire world became submerged. The only surviving European drifted on a lifeboat in the flood and used all his energy to write down the events of the final days, so that a later humanity would know that it had been his fatherland that had outlasted its final enemies by hours and had thus secured the victory laurels for itself.

All of a sudden a ponderous vessel, black and gigantic, appeared on the gray horizon and gradually approached the exhausted man. Before he fainted, he had the satisfaction of recognizing the ancient patriarch, with his wavy silver beard, standing on board the houseboat. Then a tremendous black African fished the drifting man out of the water. He was still alive and regained consciousness. The patriarch gave him a friendly smile. His work had been

successful: One type of each of the species living on earth had been saved.

While the ark sailed gently with the wind and waited for the muddy water to settle, life became merry and gay on board. Large fish followed the boat in dense schools. Birds and insects sprawled in lively, dreamlike flocks over the roof. Every animal and every human rejoiced fervently at having been saved and chosen for a new life. The colorful peacock screeched its morning call shrilly and clearly over the water. The elephant laughed and sprayed a bath for himself and his wife, with his trunk raised high. The lizard sat glittering in the sunny joists. The Indian fetched sparkling fish out of the endless flood with a quick thrust of his spear. The African rubbed fire on the hearth out of dry wood and slapped his fat wife on her clapping thighs in rhythmic beats. The Hindu stood lean and stiff with folded arms and murmured ancient verses to himself from songs about the creation of the world. The Eskimo lay steaming in the sun and perspired, laughing out of small eyes, water and fat dripping from him, while a good-natured tapir sniffed him. And the small China-man had carved a thin stick that he carefully balanced first on his nose and then on his chin. The European used his writing materials to make an inventory of the present living creatures.

Groups and friendships were formed, and whenever a quarrel was about to erupt, the patriarch settled it with a wave of his hand. Everyone was gregarious and happy. The only one who kept to himself was the European, who occupied himself with his writing.

Soon the multicolored people and animals thought up a new kind of game or tournament in which they would compete and demonstrate their abilities and talents. Each one wanted to be first, and the patriarch had to arrange everything. He separated the large and small animals, and then he set apart the people, and they all had to register and name the feat that they thought they could best accomplish. Then each one took a turn.

This splendid tournament lasted many days since each group would frequently interrupt its game and run off to watch another group. And every marvelous performance was loudly applauded by the spectators. How many wonderful things there were to see! All of God's creatures displayed their latent talents. The richness of life revealed itself. How they laughed, applauded, crowed, clapped, stamped, and neighed!

The weasel ran wonderfully, and the lark sang enchantingly. The puffed-up turkey marched splendidly, while the squirrel was incredibly nimble in climbing. The mandrill imitated the Malayan, and the baboon, the mandrill. Runners and climbers, swimmers and pilots competed tirelessly, and they were all unbeatable in their way and were given due recognition. There were animals that employed magic to perform wonders, and animals that could make themselves invisible. Many distinguished themselves through their strength; many through cunning; many through attack; many through defense. Insects could protect themselves by looking like grass, wood, moss, or stone, and others among the weak drew applause and caused the laughing spectators to flee horrible odors. Nobody was left out. Nobody was without talent. Birds' nests were woven, pasted, entwined, walled up. Predatory birds could detect the tiniest thing from scary heights.

And even the humans did their things in a superb way: The big African ran easily and effortlessly on a high beam. The Malayan made a rudder with three twists of a palm leaf and steered and turned on a tiny plank. That was worth watching. The Indian hit the smallest target with a light arrow, and his wife wove a mat out of two kinds of flax, which drew great admiration. Everyone was silent for a long time and stared as the Hindu appeared and did some magic tricks. Then the Chinaman demonstrated how one could triple the wheat harvest through hard work by pulling out the very young plants and then planting them in the same intermediate spaces.

The European, who was not very popular, had aroused the resentment of his kin many times because he found fault with them and judged them with harsh condescension. When the Indian shot down a bird from up high in the blue sky, the white man had shrugged and asserted that one could shoot three times as high with twenty grams of dynamite! And when the people challenged him to prove it, he had not been able to do it, but he responded, of course, that if he had this and that and some ten other things, he could certainly do it. He had also mocked the Chinaman and said the replanting of young wheat could certainly be accomplished through endless hard work, but such slavish work would definitely not make people happy. The Chinaman, however, had been roundly applauded when he maintained that people are happy when they have something to eat and pay their respects to God. Here, too, the European had simply laughed and sneered.

The merry tournament continued, and in the end all the humans and animals revealed their talents and artistic abilities. The impression they left was great and joyful. Even the patriarch laughed into his beard and said praisingly, "May the water subside and may a new life begin on this earth, for each colorful thread in God's robe is still present, and nothing is lacking for the foundation of infinite happiness on earth."

The only one who had not performed a feat was the European,

and now all the others insisted strongly that he step up and do his own thing, so that they all could see whether he, too, had a valid claim to breathe God's beautiful air and sail in the patriarch's ark.

The man refused to do anything for a long time and searched for excuses. But then Noah himself placed his finger on his chest and warned him that he had better obey.

"I, too," the white man began, "I, too, have developed a talent with great proficiency and have practiced it. My eyes are not as good as those of other creatures, nor my ears, nose, or hands. My talent is of a higher kind. My gift is the intellect."

"Show us!" the African cried out, and everyone crowded around the European.

"There is nothing to show," the white man said calmly. "You have not really understood me. My mind is what distinguishes me from others."

The African laughed cheerfully and displayed snow-white teeth. The Hindu curled his lips with sarcasm. The Chinaman smiled cleverly and good-naturedly to himself.

"Your mind?" he said slowly. "Well then, please show us your mind. Up to now you haven't shown a thing."

"There is nothing to be seen," the European retorted gruffly, in self-defense. "My gift and uniqueness consist in this: I store images of the external world in my head, and out of them I am able to produce new images and arrangements only for myself. I can conceive the entire world in my mind. That is, I can create it anew."

Noah placed his hand over his eyes.

"Permit me," he said slowly, "but what good is all this? To create the world again that God already created, and entirely for yourself alone inside your head—what use is this?"

Everyone applauded and erupted with questions.

"Wait!" shouted the European. "You really don't understand me. You cannot show the work of the mind so easily as you can show any kind of manual dexterity."

The Hindu smiled.

"Oh yes, you can, my white cousin. Yes, you can. Show us just once the work of your mind. For instance, let us try addition. Let us have a contest to see who can add better! For instance: A couple has three children, of which each one marries and has a family. Each of the young couples has a child every year. How many years must pass before they have one hundred children in all?"

Everyone listened with curiosity. They began to count frantically on their fingers. The European began to calculate. But one moment later the Chinaman announced that he had found the solution.

"Well done," the white man admitted, "but those things involve mere adroitness. My mind is not to be used for such clever tricks but to solve great problems on which the happiness of humankind depends."

"Oh, that pleases me," Noah encouraged him. "It is certainly better than all the other skills if you can use your mind to find happiness for humankind. You are right. Tell us quickly what you have to teach us about human happiness. We'll all be grateful to you."

Captivated and breathless, everyone waited for the white man to open his mouth. Now it came. He would be revered if he could demonstrate how human happiness could be attained. They would forget every nasty word they had said about him, for he would be such a wizard! Why should he need the art and skill of the eye, ear, and hand? Why should he need hard work and addition if he knew such other things!

The European, who until now had displayed an arrogant countenance, gradually became embarrassed when he was faced with all this reverential curiosity.

"It's not my fault," he said hesitatingly, "but you still don't understand me! I didn't say that I know the secret of happiness. I only said that my mind works on problems whose solutions foster the happiness of humankind. It will take a long time before that can be accomplished, and neither you nor I will ever see the results. Many generations will brood about these difficult questions for years to come!"

The people stood wavering and distrustful. What was the man saying? Even Noah looked to the side and knit his brow.

The Hindu smiled at the Chinaman, and when all the rest were uncomfortably silent, the Chinaman said in a friendly manner, "My dear brothers, our white cousin is a buffoon. He wants to tell us that work happens in our heads, and that the results will perhaps only be seen at one time by the great-grandchildren of our great-grandchildren. I propose that we acknowledge him as a buffoon. He tells us things that we really can't understand, but we all sense that these things, if we were really to understand them, would provide us with the opportunity to laugh ad infinitum. Don't you also feel that way? Good, then three cheers for our buffoon!"

Most of them agreed and were happy to see this irritating story brought to an end. However, some were angry and disturbed, and the European remained standing alone, without any consolation.

That evening, the African went with the Eskimo, the Indian, and the Malayan to the patriarch and spoke as follows: "Honored father, we have a question that we'd like to address to you. We don't like this white fellow who made fun of us today. I ask you to think about it: All the human beings and animals, each and every bear and flea, pheasant and dung beetle and every sort of human, we have all had something to show with which we have honored God and protected, elevated, or adorned our lives. We have seen marvelous talents, and many were laughable. But each tiny animal at least demonstrated something gratifying and nice, while the pale man, who was the last to be fished from the water, had nothing to give but peculiar and haughty words, insinuations, and jokes that nobody understands. Nor did he provide any pleasure. Therefore we ask you, dear father, whether it is right in any way that such a creature should be allowed to help establish a new life on this dear earth. Couldn't that lead to disaster? Just look at him. His eyes are turgid, his brow is full of furrows, his hands are pale and weak, his face looks sinister and sad. There is never a bright sound when he speaks. There is certainly something wrong with him. God only knows who sent this fellow to our ark!"

The wise patriarch lifted his clear eyes in a friendly way to the questioners.

"Children," he said softly and full of kindness so that their demeanor immediately became brighter, "dear children! You are right, and yet you are also wrong! Indeed, God has already given His answer before you even asked your question. Of course, I must agree with you—the man from the land of war is not a very pleasant guest, and it is difficult to grasp why such odd people must be here. But God, who created this species at one time, certainly knows why He did it. You all have a great deal to forgive these white men. They are the ones who ruined our poor earth and made it into a criminal court once again. But look, God has given a sign of what He has in mind for the white man. You all, you Africans and you Eskimos and you Indians, you all have your dear wives with you for the new life on earth that we hope to begin soon. Only the man from Europe is alone. I was sad about this for a long time, but now I believe I surmise the meaning in this. This man has been preserved for us as a warning and motivation, perhaps as a ghost. However, he cannot propagate himself, unless he is to dip into the stream of multicolored humankind. He will not be allowed to ruin your lives on the new earth. Rest assured!"

Night fell, and the next morning the small and sharp peak of the holy mountain could be seen above the water in the east.

THE EMPIRE

~~~❧❧~~~

There was once a large, beautiful, but not very rich country, and the people who lived there were good, strong, humble, and satisfied with their lot. There was not much wealth and extravagant living to be found there, nor much elegance and splendor. At times the richer neighboring countries regarded the people in this large country with condescension or mock sympathy.

However, there are things one cannot buy with money that are cherished by people, and these things can flourish among folk who are otherwise not known for anything special. Indeed, they prospered so well in this poor country that, in time, it became famous and respected in spite of its meager power. Such things as music, poetry, and intellectual knowledge thrived, and just as one does not demand that a wise man, preacher, or poet be rich, elegant, or adept in society, yet still honors such people in their way, so the more powerful people did likewise with this strange poor folk. They shrugged their shoulders about their poverty and their somewhat ponderous and clumsy way of doing things in the world, and they spoke with fondness and admiration about their thinkers, poets, and musicians.

And though the country of ideas did indeed remain poor and was often oppressed by its neighbors, it generated a constant, gentle, fecund stream of warmth and intellectual energy that flowed to its neighbors and the entire world.

One thing, however, could not be forgotten; it was a circumstance that caused this folk not only to be mocked by strangers but to suffer and feel pain. For years the many different tribes of this beautiful country had not been able to get along with each other. There had been constant disputes and jealousy. And whenever the best men of this folk proposed the idea of uniting the tribes and collaborating, the very thought that one of the many tribes or its prince might rise above the others and assume leadership was so repulsive to most of the people that they could never come to an agreement.

One time a victory over a foreign prince and conqueror, who had drastically subjugated the country, seemed at last to present a propitious opportunity for bringing about unification. But once again the tribes quarreled among themselves. The many petty princes resisted the creation of treaties, and the subjects of these princes had received so many privileges from them in the form of offices, titles, and colorful little ribbons that they were generally satisfied and not inclined to accept change.

In the meantime the Great Revolution occurred and moved throughout the entire world—that strange transformation of human beings and things. It arose like a ghost or malady from the smoke of the first steam machines and transformed life all over the place. The world became full of work and industry. It came to be ruled by machines and was continually propelled to accomplish new kinds of work. Great dynasties sprang up, and that part of the world that had invented the machines assumed even more control over the world than it had previously had, and it divided the rest of the world among its powerful leaders; whoever had no power went away empty-handed.

Even the country that is the subject of this story was affected by this wave of change, but its part in everything remained modest, as befitted its role. The goods of the world seemed once more to be divided, and the poor country seemed once again to come up empty-handed.

All of a sudden, however, things took a different turn for the country. The old voices that had sought unification of the tribes had never become silent. A great, mighty statesman appeared on the scene. A successful and completely glorious victory over a large neighboring country strengthened and united the entire land, whose tribes now all came together and established a great empire. The poor land of dreamers, thinkers, and musicians had aroused itself. The country was magnificent. It had become united and began its career as an equal power among its great older brothers. Outside in the wide world, not much more remained to rob and acquire. The young power found that the portions had already been distributed. But the spirit of the machine, which had only recently taken hold in this country, flowered now astonishingly quickly. The entire country and its people changed rapidly. The country became great. It became wealthy. It became powerful and feared. It acquired more wealth, and it surrounded itself with a triple protection of soldiers, cannons, and fortresses. Soon the neighbors, who were disturbed by the young nation, showed signs of distrust and fear, and they too began to build stockades and to get cannons and warships ready.

However, this was not the worst of it, for all the countries had enough to pay for all these enormous protective walls, and nobody thought about war. They only armed themselves "just in case"—because rich people like to see steel walls around their money.

Much worse was what went on within the young empire. This folk, which had been both mocked and honored in the world for such a long time, which had been devoted to intellectual pursuits and not to money, this folk realized now what a nice thing it is to have money and power. Therefore the people built and saved, developed their commerce, and loaned money. All they thought about was how to get rich fast, and whoever had owned a mill or a forge now had to have a factory quickly, and whoever had three workers now had to have ten. In fact, many were able to employ hundreds and thousands. And the faster the many hands and machines worked, the faster the money accumulated—especially for those individuals who were adept at accumulating. Many, many workers were no longer apprentices and co-workers of a master; rather, they suffered under conditions of drudgery and slavery.

It was the same in other countries. There, too, the workshop became a factory; the master, a ruler; the worker, a slave. No land in the world could avoid this fate. But destiny played a mean trick on the young empire, in that this new spirit and force in the world prevailed when the empire was beginning its ascent as a nation. It did not have a long history or old wealth. It plunged into this new epoch rashly, like an impatient child. It had its hands full of work and full of gold.

Of course, some individuals admonished and warned the people that they were taking the wrong path. They recalled the earlier times, the modest quaint fame of the land, the cultural mission that it had managed, the constant noble and spiritual stream of thoughts, of music and poetry that it had previously bestowed upon the world. In response, the people just laughed while they enjoyed the happiness of their new wealth. The world was round and turned, and if their grandparents had written poems and philosophical works, that was very nice indeed, but the grandchildren wanted to show that they were capable of doing other things here in this country. And so they hammered away and rooted up the ground to build thousands of factories, new machines, new railroads, new commodities, and just in case, also new weapons and cannons. The rich withdrew from the rest of the people. The poor workers saw themselves abandoned and no longer thought about the folk of which they were a part. Instead, they too worried, thought, and strove for themselves alone. And the rich and the powerful, who had procured all the cannons and guns to be used against outside enemies, were glad about the precautions they had taken, for there were now enemies within the country that were more dangerous.

All this came to an end in the Great War, which caused such terrible havoc and destruction in the world and among whose ruins we are now standing, bewildered by its noise, embittered by its senselessness, and sick from its streams of blood that flow through all our dreams.

And the War, which had begun with the sons of the young flowering nation going into battle with enthusiasm, indeed with high spirits, ended with the empire's collapse. It was defeated, horribly defeated. Moreover, the victors demanded heavy reparations from the defeated people, even before peace could be discussed. For days on end, while the beaten army retreated, the soldiers were compelled to watch the great signs of their previous power being transported in long trains right in front of their eyes from the homeland to the land of the victorious enemy. Machines and money poured out of the defeated land into the hands of the enemy.

In the meantime, however, the defeated people had come to their senses at the moment of their greatest predicament. They had banished their leaders and princes and declared themselves ready to rule themselves. Councils had been formed out of the people, and they showed their willingness to deal with their country's misfortune by using their own power and their own minds.

This folk, which had come of age after such a severe test, still does not know the direction of its path and who its leaders and helpers will be. The heavenly powers, however, know it, and they also know why they sent war and suffering to descend upon this folk and the entire world.

Out of the darkness of these days a way is glimmering, the way that the beaten people must go.

The empire cannot become a child again. Nobody can. It cannot simply give away its cannons, machines, and money and once again write poems in small peaceful cities and play sonatas. But it can take the path that the individual must also take when his life has led him to make mistakes and suffer profound torment. It can recall its previous past, its heritage and childhood, its maturation, its rise and fall, and it can find the power while recalling everything that essentially and immortally belongs to it. It must "go into itself," as devout people say. And in itself, it will find its essence undestroyed, and this essence will not want to avoid its destiny but affirm it and begin anew out of its best and most profound qualities that have been rediscovered.

And if it goes this way, and if the downtrodden people take this path of destiny willingly and sincerely, then something that once belonged to the past will renew itself. A constant silent stream will emanate from it again and penetrate the world, and those who are still its enemies today will, in the future, listen attentively to this silent stream.

THE
PAINTER

During his youth a painter by the name of Albert did not manage to achieve the success and effect with his pictures that he desired. Therefore, he withdrew from society and decided just to satisfy himself. He tried this for many years, but it became more and more apparent that he could not do this either. One time, as he sat and painted the picture of a hero, he kept thinking, "Is it really necessary to do what you're doing? Do these pictures have to be painted? Wouldn't it be just as well for you and everyone if you would merely take walks and drink wine? Aren't you just confusing yourself by painting, forgetting who you are, and passing the time away?"

These thoughts were not conducive to his work. In time Albert's painting stopped almost completely. He took walks. He drank wine. He read books. He took trips. But he was not satisfied by doing these things.

He was often compelled to think of how he had first begun painting with certain wishes and hopes. He recalled how he had felt and wished that a beautiful, powerful connection and current would develop between him and the world, that something strong and vigorous would vibrate incessantly between him and the world and generate soft music. He had wanted to express his innermost feelings and satisfy them with his heroes and heroic landscapes so that the outside world would judge and appreciate his pictures, and people would be grateful for and interested in his work.

Well, he had not found any of this. It had been a dream, and even the dream had gradually faded and become hazy. Then, wherever Albert was, traveling through the world or living alone in remote places, sailing on ships or wandering over mountain passes, the dream began returning more and more frequently. It was different from before, but just as beautiful, just as powerful and alluring, just as desirable and glimmering as it originally had been.

Oh, how he yearned to feel the vibration between himself and everything in the world! To feel that his breath and the breath of the winds and seas were the same, that brotherhood and affinity, love and closeness, sound and harmony would be between him and everything!

He no longer desired to paint pictures in which he himself and his yearning would be portrayed, which would bring him understanding and love, pictures that were intended to explain, justify, and celebrate himself. He no longer thought about heroes and parades that were to express and describe his own existence as picture and smoke. He desired only to feel that vibration, that powerful stream, that fervor in which he himself would turn to nothing and sink, die, and be reborn. Just the new dream about this, the new, reinforced yearning for this, made his life bearable, endowed it with something like meaning, elevated it, rescued it.

Albert's friends, insofar as he still had some, did not understand these fantasies very well. They saw only that this man lived more and more within himself, that he spoke more quietly and strangely, that he was away a great deal, that he took no interest in what was lovely and important for other people, took no interest in politics or business, in shooting matches or dances, in clever conversations about art, or in anything that gave his friends pleasure. He had become an odd person, somewhat of a fool. He ran through the gray, cool winter air and breathed in the colors and smells of this air. He ran after a little child who sang *la la* to himself. He stared for hours into green water, at a bed of flowers, or he absorbed himself, like a reader in his book, in reading the lines and cuts in a little piece of wood, in a root or turnip.

No one was concerned about Albert. At that time he lived in a small city in a foreign country, and one morning he took a walk down a street, and as he looked between the trees, he saw a small lazy river, a steep yellow clay bank, and bushes and thorny weeds that spread their dusty branches over landslides and bleak stones. All at once something sounded within him. He stood still. He felt an old song from legendary times strike up again in his soul. The yellow clay and dusty green, or the lazy river and steep parts of the bank, some combination of the colors or lines, some kind of sound, a uniqueness in the random picture was beautiful, was incredibly beautiful, moving, and upsetting, spoke to him, was related to him. And he felt vibrations and the most fervent connection between forest and river, between river and himself, between sky, earth, and plants. All things seemed to be set there unique and alone so that they could be reflected just at this moment, coming together as one in his eye and heart, so they could meet and greet each other. His heart was the place where river and grass, tree and air could unite, become one, enhance one another, and celebrate the festivals of love.

When this thrilling experience had repeated itself a few times, the painter found himself enveloped by a glorious feeling of happiness, thick and full, like a golden evening or a garden fragrance. He tasted it. It was sweet and thick, and he could no longer bear it. It was too rich. It became ripe and was filled with tension. It aroused him and made him almost anxious and furious. It was stronger than he was, tore him away. He was afraid that it would drag him down with it. And he did not want that. He wanted to live, to live an eternity! Never, never had he wished to live as intensely as he did now.

One day he was silent and alone in his room as though he had just been intoxicated. He had a box of paints standing in front of him and had laid out a piece of cardboard. Now, for the first time in years, he was sitting and painting again.

And it stayed that way. The thought—"Why am I doing this?"—did not return. He painted. He did nothing more except see and paint. Either he went outside and became lost in the pictures of the world, or he sat in his room and let the fullness stream away again. He composed picture after picture on cardboard, a rainbow sky with meadows, a garden wall, a bench in the woods, a country road, also people and animals, and things that he had never seen before, perhaps heroes or angels, who, however, became alive like wall and forest.

When he started circulating among people again, it became

known that he had resumed painting. People found him quite crazy, but they were curious to see his paintings. He did not want to show them to anyone. Yet they did not leave him in peace. People pestered and forced him until he gave an acquaintance the key to his room. He himself departed on a journey. He did not want to be there when others saw the paintings.

People came, and soon there was a great hue and cry. They had discovered a spectacular genius, to be sure, an eccentric, but one who was blessed by God, and they began using sayings to describe him that are used by experts and speakers.

In the meantime Albert had arrived in a village, rented a room from farmers, and unpacked his paints and brush. Once again he went happily through valleys and mountains and later reflected all that he experienced and felt in his paintings.

One day he learned from a newspaper that many people had seen his paintings back home. In a tavern while drinking a glass of wine, he read a long, glowing report in the newspaper of the major city. His name was printed in big letters in the heading, and there were numerous fat words of praise throughout the article. But the more he read, the stranger he felt.

"How splendid the yellow of the background shines in the picture with the blue lady—a new, incredibly daring and enchanting harmony!"

"The art of the expressions in the still life with roses is also wonderful. Not to mention the series of self-portraits! We may place them alongside the great masterpieces of psychological portrait art."

Strange, strange! He could not recall having ever painted a still life with roses, or a blue lady, and as far as he knew, he had never made a self-portrait. On the other hand, the article did not mention the clay bank or the angels, the rainbow sky or the other pictures that he loved so much.

Albert returned to the city. He went to his apartment dressed in his traveling clothes. People were going in and out. A man sat by the door, and Albert had to show a ticket in order to enter. Of course, he recognized his paintings. Someone had, however, hung placards on them, unknown to Albert. "Self-portrait" could be read on many of them, and other titles. He stood contemplatively awhile before the paintings and their unfamiliar names. He saw it was possible to give these paintings completely different names than he had done. He saw that he had revealed something in the garden wall that seemed to be a cloud to some, and that the chasms of his rocky landscape could be the face of a person for others.

Ultimately, it was not all so important. But Albert desired most of all to leave again quietly and to travel and never return to this city. He continued to paint many pictures and gave them many names, and he was happy with whatever he did. But he did not show his paintings to anyone.

THE
FAIRY TALE
ABOUT THE WICKER
CHAIR

A young man sat in his solitary attic. His greatest desire was to become a painter, but first he had to overcome quite a few obstacles. To begin with, he lived peacefully in his attic, grew somewhat older, and became accustomed to sitting for hours in front of a small mirror and experimenting with painting self-portraits. He had already filled an entire notebook with such sketches, and he was very satisfied with some of them.

"Considering that I never went to art school," he said to himself, "this sketch has turned out rather well. And that is an interesting wrinkle there next to the nose. You can see that I'm something of a thinker or something similar. I need only to lower the corner of the mouth a little. Then I'd have my own special expression, quite melancholy."

But when he reexamined the sketches sometime later, most of them no longer pleased him. That was irritating, but he concluded from this that he had made progress and was now placing greater demands on himself.

The young man did not live in the most desirable attic, nor did he have a very agreeable relationship with the things lying and standing around this attic. However, it was not a bad relationship. He did them no more or less harm than most people do. He hardly noticed the objects and was not very familiar with them.

Whenever he failed to paint a good self-portrait, he read for a while from books and learned what had happened to other people who, like him, had begun as modest and completely unknown painters and then had become very famous. He liked to read such books and read his own future in them.

So one day he was again somewhat sullen and depressed and sat at home reading about a very famous Dutch painter. He read that this painter had been possessed by a true passion. Indeed, he was frenetic and completely governed by a drive to become a good painter. The young man found that he had many traits in common with this Dutch painter. As he read further, he also discovered many that did not exactly fit him. Among other things he read that whenever the Dutchman had not been able to paint outside due to bad weather, he had painted everything inside, even the tiniest object that met his eyes, unflinchingly and passionately. One time he had painted a pair of old wooden shoes, and another time an old crooked chair—a coarse, rough kitchen and peasant chair made out of ordinary wood, with a seat woven out of straw, quite tattered. The painter had painted this chair, which nobody certainly would have considered worth a glance, with so much love and dedication and with so much passion and devotion that it became one of his most beautiful pictures. The painter's biographer found many wonderful and appropriately touching words to say about this painted straw chair.

Here the reader stopped and contemplated. That was something new that he had to try. He decided immediately—for he was a young man who made very rash decisions—to imitate the example of this great master and to try this way to greatness.

He looked around in his attic and realized that he had actually not paid much attention to the things among which he lived. He did not find a crooked chair with a seat woven out of straw anywhere; nor were there any wooden shoes. Therefore he was momentarily dejected and despondent, and he almost felt discouraged, as he had often felt whenever he read about the lives of great men. At those times he realized that all the little indicators and remarkable coincidences that had played roles in the lives of the others had not become apparent in his life, and he would wait in vain for them to appear. However, he soon pulled himself together and realized that it was now his task to be persistent and pursue his difficult path to fame. He examined all the objects in his little room and discovered a wicker chair that could serve him very well as a model.

He pulled the chair closer with his foot, sharpened his art pencil, took his sketch pad on his knee, and began to draw. After a couple of light first strokes, he seemed to have captured the form sufficiently, and now he inked in the thick outlines with a few firm and powerful strokes. A deep triangular shadow in a corner attracted him, and he painted it full of strength, and so he continued until something began to disturb him.

He worked a little while longer. Then he held the sketch pad away from himself and examined his sketch carefully. His very first glance told him that he had completely failed to capture the wicker chair.

Angrily he drew a new line into the sketch and fixed his eyes grimly on the chair. The sketch was still not right. It made him mad.

"You demonic wicker chair!" he screamed violently. "I've never seen a beast as moody as you are!"

The chair cracked a little and said with equanimity, "Yes, take a look at me! I am as I am, and I won't change myself anymore."

The painter kicked it with his toe. The chair swerved backward to avoid the kick and now looked completely different.

"You dumb chair!" the young man exclaimed. "Everything is crooked and wrong about you."

The wicker chair smiled a little and said softly, "That's what's called perspective, young man."

The painter jumped up. "Perspective!" he yelled furiously. "Now this clown of a chair comes and wants to play schoolteacher. Perspective is my affair, not yours. Remember that!"

The chair said nothing more. The painter stomped loudly back and forth a few times until someone began pounding beneath the floor with a cane. An elderly man, a scholar, lived under him, and he could not bear the noise.

The young man sat down and looked at his last self-portrait. But it did not please him. He found that he looked more handsome and interesting in reality, and that was the truth.

Now he wanted to read his book again, but there was more in the book about the Dutch straw chair, which irritated him. He now felt that the writer had really made much too much of it, and after all . . .

The young man looked for his artist's hat and decided to go out. He remembered that he had long ago been struck by the fact that painting was not very fulfilling. One had nothing but bother and disappointments, and in the end even the best painter in the world could portray only the simple surface of objects. For a man who loved the profound aspects of life, it was no profession for him in the long run. And once more he seriously thought, as he had done many times, about following an even earlier inclination and becoming a writer instead of a painter. The wicker chair remained behind in the attic. It was sorry that its young master had gone. It had hoped that a decent relationship could finally develop between the two of them. It would have liked at times to speak a word, and it knew that it certainly had many valuable things to teach a young man. But unfortunately nothing ever came of this.

IRIS

ᵕ⤸⤷ᵕ

During the spring of his childhood, Anselm used to run joyfully in the green garden. One of his mother's flowers was called the blue flag, and he was especially fond of it. He used to press his cheek against its tall bright green leaves, touch and feel its sharp points with his fingers, and smell and inhale its wonderful blossoms. Long rows of yellow fingers rose from the pale blue center and stood erect. Between them a light path ran deep down into the calyx and into the distant blue mystery of the blossom. He loved this flower very much and used to stare inside it for moments on end. At times he envisioned the delicate yellow members like a golden fence standing at a king's garden, and at other times they looked like a double row of beautiful dream trees, and no wind could sway them. The mysterious path into the inner depths ran between them, interlaced with living veins that

were as delicate as glass. The vault spread itself out enormously, and
the path lost itself infinitely deep between the golden trees in the
caverns. Above the path the violet vault bowed majestically and
spread thin magic shadows over the silent miracle that was antici-
pated. Anselm knew that this was the mouth of the flower, that its
heart and its thoughts lived behind the splendid yellow protrusions
in the blue cavern, and that its breath and its dreams streamed in and
out along this glorious bright path with its glassy veins.

Next to the large blooming flowers stood small blossoms that
had not yet opened. They were on firm ripe stems in small chalices
with brownish-green skin. The young blossoms forced themselves
quietly and vigorously from these chalices, tightly wrapped in light
green and lilac. Then the young deep violet managed to peer forth
erect and tender, rolled into fine points. Veins and hundreds of lines
could already be seen on these tightly rolled young petals.

In the morning, each time Anselm came out of the house,
drawn from sleep and dreams and faraway places, the garden stood
waiting for him. It was always there and always new. If yesterday there
had been the hard blue point of a blossom tightly rolled and staring
out of a green husk, there was now a young petal that hung thin and
blue as the sky with a tongue and a lip, searching and feeling for its
form and arch, about which it had been dreaming for a long time.
And right at the bottom, where it was still engaged in a quiet struggle
with its sheath, a delicate yellow plant with bright veins, one could
sense, was preparing its path to a distant fragrant abyss of the soul.
Perhaps it would open at noon, perhaps in the evening. A blue silk
tent would arch over the golden dream forest, and its first dreams,
thoughts, and songs would emanate silently out of the magical abyss.

Then a day would come when the grass was filled with nothing but bluebells. Then a day would come when suddenly a new tone and fragrance enveloped the garden. The first tea rose would hang, soft and golden-red, over the scarlet leaves soaked in sun. Then a day would come when there were no more blue flags. They would be gone. There would be no more path with a golden fence that led gently down into the fragrant mysteries. Stiff leaves would stand sharp and cool like strangers. But red berries would ripen in the bushes, and new, incredible butterflies would fly freely and playfully over the star-shaped flowers, red-brown butterflies with mother-of-pearl backs and hawk moths with wings like glass.

Anselm talked to the butterflies and the pebbles. The beetles and lizards were his friends. Birds told him bird stories. Ferns showed him secretly the brown seeds they had gathered and stored under the roof of the giant leaves. Pieces of green sparkling glass that caught the rays of the sun became for him palaces, gardens, and glistening treasure chambers. If the lilies were gone, then the nasturtiums bloomed. If the tea roses wilted, then the blackberries became brown. Everything fluctuated, was always there and always gone, disappeared and reappeared in its season. Even the scary strange days, when the cold wind clamored in the pine forest and the withered foliage clattered so pale and dead throughout the entire garden, even these days brought still another song, an experience, or a story with them until everything subsided again. Snow fell outside the windows and forests of palms grew on the panes. Angels with silver bells flew through the evening, and the hall and floor smelled from dried fruit. Friendship and trust were never extinguished in that good world, and when once snowdrops unexpectedly shone next to the black ivy leaves and the first early birds flew high through new blue heights, it was as if everything had been there all the time. Until one day, once again, the first bluish point of the bud peered out from the stem of the blue flag, never expected and yet always exactly the way it had to be and always equally desired.

For Anselm, everything was beautiful. Everything was welcome, familiar, and friendly, but the most magical and blessed moment for the boy came each year when the first blue flag appeared. At one time in his earliest childhood dream, he had read the book of wonders for the first time in its chalice. Its fragrance and numerous undulating shades of blue had been for him the call and the key to the creation of the world. The blue flag accompanied him through all the years of his innocence. It had renewed itself with each new summer, had become richer in mystery and more moving. Other flowers had mouths, too. Other flowers also diffused fragrance and thoughts. Others also enticed bees and beetles into their small sweet chambers. But the boy adored the blue flag or iris more than any other flower, and it became most important for him. It was the symbol and example of everything worth contemplating and everything that was miraculous. When he looked into its chalice and, steeped in thought, followed that bright dreamlike path between the marvelous yellow shrubs toward the twilight deep inside the flower, then his soul looked through the gate where appearance becomes an enigma and seeing becomes a presentiment. Even at times during the night he would dream about the chalice of the flower and see it enormously opened in front of him like the gate of a heavenly palace, and he would enter riding on a horse or flying on swans, and the entire world would ride and fly and glide gently with him, drawn by magic down into the glorious abyss where every expectation had to be fulfilled and each presentiment had to become true.

Every phenomenon on earth is symbolic, and each symbol is an

open gate through which the soul, if it is ready, can enter into the inner part of the world, where you and I and day and night are all one. Every person encounters the open door here and there in the course of life, and it occurs to everyone at one time or another that everything visible is symbolic and that spirit and eternal life are living behind the symbol. Of course, very few people go through the gate and abandon the beautiful phenomenon of the outside world for the interior reality that they intuit.

It thus appeared to the young boy Anselm that the chalice of his flower was the open, silent question toward which his soul was moving in growing anticipation of a blessed answer. Then the lovely multitude of things drew him away again, in conversations and games with grass and stones, roots, bushes, animals, and all the friendly aspects of the world. He often drifted off and sank into deep contemplation of himself. He would abandon himself to the marvelous features of his body, feel his swallowing with closed eyes, his singing, the strange sensations as he breathed, the feelings and imaginings in his mouth and throat. He also groped there for the path and the gate through which one soul can go to another. With amazement he observed the meaningful and colorful figures that often appeared to him out of the purple darkness when he closed his eyes, with spots and half circles of blue and deep red and bright glassy lines in between. Sometimes Anselm experienced a glad and shocking jolt as he felt the hundreds of intricate connections between eye and ear, smell and taste, felt for beautiful fleeting moments sounds, tones, letters of the alphabet that were related and similar to red and blue, to hard and soft, or he was amazed upon smelling a plant or peeled-off green bark at how strangely close smell and taste were and how often they fused and became one.

All children feel this way, although they do not feel it with the same intensity and sensitivity. And with many of them all of this is already gone, as if it had never existed, even before they begin to learn how to read the alphabet. For others, the mystery of childhood remains close to them for a long time, and they take a remnant and echo of it with them into the days of their white hair and weariness. All children, as long as they still live in the mystery, are continuously occupied in their souls with the only thing that is important, which is themselves and their enigmatic relationship to the world around them. Seekers and wise people return to these preoccupations as they mature. Most people, however, forget and leave forever this inner world of the truly significant very early in their lives. Like lost souls they wander about for their entire lives in the multicolored maze of worries, wishes, and goals, none of which dwells in their innermost being and none of which leads them to their innermost core and home.

The summers and autumns of Anselm's childhood came softly and went without making a sound. Time and again the snowdrops, violets, lilies, periwinkles, and roses bloomed and withered, beautiful and sumptuous as ever. He experienced it all with them. Flowers and birds spoke to him. Trees and springs listened to him, and he took his first written letters and his first problems with friends in his customary old way to the garden, to his mother, to the bright multicolored stones alongside the flower beds.

But one time a spring arrived that did not sound or smell like all the earlier ones. The blackbird sang, and it was not the old song. The blue iris blossomed, but there were no dreams and no fairy-tale figures wandered in and out along the golden-fenced path of its chalice. The hidden strawberries laughed from their green shadows, and the butterflies glittered and tumbled over the high lilies, but nothing was as it used to be. The boy was concerned with other things, and he had many quarrels with his mother. He himself did not know what the matter was or why it continued to disturb him. He only saw that the world had changed and that the friendships of earlier times had dissolved and left him alone.

A year went by like this, and then another, and Anselm was no longer a child. The brightly colored stones around the flower beds bored him. The flowers were mute, and he stuck the beetles on pins in a box. His soul had taken the long hard detour, and the old joys were vanquished and withered.

The young man rushed impetuously into life, which now seemed to him to have really begun. The world of symbols was blown away and forgotten. New wishes and paths enticed him. An aura of childhood could still be seen in his blue eyes and soft hair. However, he did not appreciate being reminded of it, and he cut his hair short and assumed as bold and worldly a posture as he could. His moods kept changing as he stormed through the scary pubescent years, at times a good student and friend, at other times lonely and shy. During his first youthful drinking bouts, he tended to be wild and boisterous. He had been compelled to leave home and saw it only when he returned on short visits to his mother. He was changed, grown, well dressed. He brought friends with him, brought books with him, always something else, and when he walked through the old garden, it appeared to him to be small and silent as he glanced about distractedly. He no longer read stories in the colorful veins of the stones and leaves. He no longer saw God and eternity dwelling in the mysterious blossoms of the blue iris.

Anselm went away to high school and then college. He

returned to his home city with a red cap and then with a yellow one, with fuzz on his upper lip and then with a young beard. He brought books in foreign languages with him, and one time a dog. Soon he carried secret poems in a leather case in his breast pocket, then copies of ancient proverbs, and finally pictures of pretty girls and their letters. He came back from trips to foreign countries and took voyages on large ships across the sea. He returned and was a young teacher, wearing a black hat and dark gloves, and the old neighbors tipped their hats to him as he passed and called him professor, even though he had not yet become one. Once again he returned wearing black clothes, slim and somber, and walked behind the slow hearse upon which his old mother lay in the coffin adorned with flowers. And then he rarely returned.

Now Anselm lived in a big city, where he taught students at the university and was regarded as a famous scholar. He went about, took walks, sat and stood exactly like other people of the world. He wore a fine hat and coat, was serious or friendly, with lively and sometimes tired eyes. He was a gentleman and a scholar, just as he had wanted to become. But now he felt the exact same way that he had felt when his childhood came to an end. All of a sudden he felt the impact of many years sliding by that left him standing strangely alone and discontent in the middle of the world that he had always strived to attain. He was not genuinely happy as a professor. He was not deeply gratified to be greeted by the people of the city and the students who showed him great respect. Everything seemed dull and lifeless. Happiness lay once again far away in the future, and the way toward it seemed hot and dusty and ordinary.

It was during this time that Anselm made frequent visits to the house of a friend whose sister attracted him. He no longer felt at ease running after pretty faces. Here, too, he had changed, and he felt that happiness had to come for him in some special way and did not lie waiting for him behind each and every window. He liked the sister of his friend very much, and he often suspected that he was truly in love with her. But she was an unusual girl. Every one of her moves and words was unique and marked in a certain way, so that it was not always easy to keep pace with her and find the same rhythm. Sometimes in the evening, when Anselm walked back and forth in his lonely apartment and listened attentively to his own footsteps echoing through the empty rooms, he would argue with himself about this woman. She was older than the wife he had desired. She was very peculiar, and it would be difficult to live with her and to pursue his scholarly goals, for she did not like to hear anything about academics. Also, she was not strong and healthy and could not put up with parties and company very well. She preferred most of all to live with flowers and music and to have a book, in quiet solitude. She waited for someone to come to her, and she let the world take its course. Sometimes she was so fragile and sensitive that when anything strange happened to her, she easily burst into tears. Then there were times when she would glow quietly and softly in happy solitude, and anyone who saw this felt how difficult it would be to give something to this strange beautiful woman and to mean something to her. Sometimes Anselm believed that she loved him, and at other times it seemed to him that she did not love anyone. It appeared that she was just tender and friendly with everyone and wanted nothing from the world but to be left in peace. However, he wanted something more from life, and if he were to marry, then there had to be life and excitement and hospitality in his home.

"Iris," he said to her, "dear Iris, if only the world had been differently arranged! If there were nothing at all but a beautiful, gentle world with flowers, thoughts, and music, then I would wish for nothing but to be with you my entire life, to listen to your stories, and to share in your thoughts. Just your name makes me feel good. Iris is a wonderful name. But I have no idea what it reminds me of."

"You certainly know," she responded, "that the blue flag flower is called iris."

"Yes," he responded with a feeling of discomfort. "Of course, I know it, and just that in itself is very beautiful. But whenever I say your name, it seems to remind me of something else. I don't know what it is, but it's as if it were connected to some very deep, distant, and important memories, and yet I don't know what they could be and haven't found the slightest clue."

Iris smiled at him as he stood there helplessly, rubbing his forehead with his hand.

"That's how I feel," she said to Anselm in her voice that was as light as a bird, "whenever I smell a flower. Then my heart tells me each time that a memory of something extremely beautiful and precious is connected to the fragrance, something that had been mine long ago and became lost. It's also the same with music, and some-times with poems—all of a sudden something flashes, just for a moment, as if all at once I saw my lost home below in a valley, and then it immediately disappears and is forgotten. Dear Anselm, I believe that we are on earth for this purpose, for contemplating and searching and listening for lost remote sounds, and our true home lies behind them."

"How beautifully you put all this!" Anselm complimented her, and he felt something stir in his own breast almost painfully, as if a hidden compass there were pointing persistently to its distant goal.

But that goal was completely different from the goal he sought, and this hurt. Was it worthy of him to gamble away his life in dreams by chasing after pretty fairy tales?

One day after Anselm had returned from a lonely journey, he found the stuffy atmosphere in his barren study to be so cold and oppressive that he rushed over to his friend's house and asked the beautiful Iris for her hand.

"Iris," he said to her, "I don't want to continue living like this. You've always been my good friend. I must tell you everything. I must have a wife, otherwise I feel my life will be empty and without meaning. And whom else should I wish for my wife but you, my dear flower? Will you accept, Iris? You'll have flowers, as many as I can find. You'll have the most beautiful garden. Will you come and live with me?"

Iris looked at him for a long time, calmly and straight into his eyes. She did not smile or blush as she answered him with a firm voice.

"Anselm, I'm not astonished by your proposal. I love you, although I had never thought of becoming your wife. But look, my friend, I'd make great demands on the man I marry. I'd make greater demands than most women make. You've offered me flowers, and you mean well. But I can live without flowers and also without music. I could do without all of this and much more if I had to. However, there's one thing I can't and won't do without: I can never live, not even just for a day, if the music in my heart is not at the core of everything I do. If I am to live with a man, then it must be one whose inner music harmonizes perfectly in a delicate balance with mine, and his desire must be to make his own music pure so that it will blend nicely with mine. Can you do that, my friend? If you do, you'll probably not achieve fame and reap any more honors. Your house will be quiet, and the wrinkles that I've seen on your forehead for many years will have to be erased. Oh, Anselm, it won't work. Look, you're one of those who must study so that more and more wrinkles appear on your forehead, and you must constantly create more and new worries for yourself. And whatever I may mean and am, well, you may certainly love and find it pretty, but it is merely a pretty toy for you, as it is for most people. Oh, listen to me carefully: Everything that you now consider a toy is for me life itself and would have to be the same for you, and everything about which you worry and for which you strive, I consider a toy and not worth living for. I'm not going to change, Anselm, for I live according to a law that is inside me. Will you be able to change? And you would have to become completely different, if I were to become your wife."

Anselm stood and could not utter a word, for he was startled by her willpower, which he had thought was weak and whimsical. He was silent, and without realizing it, he crushed a flower he had picked up from the table with his shaking hand.

When Iris gently took the flower out of his hand, it felt in his heart like a severe reproach, but then she suddenly smiled brightly and lovingly as though she had unexpectedly found a way out of the darkness.

"I have an idea," she said softly, and blushed as she spoke. "You'll find it strange. It will seem like a whim to you. But it's not a whim. Do you want to hear it? And will you agree to follow it and allow it to decide everything between you and me?"

Without understanding her, Anselm glanced at Iris with a worried look in his pale features. Her smile compelled him to trust her, and he said yes.

"I'd like to set a task for you," Iris said, and she became serious again very quickly.

"Very well, do it. It's your right," her friend conceded.

"I'm serious about this," she said. "And it is my final word. Will you accept it as it comes straight from my heart and not haggle and bargain about it, even if you don't understand it right away?"

Anselm promised. Then she stood up and offered him her hand as she said, "You've said to me many times that whenever you speak my name, it reminds you of something that you've forgotten, something that was once very important and holy to you. That's a sign, Anselm, and that's what has drawn you to me all these years. I also believe that you've lost and forgotten something important and holy in your soul that must be wakened again before you can find your happiness and attain your destiny. Farewell, Anselm! I'm giving you my hand and asking you to go and find whatever it is in your memory that is linked to my name. On the day that you rediscover it, I'll become your wife and go with you wherever you want, and your desires will be my very own."

Anselm was dismayed and confused and wanted to interrupt her and reproach her for making such a whimsical demand. But with one clear look, she admonished him and reminded him of his promise, and he kept quiet. He took her hand with lowered eyes, pressed it to his lips, and departed.

Anselm had undertaken and completed many tasks in his life, but none had been as strange and important and thus as discouraging as this one. Day after day he ran around and thought about it until he became tired, and time and again he would arrive at a point when he cursed the entire quest and angrily and desperately tried to dismiss it from his mind as the whim of a female. But then something deep within him would oppose this, a very slight mysterious pain, a very soft, barely audible warning. This faint voice in his own heart conceded that Iris was right, and it made the same demand that she did.

But this task was much too difficult for the learned man. He was supposed to remember something that he had long since forgotten. He was supposed to rediscover a single golden thread from the cobweb of buried years. He was supposed to grasp something with his hands and bring it to his beloved, something that was nothing but a drifting bird call, something like a pleasant or sad feeling that one has while listening to music, something thinner, more fleeting and more ethereal than an idea, something more transitory than a nocturnal dream, more shapeless than a morning mist.

Sometimes when he despairingly tossed his search to the winds and gave up in a terrible mood, he would unexpectedly be stirred by something like a breath of air from distant gardens. He would whisper the name *Iris* to himself, ten times and more, softly and playfully, like one testing a note on a taut string. "Iris," he whispered, "Iris," and he felt something move within him with a slight pain, as in an old abandoned house when a door opens and a shutter slams without cause. He examined memories that he thought he had ordered neatly within himself, and he made strange and disturbing discoveries in the process. His treasure of memories was infinitely smaller than he had imagined. Entire years were missing and stood empty, and when he tried to recall them, they were like blank pages. He found that he had great difficulty conceiving a clear picture of his mother once again. He had completely forgotten the name of a girl whom he had ardently pursued for one year during his youth. He recalled a dog that he had once bought on an impulse during his student years and that he had kept for some time. It took him some days before he could remember the name of the dog.

With growing sorrow and fear, the poor man painfully saw how wasted and empty the life that lay behind him had become. It no longer belonged to him but was strange and disconnected, like something once memorized that could be recalled only with difficulty in the form of barren fragments. He began to write. He wanted to write down, year by year, his most important experiences in order to get a firm hold on them again. But what were his most important experiences? Becoming a professor? Receiving his doctorate? His high school or university days? Forming short attachments and liking different girls in forgotten times? Terrified, he looked up. Was that life? Was that all? He slapped his forehead and could not stop himself from laughing compulsively.

Meanwhile time flew. It had never flown by so quickly and relentlessly! A year was gone, and it seemed to him that he was in exactly the same position that he had been when he left Iris. However, he had changed a great deal during this time, something that everyone saw and knew except him. He had become both older and younger. He had become practically a stranger to his acquaintances, who regarded him now as absentminded, moody, and odd. He gained the reputation of a strange eccentric, and people said it was a shame about him, but he had remained a bachelor too long. Sometimes he forgot his responsibilities at the university, and his students waited for him in vain. Sometimes, steeped in thought, he would meander down a street and walk by houses, brushing the dust from the ledges with his tattered coat as he passed. Many thought he had taken to drink. Other times he would stop right in the middle of a lecture in front of his students and try to remember something. Then his face would break into a childlike smile that was very soft and unusual for him, and he would continue his lecture in a warm and moving tone that stirred the hearts of many of his students.

After years of searching hopelessly for the fragrances and scattered traces of his remote past, Anselm had developed a new sensitivity that he himself could not recognize. It seemed to him more and more frequently that behind what he had previously called memories were even more memories, like an old painted wall where sometimes even older pictures lie concealed behind the old ones that have been painted over. He wanted to recall something like the name of a city where he had once spent some days as a traveler, or the birthday of a friend, or anything at all, and as he now dug up and rummaged through a small piece of the past as though it were debris, something entirely different occurred to him in a flash. A breeze surprised him like an April morning wind or like a misty day in September. He smelled a fragrance. He tasted a flavor. He felt dark tender sensations here and there on his skin, in his eyes, in his heart, and gradually it became clear to him: There must have been a day one time, blue and warm, or cool and gray, or some kind of day, and the essence of this day must have been caught within him and clung there as a dark memory. He could not determine exactly the spring or winter day that he distinctly smelled and felt in the real past. He could not name or date it. Perhaps it had been during his student days. Perhaps he had still been in the cradle, but the fragrance was there, and he felt something within him that he did not recognize and could not name or determine. Sometimes it seemed to him as though these memories reached back beyond life into a previous existence, although he smiled at the thought.

Anselm found many things during his helpless wanderings

through the caverns of his memory. He found many things that moved and gripped him, and many things that scared him and made him anxious, but he did not find the one thing that signified the name Iris for him.

One time, in the midst of his torment over not being able to find his goal, he went back to visit his old home city, saw the woods and streets, the paths and fences again, stood in the old garden of his childhood, and felt the waves surge over his heart. The past enveloped him like a dream. Sad and silent, he returned to the city and told everyone that he was sick and had all visitors sent away.

However, one visitor insisted on seeing him. It was his friend, whom he had not seen since the day he had asked Iris to become his wife. This man came and saw Anselm sitting in a neglected condition in his dismal apartment.

"Get up," he said to him, "and come with me. Iris wants to see you."

Anselm jumped up.

"Iris! What's wrong with her? Oh, I know, I know!"

"Yes," said his friend. "Come with me. She's going to die. She's been sick a long time."

They went to see Iris, who lay on a sofa, light and slender like a child, and she smiled cheerfully with magnified eyes. She gave Anselm her soft white child's hand, which lay like a flower in his, and her face was as though transfigured.

"Anselm," she said, "are you angry with me? I set a hard task for you, and I see you've kept your pledge. Keep searching and keep going until you reach your goal! You thought you were doing it for my sake, but you've really been doing it for your own. Do you know that?"

"I suspected it," Anselm replied, "and now I know. It is a long way, Iris, and I would have turned back some time ago, but I can no longer find my way back. I don't know what will become of me."

She peered into his sad eyes and gave him a slight and consoling smile. He bent over her thin hand and wept for a long time, so that her hand became wet from his tears.

"What will become of you?" she said with a voice that was only like a glimmer of memory. "You must not ask what will become of you. You have searched a great deal in your life. You have sought honor and happiness and knowledge, and you've sought me, your little Iris. All these things were only pretty images, and they abandoned you as I must leave you. I, too, have experienced this. I always searched, and I kept finding lovely and beautiful pictures, and they kept fading and vanishing. Now I have no more pictures. I'm no longer searching. I've returned home and have only one more step to take, and then I'll be home. You, too, will arrive there, Anselm, and you won't have any more wrinkles on your forehead."

She was so pale that Anselm cried out in desperation. "Oh, wait, Iris! Don't go yet! Give me a sign that I won't lose you entirely!"

She nodded and reached into a glass next to her bed and gave him a fresh blue iris in full bloom.

"Here. Take my flower, the iris, and don't forget me. Search for me, search for the iris. Then you'll come to me."

Weeping, Anselm held the flower in his hands. And weeping, he took his leave. When his friend sent news of Iris's death, he came again and helped adorn her coffin with flowers and lower it into the earth.

Then his life fell to pieces around him. It seemed impossible for him to continue spinning his thread. He gave everything up. He left his position at the university and the city and vanished. He was seen here and there. One time he appeared in his home city and leaned over the fence of the old garden, but when the people asked after him and wanted to look after him, he disappeared into thin air.

He continued to be fond of the blue flag. Whenever he saw these flowers growing, he bent over one, and when he stared into its chalice for a long time, it seemed as though the fragrance and presentiment of all the past and future fluttered toward him out of its blue depths. But he would sadly continue on his way because fulfillment did not come. It was as though he were listening at a half-opened door and heard the most lovely secret breathing behind it, and just when he thought that everything would now be given to him and fulfilled, the door slammed shut, and the wind of the world swept coolly over his loneliness.

His mother spoke to him in his dreams, and now for the first time in years, he felt her body and face very clearly and nearby. And Iris spoke to him, and when he awoke, something continued to ring in his ears, and he would try to recall it the entire day. He did not have a permanent home. He traveled as a stranger through the land, slept in houses and woods, ate bread or berries, drank wine or the dew from the leaves of the bushes.

He was oblivious to everything. Many people considered him a fool. Many thought he was a sorcerer. Many feared him. Many laughed at him. Many loved him. He learned to do things he had never been able to do before—to be with children and take part in their strange games, to talk to a broken twig and a little stone. Winters and summers flew by him. He looked into the chalices of flowers and into brooks and lakes.

"Pictures," he sometimes said to himself. "They're all just pictures."

But he felt something essential inside him that was not a picture, and he followed it. And at times this essence within him would speak, and its voice was that of Iris and that of his mother, and it was consolation and hope. He encountered miracles, and they did not surprise him. And one winter he walked in the snow through a field, and ice had formed on his head. And in the snow he saw an iris stalk standing stiff and slender. It was bearing a beautiful solitary blossom, and he bent over it and smiled, for now he realized what the iris had always reminded him of—he recognized the childhood dream again and saw the light blue path that was brightly veined through the golden pickets leading into the secret heart of the flower, and he knew that everything he had been seeking was there, that this was the essence and no longer a picture.

And once again he was struck by memories. Dreams guided him, and he came upon a hut, where he found some children who gave him milk, and as he played with them, they told him stories. They told him that a miracle had occurred in the forest where the charcoal burners worked. These men had seen the gate of spirits standing open, the gate that opened only once every thousand years. He listened and nodded while envisioning the lovely picture and continued on his way. Ahead of him was a bird singing in the alder bush. It had a strange, sweet voice like the voice of the dead Iris. He followed the bird as it flew and hopped farther and farther over a brook and deep into the forest.

When the bird stopped singing and could no longer be heard or seen, Anselm stopped and looked around him. He was standing in a deep valley in the forest. Water ran softly under wide green leaves. Otherwise everything was quiet and full of expectation. But the bird kept singing inside him with the beloved voice and urged him on

*I*RIS

until he stood in front of a stone wall covered with moss. A small, narrow gap in the middle of the wall led into the interior of the mountain, and an old man was sitting in front of it. As soon as the man saw Anselm approaching, he stood up and yelled, "Go back! Go back! This is the gate of the spirits. No one has ever returned after entering it."

Anselm looked up into the rocky entrance. He noticed a blue path that lost itself deep inside the mountain, and golden pillars that stood close together on both sides. The path sank downward as though into the chalice of an enormous flower.

The bird was singing brightly within his breast, and Anselm walked by the guard into the gap between the golden pillars, into the blue mystery of the interior. He was penetrating into Iris's heart, and it was the blue flag in his mother's garden into whose blue chalice he floated, and as he quickly approached the golden twilight, all memory and knowledge came to him at once. He felt his hand, and it was small and soft. Voices of love sounded nearby and familiar in his ears, and the glistening golden pillars sparkled as they had in the remote past, during the spring of his childhood.

And the dream that he had dreamed as a small boy was also there again, his dream about entering into the chalice, and behind him the entire world of pictures came and glided with him and sank into the mystery that lies behind all images.

Anselm began to sing softly, and his path sloped gently down into home.

•

About the Translator

~~✧~~

*J*ack Zipes is professor of German at the University of Minnesota in Minneapolis, and has previously held professorships at New York University, the University of Munich, the Free University of Berlin, the University of Frankfurt, the University of Wisconsin–Milwaukee, and the University of Florida. In addition to his scholarly work, he is an active storyteller in public schools and has worked with children's theaters in France, Germany, Canada, and the United States. His major publications include *The Great Refusal: Studies of the Romantic Hero in German and American Literature* (1970), *Political Plays for Children* (1976), *Breaking the Magic Spell: Radical Theories of Folk and Fairy Tales* (1979), *Fairy Tales and the Art of Subversion* (1983), *The Trials and Tribulations of Little Red Riding Hood* (1983, 2nd rev. edition 1993), *Don't Bet on the Prince: Contemporary Feminist Fairy Tales in North America and*

ABOUT THE TRANSLATOR

England (1986), *The Brothers Grimm: From Enchanted Forests to the Modern World* (1988), *Spells of Enchantment: The Wondrous Tales of the Western World* (1991), *The Outspoken Princess and The Gentle Knight* (1994), and *Fairy Tale as Myth/Myth as Fairy Tale* (1994). He co-edits *The Lion and the Unicorn*, a journal dealing with children's literature, and has written numerous articles for various publications in the United States, Great Britain, Germany, Canada, and France. In addition to this translation of Hesse's fairy tales, he has translated and edited *The Complete Fairy Tales of the Brothers Grimm* (1987) for Bantam.